E.D. HACKETT

A Match Made in Ireland

A Romantic Women's Fiction Novel

Candace,
Enjoy!
ED Hackett

It's the
little
things

E.D. Hackett-Fiction Author

This novel is dedicated to the true Galway Girls of 2002. Hanna, Cate, and Kat, may we never forget the memories we shared.

Acknowledgement

This novel had been sitting on my heart for years, and one day it spilled out of my fingers and onto the paper.

Thank you to my family, critique group, beta readers, and author friends who listened to me question my story, help to make it stronger, and encourage me to keep going. Without your support, this dream to be a writer would have died a long time ago.

Nicky, from Granite Editorial, your feedback on my writing and the Irish culture has made this story a million times stronger and more authentic. Thank you. I will forever remember what a third leg and digestives really mean.

Maryann Haraldsen, once again, your cover is beautiful.

Thank you to Willie Daly for allowing me to use your name as the Irish Matchmaker. The Lisdoonvarna Matchmaking Festival occurs every September in County Clare. For those who attend, I wish you luck finding true love.

Lastly, thank you to my readers. I hope you fall in love with Rory and

Jaime's story.

I

Part One

Living the Dream
August 2002

Chapter 1:

I knew my life was about to change, but I believed it would be transient, morphing back into my natural state like a rubber band that had been stretched, and flung across the room, yet outwardly looking no different after its journey. Looking through the small, oval window, I said goodbye to the old me, and snuggled back against the overstuffed leather chair.

People outside hurried on the tarmac, and people inside scrambled to find their seats. A line of luggage squeezed through the tiny aisle and found its way to the overhead compartments for the six-hour journey across the Atlantic.

The seat beside me remained empty, and I stretched my legs around my extra-large pocketbook. Pulling it closer to my feet, I dug out my Ireland guidebook and flipped through the pages. Reviewing my wishlist and dreaming about the incredible sights and picturesque scenery, I catapulted into a utopia of sorts.

Planning this semester precisely and intentionally, I had relied on the internet, the library, and friends and family to create a detailed route for every weekend excursion. Only this weekend and the last weekend were left open for the nonnegotiable trip to and from America. All major cities, plus the quaint towns dotted along the way were starred, highlighted, and flagged within the pages of my semester bible. This book had stayed with me morning, noon, and night since my study abroad application was accepted six months ago.

Checking my watch, I pulled a paper-thin blanket over my legs and smiled. The flight was due to leave in four minutes. My stomach tumbled at the thought of leaving my friends and my boyfriend for what might feel like an eternity, but I pushed aside images of missing out and instead embraced the hope of infinite new experiences.

The flight attendant walked by and smiled. I admired her splattered freckles, ivory skin, and strawberry-blonde hair that reminded me of summer. I pulled my own straight, jet-black mop into a messy bun behind my head and continued to look around the plane. "Few moments to go," she said, and my heart jolted with excitement. I turned to grin at the passenger two seats away, but he remained stoic, his eyes never leaving his book.

Undeterred, I leaned across the empty seat between us. "What are you reading?"

He placed the book face down on his lap and turned to me. "Just something I picked up at the book kiosk."

I glanced at the book, not recognizing the cover, and then at him. "It looks good."

He didn't respond.

"Have you ever been to Ireland?" I leaned against my seat and readjusted my blanket.

He rubbed his eyes. "Yes, often for business. Now, if you'll excuse me, I have a book to get back to."

I pulled back and my shoulders tightened, surprised by his stern words softened with an apologetic smile. "Oh, yes, sorry. Enjoy." I returned to the window and checked my watch. *We were supposed to leave three minutes ago.* Glancing around the plane, the flight attendants huddled near the front. Nothing seemed amiss, so I flipped through my book again.

I couldn't wait to get away from my parents and take a break from college. I was due to graduate in less than two years and deserved a four-month vacation from my normal, everyday life. Some of my friends took a year off after high school, but when I approached the subject with my parents, they quickly dismissed me. Now, I was free. I flipped through my book and imagined myself among the photographs of abandoned castles and flocks of sheep, while living my best life.

The numbers on my watch taunted me, a reminder that the flight should have departed six minutes ago. *What is the hold-up?* I glanced again at the flight attendants, and the woman with the strawberry-blonde hair opened the door. A man with flaming red hair and an overgrown crimson beard cruised down the aisle, scanning the numbers above the seats. He stopped directly in front of my row and shoved his backpack into the overhead bin above me, then slammed the lid down. I closed my eyes. *Please, don't sit here.* Clothing brushed against my arm, and I squeezed closer to the window as his arms flailed while taking off his sweatshirt.

When I opened my eyes, big sneakers pushed against my bag. I scanned up and noticed grass-stained knees and random holes decorating his pants. My eyes moved to his face, and he grinned at me with crooked front teeth, scrunched eyes, and bushy red eyebrows. A plethora of freckles sprayed his cheeks, morphing into the perimeter of his beard.

"Hello," he said. "Would you mind moving your bag a bit?" He pointed down, and my eyes followed. It sat slightly tilted toward his foot but leaned mostly on my side.

Tossing him a polite grimace, I moved it over some more. "Sorry about that," I said, rising to a sitting position.

"No worries." He widened his legs and his knee pressed against mine, pushing me and my bag toward the airplane wall. I clenched my jaw and tapped my toe before tilting my hips toward him.

"You know," I said, "it's a long flight, and I'd appreciate a little space. I'm practically kissing the window." For extra theatrics, I tipped my head and it clunked against the glass.

"No worries." He completed one last leg stretch before sitting upright and reaching down to move my bag back to its original resting place.

The captain's Irish lilt permeated the plane over the loudspeaker. "Attention travelers. My name is Michael, and I am your captain. We have a six-hour flight ahead of us and will arrive in Shannon around six a.m. Irish time. The weather forecast is chilly with rain. Sit back, relax, and enjoy the ride. Your adventure awaits."

The airplane tiptoed toward the runway, then shot like an arrow. I clutched my book and held it to my chest. My eyes fixated on the steady and blinking lights that illuminated the runway until the plane lifted and the lights turned to distant glitter.

I turned toward my new neighbor in the middle seat to share my excitement, but his eyes were closed, and his headphones were on, so I pulled out a notebook and listed all the places I wanted to see.

I couldn't wait to see the new person I would become at the end of my Irish fall.

Chapter 2

M y butt hurt, and my knees ached. I needed to get up, but the guy in the middle was sleeping. He had stopped snoring about an hour ago, but his eyes remained shut. The guy next to him was almost done with his book, the stretched spine dying for closure. I didn't want to disrupt either one of them, so I shifted my weight and leaned toward the window, noticing the faint wispy clouds obscuring my view from the night sky.

I spied the flight attendant at the head of the plane, preparing the food carts. It was ten p.m., Boston time, and I was starving. When she finally approached and placed our trays in front of us, the guy in the middle removed his headphones and stretched. His right arm shot out in front of me and hit my tray on the way down. My full cup tipped against his outstretched hand, and cola poured off the tray and down my leg.

"Feck!" He placed the napkins from his tray on the puddle of brown bubbles.

"Uh," I grumbled. My wet leg turned sticky, and with each move, a Velcro-sound ripped through the cabin. Too close, his tray obstructed my arm from cleaning the mess, so I sat there and did nothing. "It's okay," I said. "I wasn't hungry, anyway."

My chicken swam in soda, but the flight attendants were already two-thirds of the way back. "Oh no! My book." My pitch dropped in sadness as soda trickled from the pages of my guidebook onto my lap.

He handed me his napkins and I squeezed the book, watching the brown liquid saturate the square napkin from one corner to the other.

"Sorry," he mumbled.

"It's okay." I flipped through the book, and scowled at the swollen, stained pages. Yellow highlighter and black ink bled up and down the text. "It's just my guidebook. I can get another."

I didn't know why I was considering this guy's feelings when I was disappointed and starving. Had he been a gentleman, he would have given me his dinner, but instead he dove right in, elbowing me every time he tried to cut his food. It smelled delicious for airplane food, and my stomach rumbled. I leaned around the soppy tray and fumbled through my purse, removing the small bag of trail mix I had purchased at the airport store.

"Are you allergic to nuts?" I asked.

He shoved a potato wedge in his mouth and shook his head no. "Yer good."

Before I put the first peanut in my mouth, his tray was empty.

"You gonna eat that?" He pointed to my roll, protected by a wax bag from the soda. I raised my eyes to the ceiling and handed it to him. "Thanks."

Watching him rip open the bag, smear butter on the inside, and shove it in his mouth, I squinted my eyes and scrunched my nose. *This guy is an animal, like he hasn't eaten in days.* Crumbs rested along the small hairs growing out of his lower face and I rubbed my chin to alert him to the crumbly food.

"Whatcha doing in Ireland?" he asked, wiping his chin.

"Excuse me?"

"You're American, right? Whatcha gonna do over here?"

I straightened my back and held up the book. "Study abroad."

"Figured so much. A pretty girl like you, traveling alone, with a travel guide." He shifted his torso, and faced me.

I felt my chest tighten, unsure how much information I should give this guy. He didn't appear threatening, but he was right. I was traveling alone.

"What about you?" I changed the subject.

He stretched his arms in front of him. "Heading home."

"Were you visiting family?" I asked.

"Nah, visiting America."

I looked out the window and noticed a brightening along the horizon. "Two more hours," I said under my breath.

The flight attendants strolled up the aisle and removed all the trays. "Sorry," I said, motioning to the brown lake on my tray. I picked it up and handed it to her, careful not to let a drop spill on my two airplane friends.

Her eyes widened. "Oh, would you like another meal?"

I shook my head. "No, thank you."

"Would you like a clean seat? We have a few empty seats throughout the aircraft."

I wanted to get away from this guy, but we were closer to landing than take-off, and I didn't want to leave my luggage unsupervised. "That's okay. Thank you."

As she walked away, the guy beside me elbowed me in the ribs.

"Ouch." Rubbing my side, I narrowed my eyes.

"Why'd you say no to the food?"

"Because I have nowhere to put it. My tray is still swimming. Hopefully she'll come back with a pile of napkins."

"You could have used my tray. She offered you free food. You should always take free food. I would've eaten it if you didn't want it." He leaned back and pulled his headphones over his ears.

I shook my head in disbelief. *Who does this guy think he is?* Focusing my attention on the sky, I ignored his lame head bopping to whatever music he was playing. As his shoulders shook to the beat, his arms brushed against mine and I couldn't help but notice the goosepimples that rose from my skin.

Over the next hour, I watched the sky transition from pewter to tangerine and strawberry. It was only eleven p.m., Boston time, but four in the morning in Ireland. The ocean water flowed below us, and the blue waves eventually transitioned to round green hills.

My heart thumped in my chest, and excitement brewed up from my toes. *I am in Ireland!* I pinched my arm and embraced the pain. *Yep, I'm definitely here.*

The guy beside me leaned over to see the landscape out the tiny window, obscuring my view. The scent of his soap caused me to shiver. Squeezing against the seat to give him more room, I pursed my lips, and waited for him to return to his seat. *This guy is so rude.* His knee pushed against mine, and I did everything I could to slink away from him.

"Ah-hem," I roared into his ear. He turned toward me, and his light brown eyes remained inches from mine. The deep amber color glistened under the muted light, and my stomach fluttered when laughter flashed from his eyes to mine. I fought the urge to smile. "Do you mind?"

"Almost home." He grinned like he had a secret he was dying to share, and leaned back in his seat.

"Thanks, a little space would be nice." I flapped my arms like a chicken, demonstrating my personal bubble.

His left freckled arm flapped in response. "Sorry about that. Airplanes are tight."

The butterflies inside took flight, and I questioned if they were due to anticipation or attraction. *This guy might have been cute if he wasn't so damn annoying.*

Chapter 3

A crowd of strangers swept me along the concourse. It seemed they knew where they were going, so I fell into the current they controlled, and it led me straight to customs. Watching the guy with the red hair march past me to the green channel, I envied the speed his line moved. I debated following him, but most of my flight remained at the red channel, and I needed to stick with my fellow Americans.

Shannon Airport looked like any other airport, except for signs in English and Gaelic. Looking out the floor-to-ceiling windows, you would think you were in Chicago, Boston, or Baltimore. There were no signs of Irish life except for the traditional music blasting through the overhead speakers.

I snaked through the immigration line with other foreigners, where we pushed through the turnstiles like cattle. My hand shook as I gave my passport to the attendant.

"What're you doing here?" A short man with thin, straight hair asked.

"College for a semester." My voice shook, fearful that he'd find a reason to send me back to America.

"When are you going home?"

"Um, right before Christmas."

He took my luggage and rummaged through it before handing it back to me.

"Welcome to Ireland, Rory Stanley."

I followed the crowd to baggage claim and spied the same red, spiky hair that ruined my flight mingling with an older couple next to the conveyor belt. As I stood behind him, watching, I thought about his life in Ireland. *Does he live nearby? Does he have any siblings?* I imagined his duplex outside the city center. I envisioned him rolling into the city on a skateboard, traipsing to the fish and chips shop or the local pub.

He appeared happy to see the couple, who I assumed were his parents. His dad hugged his shoulders, and his animated mom talked with her hands. She passed him a water bottle, and I saw his mouth sequence "thanks." Seeing them made me wonder how my parents would behave when I came home from Ireland. *Would they even be at the airport to pick me up, or would they tell me to catch a cab?*

I scanned the red-haired family and realized my parents would never come to an airport looking like them. The mom's baggy jeans, circa 1990, and ill-fitting jacket practically hid her black pocketbook, which she wore underneath her coat. The dad wore dirty jeans and had a scruffy gray and orange beard overdue for a shave, just like his son. They looked tired, but joy spread through their facial expressions and excessive hugs.

People disappeared with their luggage, and I focused on the conveyor belt. My bag may have rotated around already, but the red-haired family kept popping into my view and distracting me from what was happening around us.

Once they exited the main doors, my attention zoned in on my one suitcase. I had stuffed my duffle like a sausage, making sure to pack an extra bag for all my souvenirs. It strolled down the conveyor belt as the group of bystanders dispersed with their luggage.

I grabbed my bag, hoisted it off the belt, and wandered outside to the bus terminal. I breathed in the crisp air and held my breath until my chest ached. Dampness permeated my face, but it wasn't raining. In the distance, varying shades of green created a patchwork design against the small hills.

I pulled out my travel book and looked at the address and bus route I had scribbled on the inside front cover. Not knowing if I was in the right place, my chest tightened and my lungs constricted. Breathing deeply and searching for the bus signs, I reminded myself that I needed to be brave and fearless.

I had seen the apartment in pictures but didn't know if I had made the right choice. According to the website, we'd be living with people from our same country. I hadn't received confirmation of my roommates and prayed we'd get along. Looking at the people waiting for the bus, I fantasized about which one could be my roommate.

We loaded the coach bus and I chose a seat halfway back. Based on my ticket, I should arrive in approximately two hours. As I got comfortable against the seat of the bus, a flash of red dashed past me. I turned and saw the same crooked teeth, crinkly eyes, and spiky hair that had soaked my pants and denied me dinner just a few hours earlier.

Weird. Maybe those weren't his parents. He sat diagonally behind me, and I caught his amber eyes and smiled. He ignored me and put on his headphones, facing the dusty window.

I second-guessed myself and questioned my vision. *Maybe it's not him. Maybe I'm exhausted and seeing things.* I turned away and watched the rolling hills sprint by my window as we made our way through the country towns to the biggest city on the Atlantic coast. Chatter filled the bus as I sat in solitude, absorbing the accent and vocabulary.

Craic. Feck. Grand. Bollocks. Eejit. Feeling like an imposter while eavesdropping on the surrounding conversations, I leaned into my guidebook. After flipping from front to back to front again, I leaned back in my seat and let the lullaby of their syllables relax me. The allure to recreate myself and fit in with the locals was strong, and I wanted to use their words like they were my own.

The bus made multiple stops along the way, and my sweaty hands gripped my pocketbook as I checked the time against my ticket and against the bus station sign out my window. We were finally here.

I busied myself with my pocketbook and travel book, ensuring I had everything—w*allet, passport, travel guide. Check, check, check.* The red-haired guy slid past me with his backpack slung over his shoulder, and it fell to his elbow, smacking me in the face.

"Ow!"

Oblivious to his body in space and distracted by the music in his ears, he continued down the aisle and off the bus.

Annoyed, I rubbed my arm and waited for everyone else to depart before venturing below to grab my suitcase. By the time I got outside, the red-haired guy was gone.

Galway City bustled with people, and most appeared around my age. I scanned the street for taxis and walked down the block, quickening my pace to grab a car before it was gone.

I climbed into the taxi and pulled out my book. Hesitating, I silently reread the name of my apartment building, unsure how to pronounce it. "Beal-tane, please. Apartment 102." I didn't know if I made sense or if I just produced gibberish.

He held his hand back. "Can I see that address?"

I handed him my tourism book and prayed he wouldn't accidentally rip the wet pages.

"Ah, yes. Be-al-tin. Yes, May first. The Festival of Fire."

Unsure what he was saying, I reached between the two front seats, pointing at the address. "Um, this is where I'm going. I'm not going to a festival, I'm going to an apartment."

He handed me back my book and whipped out of the taxi terminal, zooming down the narrow but busy street.

"First time, aye?"

I wasn't sure if I should answer him truthfully. "Um, yes," I mumbled, looking out the window. A large park filled with people walking, playing games, and laying in the sunshine flew by my right side. "What's that?"

"Eyre Square. Brilliant day to be outside."

"I'll have to go there."

"Did'ja know Bealtaine is an apartment building named after the Festival of Fire? Too bad you weren't here on May 1st. It marked the first day of summer here in Ireland. You also missed the Celtic Harvest festival. The next big festival is the Lisdoonvarna Matchmaking Festival in September. Are you single?"

I spun my head to the midline of his car. "No, I have a boyfriend." I played with the ring around my finger, recalling the last time I saw Scott. He hadn't seemed too concerned that I would be gone for almost half a year. He kissed me good-bye, gave me this ring, and then told me he had to get to his soccer game, as if he were telling me he had to go to the grocery store and I would see him in a few hours, not a few months. Snapping out of my memory, I asked, "Why?"

The taxi driver shrugged. "It's a fun festival if you're single. Lots of pretty men and women. There's even a matchmaker to set you up with someone."

Before I could respond with some snarky comment about being taken, the car halted. "Here you go. The front office of Bealtaine." He enunciated each syllable of the Gaelic word, and my inner voice repeated it for future reference.

I paid the man with the euro bills I had ordered from my bank in

Boston and retrieved my bag. Unsure of how much to tip, I paid him double, silently scolding myself for not being more prepared.

A pub and a convenience store flanked the sides of the three-story apartment building that I would call home. A handful of college kids moved about the street, carrying boxes and bags, and I couldn't help but wonder if any of them were my roommates.

Suddenly hot, I fanned myself and giggled nervously. My parched mouth made it difficult to swallow. "Come on, Rory, you got this," I whispered, facing the main door. *Welcome to your new life. Welcome home.*

The receptionist in the main office checked me in and gave me a key. Standing outside my apartment, I double-checked my new address. *Yep, this was the place.* I crammed the key into the lock and shoved the door with my hip. It swung open to a long, brightly lit hallway lined with doors. As I dragged my suitcase down the hallway, incoherent noise turned into giddiness and laughter.

Following the sound into the open living room-kitchen combo, I saw two women about my age rummaging around the cabinets and drawers.

My bag rested against the kitchen island separating the two rooms. "Hi," I said. "My name's Rory." I held out my hand and approached the two women.

A tall woman with defined cheekbones and shiny brown hair grasped my hand and shook firmly. "Zoey. From Wisconsin."

She wore a long flowy skirt of earth browns and greens and a beige tank top. The wooden beads on one bracelet jangled against another bangle on her wrist, and she twirled her silver ring.

"Nice to meet you. I love your bracelet," I complimented, flashing her a polite smile.

A petite woman with curly black hair stepped forward. "And I'm Marissa." Purple and blue highlights sparkled against her dark hair from the natural light coming through the sliding glass door. She wore cat-eye glasses, a nose ring, and I could see the tip of at least one tattoo curling around her collarbone. "I'm from LA."

"Rory, from Boston," I reintroduced myself. "Have you guys been here long?"

"Not long." Marissa looked at Zoey. "Maybe an hour? We were on different flights but arrived at the same time. We realized we were roommates when we simultaneously checked in at the main office."

Zoey scanned the empty mini-refrigerator and settled for a glass of water. "Is it cool if we share a room?" she asked, pointing to herself and Marissa. "We thought it would be easier since we got here first." Zoey leaned across the island, her hip bones resting just under the lip of the counter.

My head perked up. "Does that mean I get my own room?" It sounded too good to be true.

"No, there're two bedrooms, both with two single beds. My welcome packet says a fourth will be here. Jaime, I think it was." Zoey handed me the welcome packet in the navy-blue folder that sat on the table near the phone.

I quickly scanned it and saw Jaime O'Sullivan's name listed with ours. *Jaime O'Sullivan. She sounds Irish.* "Sure, that's fine with me. Where's our room?" I followed Marissa out of the kitchen and down the hall to the first room on the right.

She opened the door to a rectangular room like any other dorm I'd lived in, and I hoped it was big enough for Jaime and I. "This is it," she said. Two single beds, two wardrobes, and two desks decorated the perimeter.

"Sweet! Our own bathroom?" I opened the door next to the desks and browsed through the tiny space. The shower was barely wide enough to fit one person, but I guessed it would do the job. Turning toward Marissa, a wide grin pressed against my cheeks.

"Yeah, so since you're first, pick a side, and Jaime will have to deal with what's left. Early bird gets the worm."

Marissa left me in my room, and I unpacked my suitcase, finding a spot for all my belongings.

That afternoon, we explored the surrounding neighborhood and shopped at the convenience store for dinner. The frozen pizza we bought didn't fit in our freezer, so we cooked it as soon as we got home. After shoving a six-pack of Guinness into the empty fridge, a quarter of our fridge space was gone.

"Shopping's gonna be tough," Marissa said, pointing to the nearly full fridge.

"Tomorrow, we should go to the grocery store. And we need to figure out how we're doing food. Are we buying our own or splitting the cost and sharing? There's not enough space to do a big grocery run, so I think we need to game plan when Jaime gets here," I said, ticking off the list I had made earlier. "I wonder what she's like."

I paused and looked at my new flatmates, realizing that I was taking over the planning. Being an only child, most of my childhood was spent in extracurricular activities, where my leadership skills developed. Overextending myself had carried on into college when I immediately jumped into every activity I could fit into my schedule. Meeting people turned to managing people, as I tried to make sure everything ran perfectly. I didn't want to be like that here, but I didn't know how to be any other way.

"What time do you think Jaime will get here?" Zoey asked, seeming unbothered by my list of questions and suggestions. I let out a small sigh of relief as she adjusted her tank top and opened a can of stout.

I shrugged. "Maybe she isn't coming. Maybe she backed out at the last minute." It was evening now, but not dark yet. "Or maybe she's coming tomorrow."

"Do you want to go out tonight?" Marissa asked. "My friend studied here last semester and said there is a fun club downtown. You'll like it if you're into electronica and dance music."

Zoey and I said nothing at first.

I mentally ran through my list of wanted experiences. Clubbing wasn't one of them, but living like a local was, so if that was where the locals were, I would be there too. "Sure, that sounds great. I've never been to a club," I said. "I'm only nineteen."

"And I've never been clubbing or to a bar...legally, that is. I have a fake ID, but every time I go, I'm hiding in the corner waiting for the bouncer to kick me out," Zoey said. "I don't have clubbing clothes. What do you even wear?"

She didn't look like the fake ID type, but reminded me of someone who listened to Phish or the Grateful Dead, hanging with a small group of friends in someone's apartment until the wee hours of morning.

"I got you. I got you both," Marissa said. "Zoey, come with me. I'm sure you have something that'll work."

The two women entered their shared room and left me in the kitchen. I cleaned the dishes, threw the trash away, straightened the counter, and checked the mini-fridge again. I visualized a half gallon of milk and three apples nestled next to the beer, with no room for anything else.

Scribbling on a piece of paper, I listed everything we needed to make our kitchen functional: *paper towels, dish soap, and trash bags*. Then I dug through my neatly folded clothes and picked out my tightest jeans and Abercrombie and Fitch t-shirt. After brushing my hair and applying a fresh coat of lipstick and mascara, I hollered to my roommates. "You guys ready? Let's live it up, Galway-style!"

Chapter 4

Zoey, Marissa, and I didn't know how to get to the city center. I pulled out my Galway map and spread it on the counter. "Here we are." I pointed to a circle I had drawn on the bus ride earlier that day. "And here's Shop Street, High Street, and Quay Street." I highlighted a direct route to the Latin Quarter.

"I don't know," Zoey said. "Maybe we should ask someone before we get lost or end up in a sketchy neighborhood."

"I don't want to stick out like a sore thumb, like a tourist who needs a map to get around," Marissa added. Both girls giggled and I folded up my map, wounded by their attack on my organizational skills.

"Fine, no map. But how will we find out where we're going?" I asked.

Marissa took my map, shoved it into my guide book and left it in my room. "We ask," she said, closing my door.

"Ask who? We barely know our own address, let alone any Irish people."

Marissa grabbed her purse and threw it over her shoulder. "We live in an apartment building filled with Irish students who know their way around. Let's go introduce ourselves."

Zoey hurried after her toward the door, and I stood, unsure of the plan. It felt more obtrusive to announce to strangers that we didn't know where we were, as opposed to looking at a map and creating a plan to prevent getting lost.

"You coming?" Zoey called through the front door.

I huffed, threw on a smile, and followed them down the hall.

We heard conversation flowing under the door to one of our neighboring apartments, and Marissa grinned. "Sounds Irish in there." She knocked and waited with a tall posture and confident smile. I shrank back a bit, in case our arrival wasn't welcome. Zoey stood between us, looking around Marissa's shoulder when the door opened.

Marissa stepped forward. "Hi, my name is Marissa, and this is Zoey, and this is Rory. We live down the hall."

"Sinead," a woman around our age said. "Want to come in?"

We followed her down the narrow hallway and saw two men and a woman hanging out on the couch and loveseat. They made eye contact, but continued with their private conversation. Their apartment was a replica of ours.

"Ronan, Owen, and Bridget," Sinead said, pointing to the others.

They turned and we waved, our bodies remaining stiff, unsure of whether we should make ourselves at home or just get the directions and go.

"Crazy question, but can you tell us how to get to the city center from here? We're walking," I said. "It's our first day." I dropped my eyes and felt a blush travel up my cheeks.

Sinead gave me a reassuring smile. "Of course."

They guided us to the main strip of pubs, restaurants, and clubs, and I jotted down keywords in my small notebook. We thanked them and strolled outside into the warm setting sun, embracing the cool Irish air.

"That wasn't too bad," Zoey said.

"Not at all. Maybe we'll see them again." Marissa led the way and my feet throbbed as we walked downhill into town. When we passed the cathedral, I made a mental note to never wear these shoes again.

The lights and music from Shop Street filtered up to us as we made our way along the river. A smattering of people roamed along the cobblestone street, and I fell into step with them. Irish mixed with American accents and live music from all the venues collected in the center of the pedestrian road, reminding me I wasn't in Boston anymore. The beautiful cacophony enhanced my mood, and I weaved my way into the pub Sinead recommended.

We approached the bar and waited for the bartender to acknowledge us. I wasn't sure what the social rules were regarding pub life, but I knew the bartender needed to get us a drink. I clutched my bag, praying he wouldn't ask for my license.

"Three smith-wicks, please," I said to the round man. My heart beat against my chest, and my chilly fingers tingled. *Please don't ask for my license.*

"Smith-wicks? We don't serve that here," he said with an Irish drawl and a goofy grin.

My face dropped, and my eyebrows furrowed. "Oh, sorry. Guinness then."

"American?" he asked, grabbing a pint glass.

My shoulders relaxed. "Yeah, how do you know?"

"It's smiticks, my love." He put the pint glasses in front of us, and the dark stout settled.

I smiled in thanks, and handed him a few euro coins. I didn't know if we were drinking Smithwicks or Guinness, but I felt too jittery to ask, so I gulped down a third of the pint. The heavy bitterness awakened my taste buds and I shuddered.

"First time?" he asked.

Raising my glass, I said, "First time. Cheers." My two roommates raised their glasses and we clinked, just how Americans do.

We stood at the bar silently taking in the scene. College kids filtered in and out, and a group of older men played the fiddle, accordion, bodhran, and banjo. A handful of people clapped their hands to the beat of the drum and I kicked my shoes off under the table, tapping my toes against the cool, wooden floor.

Wholly immersed in pub life, we forgot about the club. Hours and pints later, exhausted and soaked in beer from careless dancers, we stumbled home.

The walk back took longer than the walk down. We followed the written notes from Sinead backward and pointed out random landmarks that kept us on the right path. Now and then, we rested on a stone wall to regain our bearings.

Despite my blistered feet, I felt great. Although my roommates seemed different from those I hung out with at home, we were all going to experience Ireland together. The anticipation of adventure wove around me like a giant spiderweb. It felt uncomfortable, but I busted free and embraced the habitat where all the local creatures lived.

We sang and danced up the hills until we stumbled to Bealtaine. I tripped up the steps to the second floor and burst out laughing. Zoey's arm broke my fall, and she loosely held me upright. The lights were off, just like we had left them.

Marissa flipped the switch, and the recessed lighting in the kitchen illuminated the apartment.

"Hey!" I whispered, pointing at the dirty dishes in the sink. "Look!"

"Ooh! Is it Jaime?" Zoey matched my volume.

Marissa tiptoed around the apartment and slowly opened my bedroom door. Zoey and I peeked over her shoulder, three heads creating a totem pole in the open space. Lying in the bed next to mine was Jaime. The moonlight streaked through the window and illuminated her red hair, partially covered by her duvet.

"Okay, guys, I'm going to bed. Thanks for a fun night." I leaned over and hugged them both. "I have a roommate." I pointed and closed the door behind me.

After shedding my clothes and brushing my teeth, I climbed into my cozy bed, falling asleep with a smile.

The following day, I woke up with a blazing headache, but that wasn't the only jolt to start my morning. Staring into the bed next to me, I blinked a few times, willing the image to change.

No, it can't be.

Chapter 5

It was him. The man from the plane sat on the bed, staring at a drawing pad on his lap. The spiky red hair, the smattering of freckles, and the creased eyes triggered a series of flashbacks that ran through my mind: the lack of spatial awareness, the soda down my leg, and the stolen dinner roll.

I pulled the covers over my head, my heart racing and the pit in my stomach digging into my pelvis like a concrete boulder. I dragged the duvet below my eyes and squinted, trying not to be obvious. *Am I dreaming? Ha! Maybe I'm having a nightmare.* The same red hair, now tousled from sleep, rested against the wall. I pushed the blanket down to my shoulders and said, "Hello, again."

He looked up from his drawing pad and tilted his head to the left, tapping his pencil against his scruffy chin. "I remember you. From the plane."

I tried to smile, but my lips refused to rise. I pushed my body against the back wall and pulled the sheet closer to my armpits. "What are you doing here, if you don't mind me asking?"

"I could ask you the same thing. I live here."

My eyes bulged and I scrambled to a seated position. "You can't live here. You're a guy. This is an apartment with women. Foreign exchange students. A bunch of Americans." I spoke slowly, as if that would make him understand.

Jaime chuckled and looked down again. "Yes, I am aware, but this is my apartment now. I forgot to renew my housing paperwork last semester, and they gave my room away. This was all that was left. They told me I was living with Rory, Zoey, and Marissa. I take it you're Rory?"

I nodded.

"I thought you were an Irish lad."

I swallowed loudly, the saliva crawling down the back of my throat. Reaching across my bed to my nightstand, I downed a bottle of water. Cloudiness from the alcohol still in my system slowed down my brain's processing ability, and I struggled to understand his words. "You can't live here," I said again.

"I wish I didn't. Living with a bunch of Americans during my last year of college is the last thing I want to do, but it's that or be homeless so I'll suck it up." He returned to his drawing and spoke to his paper. "Nice to meet you, Rory." His amber eyes looked over, scanning my top half. "Fun time last night?"

My brain beat against my forehead, and I massaged my temples. "Yeah. Sorry if I woke you."

"No worries. I spent the night with my old flatmates. They live downstairs, and I came up here to crash. I didn't even hear you come in."

I grabbed the hooded sweatshirt sitting at the end of my bed, and pulled it over my body. "Are you sure they said there was nowhere else? I mean, I don't know, Jaime. You're a guy, a stranger, really, and I have a boyfriend. I don't think he will be too excited when I tell him my roommate's an Irish guy."

His liquid gold eyes looked me up and down. "I asked to be moved

27

and they put me on a waiting list if some other American no-shows, but I want my old flat and my old flatmates. Unless they can squeeze me back in there, I'm staying here. So, there it is. An Irish bloke and an American lass living together. That'll make a good story for the grandkids. Promise, you won't even know I'm here."

That eased some pressure, and I exhaled. "I guess I'll have to deal with it. Promise me you aren't a serial killer?" My straight face communicated the gravity of my question.

"Promise," he said with a small smirk.

"I've never lived with a guy before. I think we need to establish rules if we're living together. Based upon the plane, I imagine you're a bit of a slob."

He flinched and rubbed the back of his neck.

"Sorry, I didn't mean that. I meant to say you're messy."

He tapped his pencil and pursed his lips.

"We're different, you and I. That's what I mean. I'm clean and organized."

He puffed out his chest. "And I'm not?"

I shrugged. "I don't know. You knocked over my soda without thinking, took over my entire plane seat, and asked to eat my dinner. I have a feeling you're a little more...what's the word I'm looking for?" I tapped my chin, trying to think of a positive adjective for annoying. "Carefree?"

He sharpened his tone. "I'll try not to upset the apple cart and keep my side tidy."

"And no girls sleeping over. I can't handle that. I don't care if you're a male or female. I would ask that of any roommate."

He glared at me.

"What? It's a respect thing. You can sleep at their place if you have to."

Jaime ticked my demands off on his fingers. "Be clean, be tidy, no sleepovers. Anything else?"

I shook my head. "Do you have anything for headaches?"

He motioned to the bathroom. "On the sink."

I looked under the sheet and saw my underwear. *Shoot. I thought I put on my pajamas last night.* "Hey, Jaime? Will you close your eyes? I have to get my clothes on. I don't think my boyfriend, Scott, would appreciate it if I walked around half naked in front of you."

Jaime rose from his bed and my eyes zoned in on his plaid boxers. Heat rushed to my face and I forced myself to look away.

"No problem. I'll give you your space." He walked past me and I couldn't help but watch him saunter away to retrieve the medicine.

My heart thudded, and my face flushed. I couldn't take my eyes off the elastic waistband that hung just below his hips. His thick thighs and broad chest reminded me of a soccer player. *I mean, football.* My inner voice yelled at me to think of my boyfriend.

I shook my head and focused on my kind, attractive, thoughtful boyfriend. Somehow, Scott's curly brown hair morphed to red. I bit my lip and giggled.

This is going to be a crazy four months.

Chapter 6

A fter getting dressed, I marched down to the main office and pleaded my case. He's male, and I'm female; he's Irish and I am American; he's in his final year, and I'm in my junior year. The office manager invalidated every argument. "We're sorry. There is nothing we can do. Jaime has paid for his room, but that doesn't mean the room stays the same." Jaime was right. He was stuck with us for the semester, and there was nothing he or I could do about it.

After returning from the main office, I knocked on Zoey's door.

"You ready?" I called.

It was my second day in Ireland, and Zoey and I wanted to time the walk to school. Classes were starting on Monday, and I needed to be prepared.

Halfway down the hill, our conversation led to Jaime, our mysterious roommate. I told Zoey about the awful plane ride and how glad I had been to get rid of him.

"Rory, he's Irish. Think of all the benefits," Zoey said. "He knows the country, the language, culture, and hot spots. We are living with our own personal tour guide. We are so lucky."

I pulled my hood over my head to protect my hair from the chilly sprinkles falling from the gray clouds. "Yeah, great," I grumbled. "Wanna trade rooms?"

"He's not that bad. He'll protect us if anything happens."

I turned toward her. "What? He barely even knows us. Why would he protect us?"

"Because that's what roommates do. It's like siblings. They always have your back."

"Not in my experience." I thought back to my freshman year. "My old roommate, Emma, had my back until she saw me using her textbook without asking. After that, it was like she was living with a monster. She said she could never trust me again, and every movement I made, she watched me like a hawk."

Zoey half-smiled. "Don't worry. You can look at my textbooks any time you want."

"I'm just saying." My hands gestured wildly in front of my face. "Don't make assumptions. He could be a serial killer."

"We know him just as much as we know each other. Do you trust me?"

I paused, contemplating her question. "Of course."

"Why? What makes me different?"

"First impressions. When we first met, you smiled. I first met him on the airplane, he dumped my soda all over me, and invaded my personal space for six hours. It was not the experience I imagined when I had dreamed about flying to Ireland." I stuffed my hands in my raincoat pockets and squeezed a balled-up tissue.

"Well, people change. Maybe he acted that way because he didn't think he'd see you again."

"Small world, huh?"

"Where's he now? I didn't see him this morning."

"Who knows? He told me he wouldn't be around much because his old roommates live in our building."

"That could be a bonus." Zoey stopped at the entrance to the college. "Time."

I looked at my watch and pulled out my notebook, scribbling a note of the time as I said, "It took us exactly twenty-four minutes in the rain, which probably slowed us down. If we give ourselves a half hour, we'll get to class with time to spare."

The beautiful campus sparkled with pink, purple, and blue flowers that popped happiness against the drab background. I took my rain boots and socks off and walked barefoot through the lush grass, dripping with water. The chilly drops sent electric shocks up my legs, and Zoey looked at me like I had gone crazy.

"What?" I asked. "Haven't you ever danced in the rain?"

She swung her bag to her other shoulder. "Not shoeless."

"Come on, Zoey," I teased. "It's Ireland. Feel that Irish grass. Feel the history seep up from the earth into you. It's electrifying. Become one with the country."

She sighed, looked around, and dropped her bag on a patch of dry concrete.

"No one cares, Zoey. No one is paying any attention to us." I saw her glance to her left and right, before returning her gaze to me.

"Fine." She slid out of her sopping wet flip-flops and stepped onto the cool ground.

Overcome with the moment, I ran and pranced down the long green. Occasional pirouettes, leaps, and spins speckled my choreography.

"Zoey, come dance with me!"

I heard her giggle, but I didn't stop. Spinning three times with my arms outstretched and my head tilted toward the sky, I caught a rainbow breaking through the gray clouds. "Zoey, look!" I yelled into the sky and my toes slipped on a patch of wet grass. I hadn't done a split since I was eight, yet somehow my body found its way back to that position.

"Oof!" I exhaled. The sound of ripped fabric brought me abruptly back to reality and I quickly touched my rear to assess the damage. My finger escaped through a hole about two inches long and my neck and ears became impossibly hot.

"Rory?" I heard a deep, familiar Irish voice. *Oh no.*

Opening my eyes, a head of red hair and slightly crooked front teeth interrupted my view of the rainbow. "Jaime."

He pulled me up, and a sharp pain traveled through the top of my foot to my shin bone. I pulled my sodden jacket off and wrapped it around my torso, making sure the length covered my exposed underwear.

"Ah." I held onto his arm and leaned into him while I grabbed my ankle, and said, "I think I messed up my foot."

He looked down. "Yep, purple and already swollen. Let's get you to Student Health."

Zoey ran over with my shoes and pushed past Jaime and the man standing behind him, who looked on with curiosity. "Rory," she cried. "Your foot! Are you okay?"

The pain throbbed when I held my lower leg frozen, and any movement caused a lightning bolt to strike my foot from the inside out. "Eh, been better. Maybe that wasn't such a great idea."

"Doncha worry. I'll take care of you," Jaime said. "This is Owen." I recognized the short, round guy from Sinead's apartment and waved.

"Hi, Owen." I winced as the pain shot through me like an arrow. "We met at Sinead's. I'm Rory. And this is Zoey. She was there too."

"You met?" Jaime looked between Owen and I, waiting for confirmation.

"Yeah, I was at Sinead's picking up my sister's coat. She left it there," Owen explained.

"These are my new roommates," Jaime said.

"I'm Zoey," Zoey interrupted. "Nice to meet you, Owen."

"Nice to meet you, too," Owen said. "Yeah, it's best you get that looked at."

I had no choice but to let Jaime and his friend carry me to the Student Health Unit, with Zoey trailing behind.

My ankle had swelled to the size of a water balloon, squishy and tender to the touch, and was twice the size of my other ankle. The nurse reassured me it was just a minor sprain and required rest, elevation, and ice. "You won't even miss a day," she promised, as I stumbled out of her small, dark office, unsure how to walk with crutches.

"How are we going to get home?" I asked Zoey.

"Maybe we can call a taxi?"

"Nah, I can get us a ride," Jaime interrupted. "Owen, can you drive us home?"

"Sure thing." Owen's wavy brown locks framed his heart-shaped face, and his oversized soccer jersey hung past his hips. He carried the same smattering of freckles as Jaime did, and a single dimple showed on his cheek when he smiled.

"Me and Owen play Gaelic football together," Jaime said, "So you might see a lot of him. I'm sure he'll be coming around, won't you, Owen?"

"I figured you played together." I pointed to their matching maroon jerseys that said Galway across the front. "When you say football, do you mean soccer?" I asked.

"It's a cross between soccer, American football, and rugby," Owen said.

"I like your jersey," Zoey said. "We'll have to watch a game sometime."

Zoey, Owen, and Jaime fell into conversation about European football, Gaelic football, and American football, while I hobbled behind.

I followed them to a tiny Peugeot coupe, trying to catch my breath from the one-legged hike through the parking lot.

"We're getting in that?" Zoey asked. Her voice punctuated the final word, and her eyes widened. "I don't think we'll fit."

"It'll be grand," Owen said.

Jaime pushed the car's front passenger seat forward, and the headrest kissed the dusty dashboard. He motioned to the tiny space between the seat and the door frame for me to climb through. "After you."

"Gee, Jaime," I said, glaring at him, "It would be nice if I could sit in the front."

"Your leg won't fit straight out like that," he said matter-of-factly. "If you sit in the front, your leg will hang out the window."

My shoulders slumped forward, and I leaned through the tiny space into the compact car's backseat. I glanced at the space in the front, and knew if I forced myself into that cramped area, my leg would be out the window for all of Galway to see. I rolled my eyes at him and shimmied my way into the backseat and rested my crutches across my torso like a seatbelt.

Zoey climbed in beside me and squeezed under the crutches. "I feel like we're at Six Flags," she giggled. "Ready for a ride?"

My outstretched leg rested across the middle console and leaned against Jaime's shoulder. I tapped Owen from behind. "Thanks for the ride. Please go slow. I don't know if I can handle the bumps."

Owen turned in his seat and grinned. "No worries." He shifted into first gear, and his elbow crashed into the heel of my foot.

"Ow." I scowled and tried to pull my leg back, but there was no extra space.

"Sorry, but I have to change gears."

My body jerked back as he transitioned into second. We lurched to the left and then the right as he peeled out of the parking lot and onto the main road. My foot throbbed with each curve, and I pulled my eyes shut, making a pained 'o' with my lips.

The two men continued to discuss football, something I didn't know anything about, so I zoned out, praying we'd be home soon. This was not how I planned on starting my trip, and my spirits fell at my lack of control.

Owen tore into the parking lot of our apartment complex, and Jaime climbed out before pushing the front seat forward. Zoey took my crutches, and I fumbled to redistribute my weight. The coupe was so low to the ground that I nearly fell out, carefully grabbing onto Zoey's outstretched arms.

Jaime and Owen followed us up the staircase, even though I moved like a senior citizen. Zoey let us into the apartment, and I fell onto the couch, utterly exhausted. My thigh muscles burned, my armpits ached, and my head throbbed from the day's stress. *I can't believe this is happening.*

The doctor recommended I stay off my foot for up to a week. She told me minor sprains could take up to six weeks to heal, and my heart sank. Classes started Monday, and six weeks was practically half my trip. Crushed by my bad luck, I watched my guidebook and calendar go up in smoke.

Jaime and Owen stood in the kitchen while Zoey got me settled on the couch with pillows under my foot.

"Hey, Jaime? Can you get me some ice?" I called.

A bag of frozen peas hit me on the shoulder.

"Ow," I said, shooting lasers from my eyes.

"It's all we have." He and Owen walked down the hall before I could request a cup of water. I frowned at Zoey and thanked her for helping. She handed me a glass of water and a snack, and placed the television remote and my stained guidebook next to my hip before retreating to her room.

Alone on our couch, I wondered if my semester was over before it had even started.

* * *

For the next seven days, I only traveled from my bed to the couch to the bathroom. I emailed my professors, explaining my circumstances, and completed the coursework at home. Zoey and Marissa went grocery shopping, window shopping around Eyre Square, and to the coast of Salthill to watch the sun set without me. Disappointment and loneliness hovered around me every time they ticked off an item on my wishlist.

Jaime constantly popped in and out of the apartment, bringing friends in or disappearing most of the day for practice. Half the time he didn't come home at night, and I couldn't help but wonder if he had a girlfriend on the side.

"Jaime?" I called when the front door closed. "Are you there?" Facing the picture window opposite the door, I couldn't turn without twisting my back.

"Yes, your highness."

"Can you get me a blanket?"

He dropped the lightweight blanket that normally lay across my bed onto my knees. "Anything else?" The words were kind but sarcastic.

I smiled and shook my head. "Thanks."

I was out of commission and unable to assert my presence, so when I went into the kitchen and saw a sink full of dishes, I flinched but bit my tongue. When I entered our bedroom, my crutch slid on a pile of dirty clothes scattered on the floor like breadcrumbs, and I screamed in frustration. Not only was I losing control of my semester, but I was feeling out of control in my house.

I stayed on the couch as long as possible. If I didn't see the mess, I couldn't get upset; if I saw it, I couldn't do anything about it.

On exactly day seven, I stepped on my foot and slowly increased the pressure. *No pain, no pain, ow.* Consistent discomfort led to muted sparks zapping through my lower leg as I increased the weight on my foot. I thought about all the times I had felt uncomfortable—poison ivy on my hands when I went to summer camp, tweaking my back when babysitting, and having cavities filled.

Mind over matter, Rory. I survived then, and I'll survive now. I willed myself to feel better, but remained cautious. I wasn't going to be stupid, but I wasn't going to let my sore ankle keep me down any longer. *Ireland, ready or not, here I come!*

Chapter 7

Walking to school every day was beginning to bother me less and less, but I still collapsed on my bed when I got home each evening, resting my foot on three stacked pillows. Ten days after my embarrassing accident, my health battery hovered between eighty-five and ninety percent, and I was almost back to normal.

My increased mobility allowed me to snoop on Jaime's side of the room. His navy duvet remained crumpled in a ball at the far corner of his bed. Potato chip crumbs decorated his wrinkled sheets and the empty Tayto bag lay on his pillow. His desk disappeared underneath piles of books, notebooks, and garbage, all of it spilling onto the floor like an island of junk. The garbage led to a pile of dirty clothes wedged between his desk and the bathroom door.

I focused on my side and reminded myself that I was in his country and on his turf. If I wanted to remain on good terms with my Irish expert, I needed to let it go. Focusing on the invisible line running through our room, I blocked out his mess by tidying mine.

My computer sat on my desk with books and notebooks standing behind it. My pink and purple tie-dyed mouse pad was the only color emanating from the sterile office items. It was exactly how I liked it. I meant business but occasionally had fun.

On top of my books, sat a brand new Irish guidebook that Jaime had sheepishly handed to me the night before. My original, swollen copy stood by itself against the wall. A small sticky sat on my computer. **Rory, sorry I made a mess on the plane. I hope this book is just as good. Jaime**. I picked up the book and flipped through, smelling the perfect, crisp pages. Grabbing my yellow highlighter, I marked up all the places I wanted to go.

Glancing at the calendar hanging beside my bed, I viewed the rainbow that organized my future. I had filled in all my weekends according to the itinerary I had created from my original guidebook. Reviewing my progress, I saw that last weekend I should have explored Galway, but of course that hadn't happened. This weekend, I had written **Connemara**, and wondered if one of my roommates would come with me, just in case my ankle gave out.

Slinking out of my room, I hobbled down the hallway and knocked on Zoey and Marissa's door.

"Come in," I heard.

Marissa sat at her desk browsing a magazine. "I need new clothes," she said. "Do you remember seeing that strip of stores on the way to school? I wonder what they have."

"I'm not sure. We can ask Jaime."

She closed her laptop and looked at me. "What's up?"

"Are you doing anything this weekend? I wanted to go to Connemara and was wondering if you'd like to come."

"Connemara? How are you getting there?"

"I think there's a day trip on a bus tour outside of Eyre Square. We'd have to get tickets. It's less than thirty bucks for the day."

"Sure. That sounds fun."

A smile spread across my face at the prospect of having a travel buddy. "Do you think Zoey would want to come?"

"Yeah, maybe. She has class until two today."

I opened my new guidebook to Connemara and found Kylemore Abbey, the granite Victorian castle built in the 1860s. I imagined the majesty that walked through the rooms of the vast stone walls set against the regal, lush Connemara mountains.

"I'll ask her." I clapped my hands and jumped on my toes. "Marissa! It doesn't hurt anymore!" I exaggerated my movements, dancing around her room. *My sprained ankle wouldn't hold me back after all.*

I pranced into my bedroom and emailed my mom and dad, updating them on my foot, my first week of classes, and my first solidified plans to see Ireland. Even though my parents weren't together anymore, I knew better than to communicate with one of them more than the other. My mother kept tabs and often threw my choices at me, making me feel responsible for her unhappiness, while my father remained emotionless. I knew if I didn't try to maintain a relationship with my father, he'd never seek me out, so I wrote to them together to keep them both involved.

I had only heard from Scott once in the two weeks since I had arrived, and it was to ask me where I'd put his dining hall ID. I had written him an email every other day, pretending that it wasn't strange I was having a one-way correspondence with my boyfriend. I told myself he was busy, just like I was, and I needed to be patient. At the end of every email, I reminded him I missed him and hoped to hear from him soon. "I love you, Rory," I typed, before hitting send. *Maybe he'll write back this time.*

I closed the laptop and looked at the picture of us taped to the side of my wardrobe. Scott and I had gone away to the beaches of Maine this past summer and stayed at a cottage on the beach, watching the sun rise and set every day. On our last night there, the sunset was brilliant pink, he turned the camera around and attempted to take three pictures of us. The 35mm clicked, and the flash burned my eyes.

When I got the photos back, I had flipped through them, admiring our beautiful weekend away. Two of the three pictures contained half of our heads, but this one hanging in my room was perfect. My sun-kissed skin was darker than it was now, and my black hair shined. His tall, dark frame held me close, and my body pressed against him. We looked happy and in love, and I needed to remember us that way.

Later that afternoon, Zoey came home from class, dripping water all over the tile floors. "It's a little wet out there!" She tore off her raincoat and hung it over our back balcony.

"Zoey, it won't dry outside," I said. The almost black clouds threatened thunder.

She raced into her bedroom, taking long strides to limit the number and size of the puddles left in her wake. "I'm not leaving the house until tomorrow. It's fine." She returned in sweatpants and a dry t-shirt. "So much better."

Her mascara ran, creating black rivers from the base of her eyes to the corners of her mouth. Her sopping hair hung against the collar of her shirt, and a wet, upside-down-rainbow formed between her shoulder blades. She took a dishtowel and placed it over her shoulders and under her hair before sitting on the couch.

"Zoey, are you doing anything on Saturday? Marissa and I are going to Connemara. Do you want to come?"

She squeezed out her hair into the corner of the towel. Her eyebrows scrunched up, and she wiped her forehead with her bare arm. "Yeah, count me in. I'm a terrible planner. Just so you know, I'll do anything, especially if I don't have to plan or research it. It'll be a disaster if you ask me to organize something."

I sat next to her, holding my book and handed her a wet napkin. "Your eyes."

She wiped her cheekbones and looked at her fingers before cleaning her face. "Thanks."

"You're in luck because I'm the best planner there is. Any potential problem or scenario I've already thought of and solved. Marissa's coming too. It'll be our first girls' outing!" I pulled my guidebook and flipped to the already tagged page for Connemara. "This is what I'm thinking."

I reviewed the bus itinerary and showed them the pictures from my book. I couldn't stop talking about Ireland and everything I wanted to experience. The beauty and mystique had taken over my heart, and I almost wondered if I would bleed green when I went home to America.

"Is there anything specific you want to do here?" I asked, noticing her noncommittal remarks during our conversation.

"Not really. I came to Ireland for the experience. The music, the pubs, and the people. Visiting specific landmarks was never really my thing, but I'll do it. It'll be fun."

"What'll be fun?" A deep voice with an Irish brogue broke up our conversation.

Jaime's jeans dripped water from his waistband to his ankles, and the front of his pants were three shades darker than the back. His t-shirt pushed against his damp skin, and I could see the ripples of his abdominal and pectoral muscles peeking through like tiny mountains and rivers. My heart thudded, and I bit my lip to keep from smiling.

"We're planning a trip," Zoey said.

"Oh yeah? To where?" he asked.

"Connemara. Saturday. Want to come?"

He removed his shirt and wrung it out in the kitchen sink. His pale skin glistened.

I noticed no freckles across his broad shoulders and had to blink three times to reset my head. *He's filthy and lazy and totally not your type.*

43

"Connemara? Yeah, I'll come. I haven't been in a while."

Heat traveled through my core and settled in my hips. "Perfect." I waved my brand new guidebook in front of us. "And thank you."

"Eh, I owed you one."

Chapter 8

The bus to Connemara was filled with people from all countries. The combination of accents floated above our heads before escaping out the open windows as everyone got settled. I sat beside Jaime, but I didn't mind. I wanted to hear all his stories about his experiences growing up in Ireland.

The tour guide, Declan, stood at the front of the bus and pulled a microphone close to his lips. He was about as old as my father and spoke with a heavy accent. I struggled to understand him but laughed when everyone else laughed. I threw a glance at Zoey across the aisle and we both grinned.

He continued chatting about Galway City, County Galway, and the Wild Atlantic Way as the bus weaved through the narrow city streets. I looked past Jaime's shoulder and leaned against him, just like he did to me on the plane. He stuck his hand in a potato chip bag, and I reached over and stole a chip. He pulled the bag closer and eyed me.

"What?" I asked. "You don't like it when people eat your food?" I turned the corners of my mouth up slightly.

"Ha. Ha." He returned to the window and ignored my body near his.

"So, dear roomie, what do I need to know about Connemara?"

He leaned against the window and looked at me. "Well, for one thing, they speak Gaelic." He held up one finger and then two. "There's a Benedictine abbey built in the 1860s and a national park surrounded by the Atlantic Ocean on three sides." His two fingers transformed into three. "And, if you need to chat with a local, ask him about The Quiet Man. It was an American movie filmed in the 1950s and still a topic of pride today."

I raised my eyebrows, surprised by his knowledge. "Very impressive. How do you know all this?"

"It's where I grew up."

I leaned away from him. He hadn't ever opened up about his past before, and whenever I questioned him about himself, he answered with vague one-word answers. "No way!" I exclaimed. "You really are our personal tour guide for today."

He tilted his head forward and tipped his invisible hat. "At your service."

"Where in Connemara are you from?"

"Clifden. Ever hear of it?"

My mouth dropped open. "Have I heard of it? Have I—heard of it?" I felt myself become more animated at the mere mention of Clifden. I grabbed my guidebook and found the yellow tab halfway through the book. "Yes. Clifden is the first town listed under the Connemara section, and it's on my list of things to see."

"Are we seeing it today?" he asked.

"I think driving through it. I couldn't find a tour that stopped there."

He chuckled. "Feck. I hoped to hop off and stay the night."

My eyes bulged. "Really?"

He half-shrugged. "It was a thought."

We rode in silence, and the scenery transitioned from flat, rural roads to rolling hills of green, brown, and gray. The fog disguised the mountaintops, and the muted colors blended together as they sped past.

The bus pulled to the side of the road overlooking a small pond. "Snacks, sweets, and drinks," Declan said, pointing to a small country store on our left. "Take a fiver and stretch ye legs."

We climbed off the bus and stood on the side of the road overlooking the pond. The mountains reflected in the water, and I pulled my camera out. "It's beautiful," I said, gazing ahead.

It had just started to sprinkle and I shivered under the dismal sky. Marissa scanned the horizon. "You almost can't see where the trees end and the reflection begin."

We stood frozen in awe at the beauty surrounding us. I smiled wide, feeling the gentle breeze push back my hair. The robins and wrens sang and it no longer mattered that it was gray, raw, and brisk. When I inhaled the clean, misty air, my insides chilled. I had never experienced such an immersive moment in nature before, and looking at my roommates' glistening eyes, they hadn't either.

"Anyone want a drink?" Jaime interrupted the tranquil moment, and I turned and glared. "What? I'm heading into the shop to grab something. You want anything?"

"I'll go with you and get us some good snacks," Zoey said.

Marissa and I stayed at the edge of the road facing the quiet pond. "I can't believe I'm in Ireland," she said. "This feels so weird. It's different from anything I've experienced back home. I kind of like living with an Irish guy. It makes the entire semester feel more authentic."

I pictured the mountain of dirty clothes, the toothpaste-coated bathroom sink, and the messy bed. "Yeah, I guess so. I'm still not thrilled that I'm sharing a room with a guy, but it is nice knowing he's there in case something goes wrong."

"Like what?"

"Like...an intruder, or I don't know, alcohol poisoning? I'm a lightweight."

"Or when you need a quickie," Marissa said.

I smacked her playfully on the arm and fought a smile. "Um, no. He's totally not my type, and if you recall, I have a boyfriend."

She leaned forward and stamped her feet to warm up. "Sure, but your boyfriend doesn't seem too concerned that you're living with a guy."

Her words ran through my mind on repeat. I hadn't told Scott about Jaime because it hadn't come up in conversation. I planned to, but first he had to respond to my emails.

We stood in silence, staring at the water and watching the clouds roll over and away from the mountain peaks. Every way I turned, the green, luscious mountains enveloped me. I felt like a four-leaf clover hidden in a pasture of treasure.

Turning slightly, I saw fire-red hair from the corner of my eye. Jaime held two bottles of water and two bags of candy. "For you," he said, handing me one. I didn't know if it was from him or Zoey, but my heart warmed at their thoughtfulness.

"Time to go," Declan said, walking around the bus. "Time to move onto Roundstone. Everyone, on the bus."

We filed onto the bus and returned to our same seats.

"The harbor of Roundstone sits on the rugged backdrop of Errisbeg Mountain. See the village, check out the mountain, and search for a Galway Hooker." Declan burst out laughing. "Just a wee bit of Irish humor for you. A Galway Hooker is a traditional Irish fishing boat. Get your minds out of the gutter."

I leaned into Jaime and whispered, "Have you ever seen a Galway Hooker?" I couldn't stop the mischief from seeping out of my eyes and upturned mouth.

"Almost every day."

I grinned. "You'll have to show me next time you see one." Leaning across, I grabbed the unopened bag of potato chips. "I think these are mine." As I gazed out the window, I rested my body against his fuzzy sweatshirt, alerted to his warmth transferring to my chilled bones.

Living my fantasy, I wondered if I would ever be the same.

Chapter 9

The bus pulled up to Kylemore Abbey, and the Victorian granite castle nestled in the heart of Connemara towered over us. The gray slabs matched the gray sky, but despite the gloomy setting, my mouth fell open. I leaned over Jaime and pressed my face against the window, remaining still. I memorized the image of the marvelous, granite castle pressed against the green and brown mountain, focusing on every color, angle, and sensation.

"Two hours to explore the abbey," Declan announced over the loudspeaker. "Then we are onto Spiddal. Don't be late. The bus doesn't wait for anyone."

Jaime, Zoey, Marissa, and I climbed off the bus and approached the castle.

"Did you know," I said to my new friends, "that Jaime is from Connemara?"

"Do you speak Irish?" Zoey asked.

"I do. It was a required course in school. My grandparents still live here and only speak Gaelic," Jaime replied.

"Have you been to this castle a million times?" Marissa asked.

"Yes, but not during the prime tourist season. The property has

Victorian walled gardens, and my class sponsored a rosebush. Do you want to see it?"

Marissa giggled. "Do you know where it is?"

"It can't be too far," Jaime replied.

We walked through the castle, and he pointed out random facts about the architecture, history, and local area. After circling through the rooms on the first floor, we settled at a table to eat scones and drink tea. "You are quite the walking encyclopedia," I said.

"Eh, no more than any other Irish folk."

I locked eyes with his, grateful for his help. "I love hearing stories, so anytime you feel like sharing, I'm all ears."

Jaime's voice dropped to a whisper. "I have lots of stories to share." Anticipation traveled up and down my spine, and I looked away to break up the intimacy of the moment.

"Do you guys want to check out the miniature gothic church or walk the gardens?" Zoey asked.

"We only have thirty minutes." Marissa's gaze circled the room. "Do you think that's enough time?"

Jaime grinned. "Declan said two hours, but we're on Irish time. You'll soon realize if you're ten minutes late, you're early."

I couldn't help but smile at the laissez-faire approach to life.

"I say we check out the gardens." Zoey scanned the map she held in her hand. "They don't look too big."

"I don't know," I said, biting my bottom lip and picking at my cuticles. "What if we miss the bus?"

"Yeah, I don't think we have enough time." Marissa flipped her hair back and leaned on her hand.

Zoey sipped her tea quietly. "I think we should go for it. It's not like we'll visit Connemara again. We need to explore everything, while we can. Don't worry, Rory. We'll make it back in time. Marissa, I promise." Her eyes pleaded with us.

"I thought you weren't a tourism kind of girl," I said.

Zoey shrugged. "Eh? I guess the moment got to me."

"It'll be grand." Jaime gathered our dirty dishes and brought them to the dish bucket. My mouth dropped open and I quickly closed it. *Why isn't he this conscientious at home?*

"Ready?" he asked. "I'll show you the way."

Zoey and Marissa immediately followed him toward the exit.

As much as I wanted to go, I still wasn't sure, and my brain debated the pros and cons of taking such a calculated risk as I watched my friends file out the café. Reaching a decision, I grabbed my bag and raced after them. "We have to hurry! We can't be late."

We passed familiar people from the bus as we made our way outside, the crowd of tourists diminishing as we approached the garden. Jaime led us through the tall blue-green door that propelled us into another world.

Rows of color dotted my vision like paint speckles flung from a paintbrush for as far as I could see. "Wow, this is beautiful." I turned to Zoey and Marissa and saw the same glimmer of awe reflected in their pupils. "I feel like I'm in Alice in Wonderland and the Queen of Hearts is going to pop out from behind the fountain."

"Come on, let's go. It's over here." Jaime speed-walked down the recently mowed aisles and the scent of damp grass overpowered the scent of roses. Every bush looked exactly the same. He eyed them, walking up and down the row, and stopped mid-way. "Here. This is it." He pointed at a bush with magenta flowers. "This is it. I know it. We came here during fourth year. I remember that tree behind it."

I narrowed my eyes at him. *Is this all a farce?*

Looking beyond the neatly pruned bush, I saw an apple tree in the near distance. One red apple rested against the trunk and disappointment settled in my stomach. I wasn't sure what I expected, but a random bush amid an entire row was not nearly as exciting as I had anticipated in my mind.

Nerves jittered through my body, and I glanced at my American roommates. Marissa rocked back on her heels and widened her eyes at me. Zoey leaned forward and smelled the flowers, oblivious to my sweaty palms. We had followed a random Irish guy into a nearly empty garden to check out an indistinguishable bush.

"Awesome," I sputtered, and checked my watch. "We gotta go. The bus leaves in seven minutes."

"Irish time," Jaime mumbled. "They'll wait for us."

I wanted to believe him, but my life rotated around punctuality. Rolling my shoulders back, my muscles remained tight. *I'm with an Irish guy who lives in the area. I need to trust him. We'll be fine.* "Okay." Although despite what my mouth said, my body remained alert and I listened to the tick-tock of my watch.

I turned around, and Zoey and Marissa were already four steps ahead of me. "We gotta go," Marissa called behind her shoulder. "If we get there first, we'll tell the bus driver to wait."

Jaime meandered through the garden, and I followed his lead. I wanted to trust him, but my heart raced faster with every minute gone. When we exited the garden and arrived at the abbey's entrance, I couldn't find Marissa or Zoey. Scanning the crowd, I cleared my throat, trying to dislodge the giant pit resting above my trachea. "Jaime, do you see them?" My crackly voice surprised me and nervous, loud-pitched laughter escaped from my mouth.

"They're probably on the bus. We'll be there in a minute."

Perusing the parking lot, I located a handful of tour buses parked on the side. "We gotta go. We're late." I picked up my pace and lengthened my stride. Jaime remained a few steps behind, but I continued for the buses. I dodged between visitors and their incoherent chit-chat came at me from every angle. My eyes remained peeled on the buses and my gaze followed one as it crept out of the parking lot. My legs carried me forward even faster. I glanced at my watch but the numbers danced as my feet thumped against the wet ground.

"Sorry," I mumbled to the couple I nearly bulldozed, and ran off before they could reply.

When I got to the bus stop, my heartbeat throbbed against my chest and my calf muscles burned. I looked up and down, expecting to see Declan hanging outside the bus, but he wasn't there.

"Where's the bus?" Jaime asked.

I turned and narrowed my eyes. "I don't know."

I knocked on the door of the closest bus, and a short, chipper man stepped down the stairs. "Hello," he said.

"Hi, I'm looking for the bus that came from Galway. Declan was the driver. Do you know him?"

"Ah, yes, dear. Lovely bloke. He left about five minutes ago."

My eyes widened, and my heart skipped a beat. "But my roommates were supposed to ask him to wait."

"Tight schedule, ya know," the man replied.

I muttered my thanks, shocked that a company would encourage leaving tourists somewhere in a foreign country, and turned toward Jaime.

He sat on the curb, watching me.

"You," I said, pointing at him. My jaw clenched, and tension pulsated down my neck. Heat radiated through me, and I ripped my jacket off, throwing it on the ground next to him. I sat on the nylon and moved my face toward his, refusing to break eye contact. "You did this. I told you we were going to be late, but no! You said it would be grand." I tried my best Irish accent, but it fell flat, and Jaime chuckled, making my blood boil. His response ignited a fire within me, and I erupted like a volcano. "I cannot believe you did this! I knew it. I knew it!" I sat beside him and leaned forward, placing my elbow on my bent knees. I wanted to cry, but the level of rage prevented the tears filling my eyes from falling. Instead, I flared my nostrils and leaned closer. "What do we do now?"

"I have a plan. It'll be grand."

Chapter 10

I wished I had a cell phone. Our apartment had a house line, but with the cost of international calling, it made little sense to use it. I relied on email to connect with my parents and Scott, either dialing in when no one else was using it or stopping at an Internet café between classes. Back in America, I had a cell phone, but only about half the kids here seemed to have one. It would have been convenient, especially now when I didn't know where Marissa and Zoey were, but we were in the middle of nowhere.

"Do you think Marissa and Zoey are on the bus home?" I asked.

"Yeah, if they weren't, don't you think we would have seen them by now?"

"I still can't believe the bus left without us. That would never happen in America." I picked at my stubby fingernails, scraping the pink paint into tiny flakes. "I mean, if a driver left a tourist and something happened, they would be sued."

"You Americans and your suing. Over in this country, we say that you're an adult and you make your own choices. If you're stupid enough to miss the bus, that's on you."

Catching the insult, I saw red. "Are you calling me stupid?" I asked.

"It's Irish time," I air-quoted with my awful Irish accent. "I would have been there if it weren't for you."

"He probably left because it's still prime tourism time. More and more buses are on the roads, and the roads are so narrow cars have to pull over to let them pass. He probably left on time because of the traffic."

He had a point, I guess. There were so many nuances to this country, I didn't think I would ever get used to them.

Jaime stood and shoved his hand into his jacket pocket. "I'm going inside to make a call. You want to come, or will you stay here?"

I looked up at the sky. In the garden, blue had mixed with gray, but now gray mixed with black. "I'm coming with you." I hopped up and swiped my damp jeans. "I can't believe you did this to me."

Jaime ignored me, and I followed him back to the Kylemore Abbey entrance. We moved into the gift shop, and Jaime spoke to the attendant in Irish. I watched them closely, trying to infer the conversation based on facial expressions and changes in their voices.

He motioned for me to follow him, and we entered an office behind the registers. I sat in the folding chair in front of the desk, and Jaime dialed. He continued to speak in Irish, laughing, rolling his eyes, and glancing at me mid-sentence. My face flushed, assuming he was talking about me.

He hung up the phone. "I told you it'd be grand. My ma and da will be here in twenty minutes."

He moved out of the office, and I scampered behind. "What do you mean? Are they picking us up?"

Jaime ignored me until we moved through the crowd. "Yeah, picking us up. They can't drive us back to Galway until tomorrow, so we'll stay at my house until the morning."

My mouth dropped to the floor. "What? I can't stay at your house."

He shrugged. "Where else will you go? We're in the middle of

Connemara. You told me earlier you wanted to visit Clifden. Now, I can show you all the local spots. It'll be lovely."

I stared at him in disbelief, then marched back to the buses. I would beg a driver to take me back to Galway if I had to.

"Dear, all the Galway buses left already. I could bring you to Cork," one driver said.

I moved to the next bus and received the same response. It seemed my choices were Cork, Dingle, or Dublin, but where would I stay? Plodding to the grassy area away from the tourists, I clenched my fists and stomped the ground, grunting obscenities. I knew I looked like a toddler throwing a tantrum, but I didn't know what else to do.

I looked around, considering my options. *I have no choice but to follow Jaime back to his hometown. His parents are harmless. Happy and harmless. Or I can hitch a ride to another part of the country.* No option felt good, but I was stuck. Alone in a foreign country, with little money and no phone.

I trudged back to Jaime, sitting on a bench near the entrance to the abbey. "You win. I'll go with you as long as you promise we will return to Galway tomorrow."

"Tomorrow. First thing."

After an eternity, a dull, silver Ford Focus peeled into the parking lot. I recognized the woman with the curly, auburn hair behind the wheel.

"Seamus!" She stuck her arm out the window and waved.

"There's my ma," Jaime said to me.

"Shay-mus?" I asked.

"That's me Irish name, Rory. Seamus O Súilleabháin." My ears heard O'Sool-ih-vahn. Well-versed in Irish culture, I knew there were many vowels, accents, and a 'bh' in the word he just said.

"You'll have to spell that out for me later."

Climbing into the back seat and smiling politely, I greeted the woman from the airport.

"Ma, this is Rory. She's me flatmate. Rory, this is me ma. You can call her Deirdre."

Deirdre whipped her head around. The splatter of freckles and crooked front teeth matched Jaime's. "Hi, dear. Welcome to Ireland."

She pulled out of the parking lot, and we rolled through the mountains. Instead of focusing on the fiasco Jaime created with his 'Irish time', I looked on the bright side. I was going to Clifden.

Chapter 11

Deirdre pulled into a single-story home set away from the main road. The white painted concrete gave way to miniature windows, and the thatched roof reminded me of a light brown horse's mane. Images held within the pages of my guidebook flashed through my mind, and elation consumed me. *I can't believe I'm staying in an authentic Irish cottage.*

"This is it," Jaime said.

"Wow, this is beautiful." I studied the quaint home surrounded by green and gray hills.

We climbed out of the car, and I saw a large body of water in the distance behind the house. "Is that the ocean?" I asked.

"It's called Salt Lake. It eventually empties into the ocean, but not for a while," Deirdre said.

The many shades of green and blue stripes swiped across the landscape like an oil painting and it stopped me in my tracks. The rolling hills looked fluffy to the touch, and gray rocks below the clouds created a rough texture. The blue water mixed with the green reflection transported me into the images in my travel guide. "It's gorgeous. I can't believe this is your backyard," I said.

"Thanks." My ears heard 'tanks' and I smiled warmly. "Jaime says this is your first time in Ireland," Deirdre replied. Based on her intonation pattern, I didn't know if she was making a statement or asking a question.

"Yes, it's so beautiful, I am in awe." A warm blush crept up my neck, as I realized Jaime had spoken about me to his parents.

"You want true Irish life?" Deirdre asked. "You've come to the right place."

Jaime and I followed her into the house, and a small, white, fluffy dog raced to greet her. "This is Clover," Deirdre said, picking up the dog and rubbing her head. "She's a good girl."

I leaned over and gave Clover a head scratch, her soft mop-like fur tickling my fingers. "I always wanted a dog," I said to Jaime. "I never got one though. My parents said it would be too much work." My body relaxed at the cozy feel within the home, and I smelled something unfamiliar but comforting. "What's that smell? I can't seem to place it."

"Ah, that's the remnants of peat. It's been a bit nippy this past week. You get used to it."

"It smells like Ireland." I smiled at Deirdre. "Thank you for welcoming me into your home."

"Any time, dear. It's not like I could leave you at the abbey." She put down Clover, who ran to Jaime. "Connor, are you here?" Deirdre yelled into the next room. "Your da was cutting peat when I left. I suppose he's still outside."

I looked around the charming home with the tiny square rooms. The sitting room contained one loveseat, a rocking chair, and a fireplace, and the floral wallpaper reminded me of my grandmother. Jaime and I settled on the loveseat, and Deirdre asked, "Would you fancy a cuppa?"

I didn't, but I also didn't want to be rude, so I obliged. "Sure, a cuppa would be lovely." I felt like a child playing dress-up, rolling the Irish adjective and slang for tea off my tongue as if I was a local.

Deirdre entered the kitchen through the narrow doorway, and I heard her fumbling in the cabinets.

"I appreciate the place to crash," I said to Jaime.

"No worries." He flipped on the television and settled on RTE. "Wanna watch football?"

I leaned back against the couch, my shoulders melting into the body-imprinted crevices only a well-loved couch could show. Deirdre returned with a tray holding a small ceramic teapot and three miniature cups. The cups rested on saucers, and a sugar bowl and milk container sat behind it. She placed it on the rectangular coffee table in front of Jaime and me.

"So, Rory, tell me about yourself," Deirdre said.

I focused on perfecting my beverage, dropping a dash of milk and a spoonful of sugar into my cup. "Well, I am Jaime's roommate, uh, I mean flatmate. There was a bit of a mix-up, and they placed him in my apartment. There are two other American girls living there. I'm only here until Christmas, and then I'll return to Boston." The boiling water scalded my lips as I slurped my tea. I wanted to spit it out but forced myself to swallow. The heat traveled down my throat, and my eyes watered.

"Ma, are you sure you can bring us home tomorrow?" Jaime interrupted.

"Yeah. I have church in the morning. You're welcome to come, Jaime."

He made a face.

"Rory?"

I wanted to experience everything related to Ireland, but I hadn't considered attending church. I didn't know if I was ready to stick out like a sore thumb in a tiny village. "Thank you, but can I let you know in the morning?"

"Sure, that would be grand. I can bring you back after lunch if that's good for you?" She looked at me for confirmation.

"Sure, that would be great. Thank you."

"Brilliant. I'll let you relax. I know you've had a crazy day." She hummed on her way back to the kitchen.

"Oh, Deirdre?" Her name stuck to my tongue like glue, and I worried I had mispronounced it. "Can I use your phone to call my roommates? I need to let them know I'm here."

"Sure, dear."

Deirdre helped me dial the number from the kitchen's rotary phone, and Zoey answered on the first ring.

"Oh, Rory! We were so worried about you. Are you okay?" She sounded out of breath, and I heard fear hiding within her voice. "Where are you?"

I wrapped the yellow curled cord around my index finger. "I'm at Jaime's house. His mom picked us up. We'll be home tomorrow. What happened?"

"Marissa told the bus driver you were coming, but he said we couldn't wait. He told me we had to go and you should have been there on time. Marissa and I debated getting off, but what good would the four of us stranded in Connemara be? It's not like there's a hotel anywhere nearby."

"I can't believe you left me. I would have waited for you." My tone was harsher than I expected, and I wasn't sure if my words were true. After a moment of silence, I softened my voice. "It's okay, I'm not upset at you, just the situation. It could have happened to any of us."

"Sorry." Her voice dropped. "We didn't know what to do."

"It's okay. It's been a long, stressful day. How was the rest of the tour?" I asked.

"It was beautiful, but we were worried. We came home and haven't left, just in case you called."

"Well, we're here and still alive," I said. "I'll see you sometime tomorrow afternoon." I hung up the phone and looked at Deirdre.

"Your friends left you?" she asked, boiling more water for tea.

"Yep. They didn't know what to do. Maybe I would have done the same." I shrugged my shoulders and picked up my teacup.

"Hindsight is twenty-twenty, dear. I'm sure they were worried about you. Here, bring these biscuits in for you and Jaime. They're his favorite."

I placed the shortbread cookies on the coffee table, and Jaime swallowed one cookie in two bites. I watched the beige crumbs fall along his beard and into his lap.

As he whooped and hollered as the game progressed, I found myself staring out the window at the beautiful Salt Lake. I wanted to memorize the scene, and the magic called to me.

"Jaime, would you mind if I walked around outside and took some pictures?" I rose from my seat beside him and grabbed a cookie to go.

"Of course. Have fun." He remained seated at the edge of the couch with his bent elbows against both knees.

I gathered my raincoat, just in case the gray skies opened, and crept out the front door. Alone in nature, I felt free. It was as if the fairies had scooped me up and carried me to the shores of the lake. Maneuvering around boulders embedded into the greenery, I arrived at the perfect sitting stone. Facing the sunset, I pulled out my camera and took pictures from every angle. Muted colors merged in the evening sky, creating shadows of various hues along the mountains and into the water. Rugged Connemara beauty filled my viewfinder. I didn't want to forget a thing and didn't stop until my film counter hit zero.

As the sun sank behind the horizon, I gathered my raincoat and camera and walked back to the house. I stood at the door, unsure if I should knock or walk in. I opened the door and yelled, "Knock, knock!"

I entered and removed my shoes before stepping into the living room. Jaime sat on the edge of his seat, yanking on his hair.

"Hey Jaime," I said. "Is everything okay?"

He didn't look at me. "No, we're at a draw with three minutes left in the game." He placed his fingers near his mouth and bit the cuticles.

I sat beside him and waited. I had learned from Scott that the worst thing you could do was interrupt a die-hard sports fan during the clutch moments. Fifteens seconds in the game and the red team kicked a ball into the net. Jaime erupted in excitement, jumped off the couch like a rocket, and grabbed my shoulders, hugging me. "We won!" he shouted.

I laughed, feeling his strong body press against mine. His enthusiasm and joy transferred into me, and I squeezed him closer, breathing in the scent of peat smoke that was already permeating his clothes, and probably mine too.

"Oh no, Jaime." I pulled away and looked into his eyes. "I don't have clean clothes, a toothbrush or anything."

He scrunched his eyebrows and raised his shoulders. "I guess you'll have to wear some of mine or my ma's. The nearest store is closed."

My body stiffened, and I stepped back, thinking about Scott. I couldn't imagine telling him I slept at a stranger's house while wearing his pajamas. If Scott slept at another girl's house, I knew I would be upset, and I didn't want to bobble the precarious pedestal our relationship was already balancing on. As much as I couldn't lie to him, it felt like the easier option. *He'll never know. Besides, nothing is going on between Jaime and me. Red hair and freckles? Definitely not my type.* It seemed I often reminded myself he wasn't my type, and the little voice inside my head called me a liar.

My relationship with Jaime was barely a friendship, but a part of me wanted more. Confused by the emotions swirling inside, I stepped back and looked at Jaime, seeing him for what he could represent.

Questioning my past choices, I considered jumping head first into new experiences, unafraid of the consequences.

"Great," I chirped. "I'll take your comfiest shirt."

Chapter 12

"Dear, would you like more brown bread?" Deirdre asked, eyeing my empty plate like she was a mama bird fattening her chicks. She placed a slice on my plate before I could respond. Deirdre, Connor, Jaime and I sat at the small wooden table, my belly filling with Irish cuisine.

"Mm-hmm, this is delicious," I mumbled between the crumbs in my mouth. "Did you make this?" I took a bite of Irish Stew, still steaming from my bowl.

"It was my ma's special recipe. She left me her recipe tin, God rest her soul." Connor and Deirdre turned toward the crucifix above the door and signed the Sign of the Cross.

I dropped my spoon, held the hot potatoes in my mouth like a tiger trapped in a cage, and did the same. The gravy scalded my tongue. It should have hurt more, but the earlier cuppa had already killed my taste buds. Jaime took another bite of lamb.

"Brown bread is lovely with Irish Stew." Deirdre placed another slice on my plate.

I reached across Jaime and cut a pad of butter off the brick.

"Do you like it?" Connor asked. His dirt-stained flannel shirt smelled like the outdoors, and his weathered hands aged him. He took another bite of bread, and his intense eyes bore a hole into mine. Deirdre's presence comforted me, while Connor put me on edge. He reminded me of my grandfather, who my father said changed after returning from World War II. "It was like the war took a piece of his soul, and he could never find himself again," my dad used to tell me. My grandfather never laughed or smiled, and I could see that Connor had the same indifferent presence. It made my knees quiver, not knowing what he was thinking, or if I was welcome for the night.

I dipped my bread in my stew, fully melting the butter. "I've never had anything like this. It's delicious. Thank you for dinner," I said to Connor and Deirdre, wiping my lips with my napkin. My knee shook under the table and I forced another bite, even though I was full.

After dinner, I helped Jaime clear the table, and we cleaned the kitchen. His cottage didn't contain American luxuries, like a dishwasher, and I questioned my hand-washing skills.

"Do you want to scrub or dry?" he asked.

The pile of dishes haphazardly leaned toward the counter beside the sink basin, and I imagined bumping the tower and sending all their plates crashing to the floor. "I'll dry."

Jaime tossed me a towel, turned on the radio, and squeezed soap onto a sponge. He washed quicker than I dried and I struggled to keep up. For every dish I placed in the cabinet, two more dripped in the dish drain. I felt like Lucy in the chocolate factory.

"Jaime, have you ever seen *I Love Lucy*?" I asked, rubbing the towel along the basin of a glass cup.

"Nah, I don't think so. Is it an American show?"

"Yeah, it's old. We'll have to watch it sometime."

We chatted amicably about nothing in particular. I questioned him about his life before college, and he asked me about my life back home. *Maybe I overreacted on the airplane. He's not that bad. He's actually kind*

68

of cute, in that Irish way.

Distracted by my revelation, a small cup slipped out of my hand and tumbled to the ground, shattering at my feet. "Oh no, I'm so sorry!" I squatted down to pick up the pieces. My hands shook as I scooped up the tiny fragments.

Jaime bent down to help me as I stood up to throw away the glass, and my lips brushed past his scruffy beard. My body stiffened, and I watched him stand, requesting whatever pieces I still held. I smelled beer from dinner on his breath and my stomach quivered. Our hands touched, as I carefully placed the glass in a napkin in his hand, and my heart stuttered. These unexpected feelings terrified me and my muddy brain couldn't process my body's reaction. "Um, Jaime? You weren't my favorite person when we first met, and I'm sorry I judged you," I confessed.

Jaime turned the water off and tossed the sponge in the sink. Only dirty silverware in a soapy basin remained. "What do you mean?" he asked. His amber eyes looked green under the dim lights.

My chest thumped twice and then slowed down. I felt the blood rushing to my ears and I swallowed. He appeared genuinely hurt, and I regretted saying anything at all. I picked up the last cup and stuffed the wet towel into the cylinder, careful to twist. "I thought I would have a middle seat to myself."

A smile pulled against his lips. "Yeah, I squeezed in right before they locked the doors."

"And then you made a gigantic mess with my dinner. You're lucky you didn't ruin my bag!" I said, laughing. I threw the wet towel at him, and he caught it with one hand.

"It was an accident," he replied, still grinning.

His positive response to my criticism encouraged me to continue. "And you know nothing about personal space. I couldn't move because you were practically sitting on my lap."

Jaime stepped closer, and I counted the freckles scattered across his nose. "Practically. You haven't been the easiest flatmate either," he said.

"What do you mean?"

"You're the craziest flatmate I've ever had. You color code your calendar and schedule out every day in fifteen-minute intervals. You try to micromanage everyone. You even have Zoey and Marissa's schedule taped to your wall."

The corners of my mouth dropped slowly, and I pulled away. "So?" It was the best rebuttal I could form from his unexpected personal attack.

"So, you need to loosen up. Live a little."

I crossed my shoulders over my chest and widened my stance. "I live a little. I live a lot, thank you very much." I poked him on the shoulder, asserting myself.

"Oh, yeah? When's the last time you woke up and didn't know what your day would look like?"

"Today. I never imagined I'd be here in your house." Scott's face crawled toward me, and I brushed it away with a broom coated in cobwebs.

"When's the last time you danced with a stranger? Or kissed a man? Or said feck it, life's grand? And did what you wanted to do at that moment?"

I whipped around and sat at the table, thinking back to spontaneous times, but nothing emerged. "Plenty. It's none of your business how I live my life." Annoyance replaced my flirtation.

Jaime dropped into the chair next to me. "Exactly. So you live your life, and I'll live mine, and eventually, we'll find a compromise since we're living together."

I didn't reply because the conversation was over. *How dare he call me controlling? At least I'm not a slob and can tell the difference between a trash can and the floor.* My gaze flickered toward the ceiling and I stood to leave the room, but had nowhere to go.

Deirdre popped her head into the kitchen and broke the silence. "Oh, thank you," she said, noticing the empty sink. "Rory, I think we need you here more often. You're a good influence on Jaime. I can't remember the last time he cleaned the kitchen and gave me a night off."

I smiled at her and smirked at him, folding my hands and pulling back my shoulders.

"Here's a new toothbrush," she said, handing me a plastic package. "Jaime, can you show her where she'll be staying?"

"Sure, ma." He stood from the table, and I slinked behind him up the narrow wooden stairs to the second floor. He ducked through the doorway and leaned forward to prevent bumping into the slanted ceilings.

"Toilet." He opened the creaky door next to the stairs, and I peeked inside. I placed the brand new toothbrush on the sink and continued to follow him down the hall.

"This is my room, and it has a bed and a couch. Your choice. Which one do you want?"

Images of dirty sheets from before he moved, piles of dirty clothes flooding the floor, and smelly trash trapped in the room flickered in the corners of my mind.

When he opened the door, I stepped back, shocked. Standing before me was an immaculate, modern room that reminded me of a hotel suite. With fluffy pillows matching the generic bedspread, a desk, and a dresser, I could have been standing in the Marriot or the Sheraton. Beside the bed sat a fully made matching sofa bed. No matter how hard I looked, there wasn't a speck of dirt anywhere. "This is your room?" I asked, spinning in a circle.

"Yep. When I left for uni, my ma redid it in case any of our American relatives wanted to come over and visit."

"That sounds like fun."

"Yeah, so this is it. Where do you want to sleep?" he asked again.

"Sofa bed." It was closest to the door, so if I needed to make a quick escape, I'd have an advantage.

Jaime dug through his drawers and tossed a Manchester United t-shirt on the bed. "Pajamas."

I picked up the shirt and held it against my torso. The hem hung just below my hips. "Um."

"Rory," he said. "You have legs. It's not like I've never seen them before."

I gulped and forced a smile. "Right."

That night, I gripped Jaime's t-shirt, and looked at myself in the bathroom mirror. *Should I take my bra off? Usually, I'm asleep by the time he gets home and I'm gone before he wakes, but I don't know about this...*I bit my bottom lip, looking at the Manchester United shirt, and pulled it over my head before exiting the bathroom. My dirty jeans hung from my hips and I sneaked back into Jaime's room, crawling under the fluffy blanket on the sofa bed. It wasn't the first time I'd slept in my clothes, and I'm sure it wouldn't be the last.

Even though I closed my eyes, my brain remained awake like a hamster running on a squeaky wheel. The opened windows let in a slight breeze, but the silence was deafening. I wrapped the blanket tighter around my torso and rolled onto my side.

Excitement and applause traveled up the stairs and under Jaime's closed door. He and Connor stayed up to watch another football match. I knew whatever team they rooted for was doing well based upon the cheers. One cascade of disappointment rolled into the room, followed by exuberance, and then nothing. I wanted to be asleep when Jaime entered, but I couldn't relax. My legs twitched, and I flipped my pillow, squeezing and fluffing, tossing and turning.

I was still fidgeting when the door clicked open, and a slice of light shot across my face. I froze and peeked one eye open, seeing a tall, dark shadow stand in the doorway. The door closed and the light disappeared, but I followed his shadow to his bed across the room. The moonlight outlined his body, and I felt like a voyeur, peeping into his personal life.

He removed his shirt and dropped his pants before pulling up a pair of shorts. He looked around the dark room, searching for a shirt in his dresser. My heart thudded against my chest and I held my breath.

I knew we were roommates, but I had never seen him change for bed before. He spent most of his time with his old roommates or the football players, so when he stumbled home, I was fast asleep. I sometimes heard him in the bathroom, but it became routine and I never woke up long enough to say hi.

But now, here he was in the flesh, and I was wide awake. Being in his room and seeing his life more intimately made me understand him better. Despite my apprehension about staying here, sleeping in his room, and wearing his clothes to bed, I felt strangely at ease.

I lost his facial features as the clouds rolled past the moon. His eyes could have been staring into mine, or they could have been tightly closed. Not knowing made my heart race and my throat constrict. I rolled over, away from Jaime, unable to interpret my body's hypocrisy.

I thought about Scott, wondering where he was. It was a Saturday night in the middle of September, and early evening back home. I pictured him eating dinner with his friends at the busted table we picked up on the side of the road. I saw his roommate Tommy, Tommy's girlfriend, and my roommate and best friend, Marty. It looked like a double date, so I shook my head until the two women disappeared.

Every Saturday night last year, Scott hosted a poker game in his dorm room. It was risky, but he didn't have a job and needed quick money. He had always been a risk taker, pushing the boundaries, and my logic often challenged him to the point where he no longer shared certain parts of his life with me.

He lived in an apartment now and I imagined house parties with dozens of people—cash on the table, chips stacked, and cards dealt. In my mind, I watched him scoop the center chips toward him, readjust his sunglasses, and rub knuckles with Marty for good luck.

Visualizing the night made my heart hurt. I missed him, and didn't understand where we had veered off course. The summer felt normal until I left, and then it felt like I had disappeared. Or he had disappeared. I tried to contact him, but he never responded. Fear of missing out on my life back home draped over my body and a single tear dropped from my eye onto the flattened pillow.

I sniffled, but it came out more like a snort. My body froze, and I held my breath, unsure if Jaime was asleep. I heard rustling across the room.

"Good night, Rory," he whispered.

"Night." I wiped my eyes and buried my face in the pillow.

I knew this semester would be tough, but I never imagined how difficult it could be. I couldn't wait to get back to Galway and email Scott, just to remind him I was still around and thinking about him. *If only he were thinking about me.*

My jumbled thoughts numbed my brain. I closed my eyes tight and when they opened again, it was morning.

Chapter 13

The sun cascaded through the small window above Jaime's immaculate dresser, and my body relaxed under the covers when I saw his empty bed. I ran to the bathroom to prevent any uncomfortable encounters in the hallway and swapped Jaime's t-shirt for my dirty top from yesterday. It still smelled like burning peat and nature.

My body yearned for a hot, cleansing shower, but I didn't dare shower in Deirdre and Connor's home. I brushed my teeth, pulled back my hair, and returned to Jaime's room. Being alone in this strange house in a different country made me feel peculiar. *If only my parents knew. They would lecture me about being a young woman alone with a strange man and how I must always make intelligent choices.* I had never had a one-night stand, gotten blackout drunk, or even skipped a class before, but sometimes it felt like my parents assumed the worst of me, even though I never gave them any reason.

I sat on the sofa bed, trying my hardest not to snoop, but the temptation was too great. I crept over to the window and pretended to check the weather, but instead peeked down at his dresser. A picture of a younger Jaime standing with Owen and a blonde woman sat on the far corner of the clean, smooth surface, and I brought it to my face to get a better look. Owen and Jaime wore matching football uniforms and the blonde girl wrapped her arms around both of them. Her long hair and infectious smile made my heartbeat quicken and my gut clench. Surprised by my jealousy, but also curious as to who she was, I dropped the photo and headed toward the stairs.

Hints of sausage, eggs, and bacon crawled toward me from the kitchen, and my stomach growled. Moving through the hallway and down the stairs, I stepped softly, avoiding any noise that would indicate my arrival. My mouth salivated and my stomach grumbled, begging for food.

"Good morning, dear," Deirdre sang. She placed a cup of tea in front of an empty chair, and I slid into the seat, smelling the hot, malty drink. "Breakfast?" She held a plate with sausages, eggs, bacon, and butter-soaked bread.

"Yes, thank you. Morning, Jaime, morning." I made eye contact with Connor, unsure what to call him, and he tipped his head back in greeting before taking another bite of breakfast.

The plate set before me overflowed with an all-you-can-eat buffet. I took a bite of sausage and moaned under my breath with pleasure.

Jaime's eyes sparkled like the joke was on me. His stare made me shift in my seat, so I cleared my throat and asked, "How'd you sleep?"

"Great, thank you."

Jaime continued to stare at me, and I wiped my chin and ran my tongue over my top teeth, in case part of my meal hadn't made it to my stomach.

"Oh, dear," Deirdre interrupted. "Did you decide on church? We need to leave in thirty-five minutes." I heard tirty-five and smiled to myself. I still couldn't believe I was in Ireland.

I swallowed and looked at Jaime, pleading for help.

"Ma, I'm taking Rory to Clifden Castle for a few hours. She's never been to ruins before."

I looked at him, and he winked at me. This was the first time I had heard about a castle, but castles and Ireland went together like brown bread and Irish butter. It was one of the first things I had put on my to-do list, and it was about time I visited one.

"Ah, wonderful!" Deirdre clapped her hands. "Are you taking the old car?"

Snapping my head to attention mid-bite, I waited to see if he'd tell me what 'the old car' meant.

"Yeah," Jaime said.

"Be safe. And be home by one, so I can drive you back to Galway."

My watch read half-eight, and I wondered how long it would take to get there.

After breakfast, Deirdre and Connor excused themselves to prepare for church.

I looked around the now empty kitchen and leaned in toward Jaime. "A castle, huh?"

"You didn't want to go to church, did you?"

I shook my head. "Not today."

Jaime grinned. "Let's explore a castle. I saw it on your list."

My heart warmed, realizing that he noticed things about me.

About twenty minutes later, we walked behind the house. In the distance, I saw a pale-yellow Volkswagen Beetle, half immersed in bushes.

"Is that what we're driving?" I asked.

"Yeah, this was my da's car when he got his first job before I was born. He loved that car and wouldn't let my ma get rid of it. We don't use it much. Here, let me clear these branches."

I pulled at branches growing against the car door and rolled some rocks out of the way that may have caused a bumpy departure.

"Get in," he ordered, holding open the passenger side door.

Sitting against the ripped upholstery, I scanned the metal floor to avoid the small holes and flowers growing up into the car. Against my better judgment, I secured my seatbelt. This was Ireland, and I was on an adventure.

"Wow! I've always loved these cars." I balled my hand into a fist, and punched him on the arm with force.

"Ow. What'd you do that for?" He rubbed his arm and scrunched his eyebrows.

"Punch-buggy yellow. No punch-backs." I laughed at my joke. "I haven't done that in years."

"What?" he asked.

"Nothing. It's an American thing, I guess." I pulled the seatbelt across my lap. "I'm buckled." I gripped the handrest on the door and straightened my back.

"Prepare for take-off," he said, shifting the car into reverse.

We chugged out of the driveway, and my body jerked forward with every gear change until we cruised over thirty miles per hour.

"Do you drive this often?"

"Nah, it's not even registered, but no one cares. We use it when we need it. Like today."

I widened my eyes, shocked that he and his family would drive a car without proper paperwork. *My parents would kill me. Good thing they don't know.* I reminded myself that I was in Ireland and this was an opportunity I would never forget, so I swallowed down my hesitation and opened my mind to whatever Jaime wanted to show me.

Ten minutes down the twisty, narrow road, I saw a castle on a hill in the distance with the rugged Atlantic behind it.

"Wow," I muttered.

The remains of the green and gray Gothic-Revival castle shot up to the sky with dignity and grace. There wasn't another building nearby, and the ruined castle took center stage. Green vines grew up the length of the castle like the country had born ownership.

Jaime drove the car to a stone archway and parked outside the towering granite monstrosity.

"This is beautiful!" My hand rested over my eyebrows as I leaned back to scan the height of the tallest tower.

"Come with me," Jaime said, grabbing my hand.

A shot of electricity coursed into my heart, and I dropped his hand and raced in front of him. "Is it okay if we're here?" Without waiting for a response, I kept exploring.

Standing in the center of the courtyard, I spun in a slow circle, taking in the jagged walls and windows. The sunlight shot through a crucifix cut out on the side near the bay, and a rectangle of light immersed me.

"Eh, not really," Jaime said.

I turned and gawked. "What do you mean?" Images of trespassing, arrest, and being sent back to America flickered through my mind.

"It's private property, but don't worry. It's Ireland. The owners are nowhere near. Visitors can use the walkway, and if anyone asks, say we didn't know. You're American. They'll believe you, and I'll play dumb."

I bit my tongue, thinking of how I trusted Jaime yesterday, and focused my attention on the tiny details left in the deserted castle walls. *If he says we are fine, we are okay.*

"Follow me." Instead of grabbing my hand again, Jaime waved me toward the castle turrets.

He brought me to the hill's peak, looking out at the craggy ocean. "They built this castle in the early 1800s. Then the famine hit, and the castle was bought and sold multiple times. I think it's been neglected since before 1900."

"It's a beautiful building." I walked back to the cool stones and pressed my cheek against them.

Jaime settled against the castle wall and I joined him. The ocean waves lapped in the distance.

"Thank you for taking me here," I said. "It feels different exploring Ireland with a local, you know? It's like I'm not a tourist, and the entire experience feels more authentic."

"When I was in America last semester, I was lost. People weren't the nicest, and I found myself disappointed often. I didn't want you to feel that way."

My face fell. "I didn't realize you studied abroad last year. I'm sorry you had such an awful experience."

Jaime turned toward me. "No, it wasn't bad, but it wasn't what I'm used to, and I had a bit of culture shock, as well. I didn't connect with my flatmates, so I spent a lot of time exploring the city alone. I want you to have a better experience than I did."

I leaned against him and placed my hand on his. That damn jolt of electricity shot through me again, and I ignored it, leaning my head against his shoulder. "I can't wait to take a shower," I said.

In the far distance, I heard the waves crash against the surf. The bright sun beat down on my face, and the closeness of Jaime's body heightened every nerve in my body.

"Yeah, you kind of stink," he said.

Straightening my back, I turned to him with a wide grin and a slap on his thigh. "Stop!"

"Just kidding," he said. "You smell like roses."

I hit him again, threw my head back, and laughed into the Irish clouds. When I pulled my head down, he was right there. The freckles across his cheeks and forehead highlighted his eyes, and the shadows created a green shade around the edge of his pupil. I had never seen such a deep shade of green before. His captivating eyes stopped me, and my soul shed its clothes. My smile dropped, and everything felt serious, like if I said or did the wrong thing, I would ruin it forever.

The intensity drew me closer, and before I could say 'Scott' my lips were on his and my body was on fire. His soft lower lip fell into the crevice between mine, and his beard tickled my chin. I leaned into him, intensifying the waves of electricity, as his beard roughed up the delicate skin around my mouth.

Then a red flashing stop sign with blaring sirens sounded behind my eyelids. "Abort! Abort! You have a boyfriend," the siren wailed.

My eyes popped open and my breath caught in my throat. Pulling away, I stared into his hypnotizing eyes and the walls I'd built around myself melted within the inferno of my lust.

This was not good.

The moment my brain registered that I was a cheater, I pulled away like I had touched an open flame. *What am I doing? This is not me. I don't cheat. I don't stray. I'm devoted and dedicated, and committed. To everything I do. I'm not a cheater. I'm not like my dad.*

I pulled my chin into my neck and analyzed the tufts of green grass pressed against my legs. Pulling out tiny, sharp blades and creating a pile beside me, I refused to look at him.

"That was lovely," he said. He cleared his throat, and my heartbeat stuttered in response to his compliment.

I didn't look up. I couldn't. My body radiated heat, and my dry tongue stuck to my lower jaw. I forced back all the saliva I could manage and swallowed.

I squirmed under his eyes. *Please stop looking at me.*

"Was kissing an Irish bloke on your to-do list?"

A chuckle burst out of me, and I raised my eyes. "Nope. I can't say it was."

"It wasn't so bad, was it?" he asked.

I smirked. "I've had worse."

"I didn't brush my teeth this morning."

I swatted him on the arm, and the moment's intensity broke under his self-deprecating humor.

He stood up and stretched, reaching to take my hand. "You ready to go? My ma and da should be back in about forty-five minutes."

Brushing the dirt off the seat of my filthy jeans, I followed him to the car in silence. Lost in my thoughts and torn between what felt acceptable and adventurous, I wasn't sure who I wanted to be or if being myself was holding me back.

Jaime walked to the passenger door and stuck his arm through the open window. He pulled up the door lock and opened the rusty door from the inside. "After you."

I curtseyed with my invisible skirt and slid into the seat. He slammed the door shut and settled into the driver's side. "Thank you. You're quite the gentleman."

He grinned and turned the key in the ignition, but nothing happened. He tried again, and we continued to sit in silence.

"Bloody car," he said. "I told my da the battery keeps failing."

I leaned over to look at the dash, and all the lights blinked at me. "What's up?"

"We need a new battery. Can you drive a manual?"

I looked at him like he asked me to speak Gaelic. "No. Never tried."

"Okay. Well, I need you to get out and push."

I threw my head back and laughed. "You're not serious."

"If you want to get back to Galway, you need to push me down the hill so I can pop the clutch." His mischievous eyes made me giggle. I wasn't familiar with 'pop the clutch' and didn't know how pushing a two-ton object would help.

When he didn't laugh back, I rolled my eyes. "You are serious."

"Help, please." He waved at me, signaling me to get out of the car. "I can't do this without you."

I sighed and walked to the hood.

Jaime stuck his head out the window. "We have to turn the car around. You push on the bonnet and I'll turn the wheel."

I leaned on the hood and pushed with all my might. The car rolled about two inches, and my shoulders ached.

"Come on, do it again. You can do it, Rory!"

Annoyed that I was doing all the hard work, I leaned down and grunted, shifting my weight through my left leg and into the hood of the car. It crept toward the castle archway.

"Great, Rory. Now walk around to the back, and push with everything you have." Visions of me in labor and my future husband telling me to 'push with everything I have' flashed at me. In any other situation, I would have laughed at the comparison.

I widened my stance and crossed my arms over my chest. "Why am I doing this?" I called over the front windshield.

He stuck his head out the window, and I saw his face transform into a red-haired Irish setter going for a joyride. "Because you can't drive a manual. Who comes to Ireland not knowing how to drive a manual?"

I threw my arms up in the air and stomped to the back of the car. "Fine. Are you ready?"

Jaime fumbled with the gears and checked his mirrors. "Ready!"

I lunged forward, placed my hand on the metal bumper, and threw all my weight into the car. The first few inches took all my energy, but the decline helped the car pick up speed. I pushed and ran behind the vehicle until it was going so fast that it left me in the cloud of dust created by the wheels spinning along the dirt road.

The engine kicked on, and the car stopped about a hundred feet in front of me. Jaime stuck his head out the window, twisted backward, and waved. "Great job, Rory! Let's go!"

I ran to the car and slammed the door. "Good?" I asked, still unclear how he got the car running.

"Bravo, Rory." He leaned over and kissed me on the lips again. It was quick, tender, and comfortable, like we had been dating for years. I hadn't expected it, but I didn't hate it.

It seemed like a perfect ending to the crazy twenty-four hours Jaime and I had spent together.

Chapter 14

By the time Jaime and I got back to Galway, all I wanted to do was lay in my bed and recoup from the weekend. I needed quiet and alone time, but the small apartment and sharing a bedroom with the object of my anxiety kept me on guard.

Zoey and Marissa were out, and I savored the stillness. Jaime grabbed a beer and threw on the telly. "Wanna watch the match?" he asked.

I shook my head. "Can we talk for a second?" I sat next to him on the couch, carefully sitting as far away as possible without seeming to avoid him.

He kept his eyes on the television and nodded.

I wanted him to look at me because I had been practicing this speech the entire drive back from Clifden, but not making eye contact gave me the courage to spit it out. "What happened between us...the kisses... can we keep it between ourselves?" I watched his face to see a reaction, but he barely acknowledged me.

"Of course."

"I...would rather no one know. It might be weird for Marissa and Zoey to live with two people that kissed, even if it meant nothing." Still no reaction. *Am I totally overreacting?* "Thanks, Jaime." With wooden logs for legs, I stumbled to the kitchen. "Tea?" I asked, thankful for an excuse to give my heart time to slow.

"Yes to the tea, and of course. It was just a small shift and it meant nothing." He shrugged his shoulders.

"What's a shift?" I handed him a mug and sat beside him.

"It's Irish for kiss. No worries."

I drank my tea in silence, knowing that the kiss we shared brought me many worries. The thought of being a cheater mortified me, especially after what my dad put my mom through. I knew I was better than my dad, and wouldn't allow myself to stoop to his level.

Leaving my mug on the coffee table, I snuck past him and into our room. My skin felt too small for my bones, like if I put too much pressure on any joint, I would collapse to the floor. I stripped out of my clothes and took the hottest shower the pipes would allow. The tiny stand-up shower looked like a spaceship missile, and I couldn't breathe while trapped amid the hot steam. Each burning drop scorched my body, reminding me that I was imperfectly human.

When my skin resembled a cooked lobster, I wrapped the towel around my body and stepped out of the bathroom, opening the door to our bedroom. The cold air shot at me and caused me to shiver. "Oh!" My body jumped and jerked as I took in Jaime, sitting on his bed. Tightening the towel, I froze. "You scared me. Sorry, sorry. I should have gotten dressed in the bathroom." I turned to return to the sauna.

"No worries, I'm just getting my notebook." Jaime grabbed his sketch pad and left the room and I quickly locked the door behind him.

Before getting dressed, I sat at my computer and pulled up my email. Two from my parents and none from Scott. I slit my eyes at the screen and scrunched my lips. *Did he not receive them?* Anger at him for blowing me off and anger at myself for wasting my time clouded my vision.

I clicked 'new' and started one last email. **Hi Scott. It's been almost a month, and I haven't heard from you. I hope you are well and wish you the best, but I can't do this long-distance relationship anymore. Maybe we can talk when I get back, but I need space. I think of you often, but please don't contact me. Rory.** I hit send and immediately closed out my email. Yanking at the snug ring, I pulled it off my finger and tossed it in my desk drawer. Desperate to erase all the memories that I had brought with me to Ireland, I ripped the picture of Scott and me off the wall and threw it in the trash.

The weight of my break up drifted above my head and floated away, and my wooden arms and legs loosened like putty. Leaning back in the chair, I stared up at the ceiling. *Why am I not upset about this?*

Scott was my longest relationship of only eight months, but he was my only 'real' boyfriend. Everyone told me we didn't quite fit, but I knew opposites attracted. Carefree and spontaneous, he complemented my rigidity and organization. *We had worked, hadn't we?*

My parents' relationship had self-destructed when I was eight, and their marriage taught me about lack of connection and emotional instability. I learned that when you kept things inside, the days moved on autopilot, and although not exciting, you were safe and comfortable. My father never rocked the boat, even though his actions shook us up like a hurricane.

Now that Scott was a non-issue, I could just be, and that ability to be present in the moment was something I had been lacking for most of my life. *Better to break it off now. The universe is telling me to let him go and put me first...otherwise I wouldn't have kissed Jaime. Right?* The tiny voice reminded me what I had done and my body responded with a slow growing heat.

Lacing my fingers behind my head and staring at the space where our picture had hung, I pulled out an envelope of newly developed film. Flipping though, I found a picture of me and my roommates from our first weekend out, and I taped it exactly where Scott had stared back at me before.

Pulling on a clean pair of jeans and a white t-shirt, I massaged mousse into my hair, and applied some makeup. Needing to feel pretty, wanted, and worthy of love, I checked myself in the mirror and strolled into the living room. Jaime sat on the couch, exactly where I had left him when we'd had our talk.

He turned toward me and did a double take. My heart thudded against my chest, recognizing his curiosity and my desire.

"You look lovely." He patted the cushion next to him. "Wanna watch the match?"

I sat beside him, our hips touching, and I leaned into him. He draped his arm around my shoulder and pulled me closer. "Actually, you look daycent," he said.

I held my smile, unsure if I heard him correctly. "Daycent?"

"You know, daycent, like good looking. D-E-C-E-N-T."

I couldn't help but laugh and I cuddled up against his shoulder. "Decent in America means average. Are you saying I look average?" I teased.

"No, no, daycent in Ireland means attractive, good looking, beautiful."

I reveled in his warmth and continued to have a two-person debate in my mind. *What am I doing?* "Hey, Jaime." I looked up at his warm, inviting eyes. "I need to know. Why did you kiss me?"

He studied my face, and I moved to a more upright position. "I didn't. You shifted me."

"What? I did not." I pulled my head back and crossed my arms over my chest. "You shifted me in the car. You might have shifted me in front of the castle too; I don't really know. But you definitely shifted me in the car." The Irish vocabulary easily replaced my native verb as my connection to Galway grew.

"You got the car started, Rory. I was saying thanks. And that smooch at the castle? That was all you." His eyes glimmered, and I smirked at his flirtation.

"Whatever." I leaned back into him and watched the game, asking questions about rule play. I rooted for the opposite team to keep things exciting, and every time my team scored, he threw a balled-up paper towel at me.

It seemed we were back to our bantering ways.

Chapter 15

Things normalized between Jaime and me, and the animosity I had felt toward him on the plane, and that first weekend we moved in together, merged with a growing fondness I couldn't shake. He mixed me up with his crooked smile, witty outlook on life, and carefree attitude. If I compared apples to apples, he carried a lot of characteristics I had convinced myself Scott brought to our relationship. Still, Jaime was a thousand times more genuine. He made me feel good, and I knew I had made a mistake wasting my time with Scott.

"Do you have any plans this weekend?" Zoey leaned against my doorway, holding a bowl of rice and sauteed mushrooms. It had become a staple in our household since all our money went to traveling and beer.

I looked at my calendar. "Nothing Friday night. I'm here if you want to go to the pub. Saturday and Sunday I wanted to go to Killarney, and next weekend I wanted to go to Dingle. Want to come?" My eyes and fingers returned to my computer.

"I'll let you know. It depends on how much money I have. I wanted to go to Dublin for the Bank Holiday. I heard they do a big thing for

Halloween. Want to come?"

I looked at my calendar again. *Belfast. Can I get there another weekend?* I scratched my head and rubbed my forehead. "Um." I pinched my bottom lip and flipped to November. "Sure. That'd be great." Traveling was always more fun with a friend, so I crossed off **BELFAST** and scribbled **DUBLIN** onto my calendar.

"Awesome. I'm heading to class. I'll see you later." The door clicked shut, and I continued researching my Women in Ireland project. I had given myself until one o'clock to get as much done as possible, and when my watch beeped, I shut it down.

I opened my email and read a note from Marty. We'd been communicating back and forth since I arrived. She frequently updated me on Scott telling me he missed me—it would have been nice to hear that from him. All I had gotten in response to my breakup email was crickets. Even though I told him not to, I secretly wanted him to respond, baring his heart and soul and apologizing for being such a jerk, but I guess my expectations were too high.

I didn't want to complicate things, so I skirted around the Scott subject anytime Marty brought it up. He was a separate part of my life, and drama from back home didn't belong here. Plus, I had never told her about Jaime, and if Zoey and Marissa didn't know, Marty didn't need to know, either.

A grin spread across my face and I read through her email. **Hi Rory! So, I noticed that tickets to Ireland are wicked cheap next month. I hope you don't mind, but I bought a ticket. Actually, I bought two, because you know me, a complete baby when it comes to flying. Is it cool if I come to visit during Thanksgiving weekend? I don't know who else can come...maybe my sister? Please please please say it's okay because I didn't buy the cancellation insurance. Haha. Love you and miss you! –Marty.**

I couldn't believe she was coming! I hit the reply button and typed one capitalized word: **YES!**

I tapped send, shut my laptop, and danced around my room to invisible music. I vogued over to my radio and turned it on. Pop music from someone I didn't recognize sprang from the speaker and I spun in circles, moving my hips to the beat, and swinging my arms like octopus tentacles. Mid-swing, I saw a long shadow on the floor, and spun to see Jaime standing in the doorway with a wide, goofy grin radiating across his face.

Too excited to feel embarrassed, I danced over and grabbed his hands. We attempted the waltz and tango, but my feet stumbled over his.

"What's the craic?"

My arms draped around his neck, and his hands rested below my hips. I rocked him in circles, staring into his deep eyes. "My best friend is coming to visit. I can't wait for you to meet her. She's a hoot!"

"A hoot?" Jaime asked.

"A hoot! A hot sketch. You're gonna love her. But she doesn't know about you, so we are strictly roommates."

He spun me in a circle. "But that's what we are, right?"

"Yep, I am a single woman living in Ireland. What happens in Galway stays in Galway."

"Single, eh?"

"Yes, officially single." I held up my hand showing my bare finger. "I broke it off with Scott after Clifden. I don't want a boyfriend; I want to have fun. Do you want to have fun with me?" I leaned my face toward him until his lips met mine, too excited to be shocked at my own boldness.

"Yeah, that'd be grand. I guess there's nothing to tell." He pulled me closer, spun me out, and dipped me backward.

I belly-laughed as all the blood rushed to my head. Kissing him deeper, everything I knew about myself washed away in a tidal wave of Jaime bliss. It was time I threw away all the expectations the world had placed upon me and lived life for me...even if it was only for a semester. This was my time to create the life I had always wanted.

One week later, my plans to travel through the Dingle Peninsula were thwarted by time. Looking at the map, it seemed simple to get there and back. Unfortunately, there was no direct way, and all the buses out of Galway stopped in every tiny town. My 157-mile trip was due to take over seven hours to arrive, and I couldn't see myself spending that much time on a stuffy bus. I wanted to go, but not at that expense.

Flipping through my guidebook for something closer, I opened to County Clare, which neighbored County Galway. The word Doolin had been circled and highlighted and the Cliffs of Moher was starred. Surprised that I had missed such a beautiful landmark in my calendar of things-to-do, I studied the map between Doolin and Galway. It didn't look too far.

In tiny black letters, the words Lisdoonvarna jumped at me. I heard the cabbie's words in my head, *'The next festival is the Matchmaking Festival in Lisdoonvarna.'* Searching for festivals in the index, I found Lisdoonvarna's Matchmaking Festival, and flipped past the Cliffs of Moher. There it was. "For the entire month of September, come to Lisdoonvarna for the biggest matchmaking festival in Europe. Meet with Willie Daly, Ireland's premier matchmaker. To date, he has matched over 2,000 couples."

My mind wandered to Scott and the state of our relationship and lack of correspondence. My growing feelings for Jaime convoluted my logic, and I wondered if what I was doing was right. *Maybe the matchmaker could help me sort out my worries.*

Zoey and Marissa sat on the couch in our living room watching Coronation Street, the long-running British soap opera. "Hey, guys." I sat beside Zoey, and she passed me a potato chip. On the screen, a woman I didn't recognize walked past. "Who's that?"

"Lucy Richards. She's a florist and somehow connected to Peter," Marissa said. The three of us had fallen into this addictive show when we first moved in and hadn't found anything else to watch on the telly. Now at least one of us watched it daily and provided updates over dinner.

At the first commercial break, I broke up their trance. "Do you want to go to Doolin this weekend? Jaime has a football match in Cork, so it would be just us girls. I thought we could check out the Cliffs of Moher and then spend a day at the Matchmaker's Festival on our way home. This is the last weekend for the festival, and I heard it's wild."

"Would we be gone the whole weekend?" Marissa asked.

"I think so. We can go to Doolin after classes on Friday, the Cliffs on Saturday morning, head to Lisdoonvarna Saturday night, and then home by Sunday morning." The scheduling was the easy part. The follow through would be tougher with so many personalities involved.

"How much do you think it would cost? I've been going through money kind of quickly so far." Worry lines in Zoey's forehead deepened.

Mental math was not my strong suit so I guessed a generous number. "I don't know. I would say a hundred bucks, just to be safe."

"I'll go," Marissa said. "I have nothing else to do."

"Can I let you know tomorrow? I have to look at my bank account." Zoey's fingers drummed on her lap.

"Sure, of course. In the meantime, I'll do some research and buy tickets tomorrow. Zoey, let me know in the morning, okay?"

Zoey nodded and both girls turned their attention to the telly. I made my way back to my room, scouring my guidebook for hostels, cheap hotels, and bus routes. I'd be hitting two birds with one stone...the travel bug and Cupid's arrow. Maybe this matchmaker could shed some light on my ability to find love.

The next morning, Zoey had gone to school but left a note on the table: **Rory, I'm going to pass on this weekend. Thanks for the invite though! Zoey**

Underneath was a note from Marissa: **Rory, I forgot I have a project due Monday that I haven't even started yet. I'm going to stay home this weekend. Have fun! Marissa**

Frowning, I picked up both notes and contemplated my choices. *Do I travel alone or do I miss out on an opportunity to sort myself?* All I needed was a body to keep me safe, but no available person came to mind.

As much as it pained me to scrap the Cliffs of Moher from my itinerary, finding the matchmaker was more important, and this was the festival's last weekend. It was now or never. Do or die.

That afternoon, I purchased one round trip bus ticket to Lisdoonvarna for Saturday.

Chapter 16

My Saturday morning alarm blared at six a.m., jolting me upright. I had stayed in the night before while Zoey and Marissa went to some local bars and Jaime traveled to Cork with his team. Alone in our apartment, I had curled up under my duvet and thought about my feelings toward Scott and Jaime. Nervousness had turned to excitement as my thoughts transitioned to meeting a real matchmaker, unsure what to expect. I hadn't told anyone about my appointment with him because I felt silly, like I wasn't in control of my life.

Now, dragging myself out of bed, pins and needles swept through my limbs as I carried myself to the shower and down to the bus station. My father would kill me if he knew I was traveling by bus through a foreign country alone. With commitment, I reminded myself that I came to Ireland to grow, and although this solo trip wasn't originally planned, it was necessary.

The bus ride to Lisdoonvarna took a little under two hours, and I spent the time staring out the window, dreaming about creating a life over here. The slower pace, kind people, and natural beauty were the exact opposite of my experiences in Boston. Time slowed, and every moment meant more and had a greater impact than any of the fleeting moments in America.

I knew I had arrived before the bus halted on the narrow street. People of all ages filled the downtown strip, walking up and down the sidewalk and moving in and out of pubs. It wasn't even lunch yet, and the party had already started. Music beat through the closed bus windows and I swayed my head to the beat of a jig, feeling my spirits soar as all thoughts of uncertainty disappeared. This was where I belonged.

Swinging my backpack across my shoulders, I followed a dozen people off the bus and into the chaos of the bustling town. Everywhere I looked, men of all ages popped into my vision. Regardless of their age, they smiled warmly. I couldn't help but smile back, the infectious music lifting my spirits and making me forget about my uncertainty.

I roamed through the streets until I found The Matchmaker's Bar, where Willie Daly set up shop. The pub screamed fun, with its bright colored mural along the outside of the pub, decorated with images of iconic Ireland, musical instruments, and symbols of love. The entrance swam with people, and inside the bar was a sea of men and women, dancing to a band set up in the corner. Brought back to the 1950s, when dating seemed easier, I imagined my grandparents dancing at a sock hop, enjoying the night and all the possibilities it could bring. They would have loved it here.

A crowd of people stood beside the bar on the far side of the pub and a handful of men settled at tables drinking pints. Clusters of women hovered on the outskirts checking out their options.

An older man with white hair and a long beard roamed through the pub holding a thick, tattered book wrapped with twine. I didn't know if that was him, but when I had spoken to the pub owner a few days before, he said I should find the man with the Book of Love. Perhaps that old book was the book I needed.

Rather than approach him I ordered a beer and sat at the bar, watching him mingle with the guests and laugh at their stories. A tall man at least twice my age caught my eye and threaded his way through the crowd. "Hi, I'm Seamus." He stuck out his hand and I shook it. The Irish name brought my thoughts back to Jaime, and I wondered if this was a sign.

"Rory. Nice to meet you."

"Hi, Rory. Are you looking for a husband?"

I choked on the liquid swirling in my mouth and swallowed it down. He was old enough to be my father. "Ehm, no, not really."

"You know, you're a lovely lass. You may find yourself a match here. It might even be me."

I leaned back and smiled politely. "Thank you, I'll, uh, keep that in mind. But no," I reiterated, "I'm not looking for a husband."

"You know, I'm a farmer out in County Tyrone. It's north of here, in Cookstown. I'm a dairy farmer with hundreds of cows. Been in me family for generations. Very successful farm."

I nodded, trying not to be rude, but also not entertaining a continuing conversation.

He didn't seem to notice my shifting body turning away or my arms across my chest, as he continued talking. "Yeah, so I come here every year, looking for a wife. Life can be lonely when you're working all day. It would be nice to come home to a warm meal every now and then."

I choked down another sip. "I'm sorry, Seamus, but I'm actually just visiting. From America. I don't have any plans of settling here in Ireland, but it was nice meeting you." I turned before he could reply and set out to find the matchmaker. *Maybe coming here alone wasn't such a great idea.*

I felt Seamus's eyes on me as I walked away and tried to disappear amongst a group of women in the far end of the pub. When I was confident Seamus had moved onto another unsuspecting woman, I scanned the room for the older man with the ancient book.

He sat at a table with an older couple not too far from where I was standing. I slinked over to them and stood a few feet away, waiting my turn to speak with him.

The couple placed their hand on the old book and all three adults appeared to be praying or meditating. When the couple rose from the table, they hugged and moved toward the dance floor.

I stepped toward the table as he flipped through his book, the brown and yellow pages falling out of the binding and onto the pub table, which he scooped up and shoved back inside.

"Hi, are you Willie Daly? The matchmaker?" I asked. Getting closer, he gave off Santa Claus vibes with his round belly, bushy eyebrows, and rosy cheeks.

"I am. Would you like to sit down?"

He motioned at the seat across from him and I obediently sat. "My name is Rory. I'm visiting from Boston."

"What can I do for you?"

I didn't know how to respond because I didn't know how this worked. "Eh, this is my first time, so I don't know. I made an appointment for half-two. Do you want me to find you then?"

"Ah, no, this will be fine."

I fell into the chair beside him and leaned forward. "I was hoping I could meet with you and you could lead me in the right direction to find my match."

Willie closed the book and secured it with the strap. "Certainly. Please fill out this quick questionnaire." He handed me a piece of paper and a pen and waited silently for me to fill it out. On the sheet of paper I saw three sections: **Physical Attributes. Personal Attributes. Life goals.**

I wrote down the first thing that came to my mind for each section.

Taller than me. Healthy/fit. Kind. Thoughtful. Faithful. Motivated/goal-oriented. Good with money. Good with kids. Personal Goal: Marriage-house-kids. It wasn't specific but hit all the marks of what I considered the attributes a good husband would carry and how my future would unfold.

Willie stuffed it in the back half of his book without even reviewing it or asking further questions. I pushed my eyebrows together, curious about this process.

"Okay, Rory from America, your desires are now in the Book of Love. They will stay here until you find a match."

"What is the Book of Love?" I asked.

"The Book of Love is over 100 years old and belonged to my father and his father before him. This book carries the desires of all the lonely lads and lasses looking for love. It's the magic behind matchmaking."

Willie analyzed my eyes, nose, mouth, and hands, and then continued. "You will find someone but it is someone you least expect. It's actually someone you already know." His eyes rose back to mine and I couldn't look away, enchanted by his prediction. "You must open your heart to new possibilities, or love will not grasp you. When you find yourself falling, you must not doubt yourself. Open your heart and follow it. Love is right around the corner."

Disappointment crossed my face at his rather generic prophesy.

He took my hand and placed it on the Book of Love. "I want you to close your eyes for eleven seconds and think of your future. Imagine yourself with your perfect match. Keep your hand on the book so it can transfer its power to you. Ready?"

I nodded, closing my eyes.

"And go."

My mind created an image of life fifteen years from now. Standing in a yard, I saw a white cape-style home surrounded by a white picket fence, creating a perfect square. A child ran through the grass and was placed on a swing set by a man without a face. He wore a baseball cap, and I couldn't see his hair. He was goofy, pushing a boy on the swing, both laughing with joy. I saw myself looking at him lovingly, appreciating him for being so different from me. My child had dark hair that shined red in the light and a smattering of freckles across his nose. The man chased the toddler up and down the slide. I smiled at the two of them, observing the relationship and feeling thankful that he was nothing like my father.

"And open." Willie's words broke me from my fantasy and I smiled.

"Thank you." I pulled my hand away from the book and placed it in my lap.

"You will find your match within six months. Just remember, Rory, you must keep your heart open."

I placed a few coins on the table, thanked him for his time, and walked outside, considering Willie's words. *You will find your match within six months.* That seemed pretty sudden, when I had limited experience in the area of love. Although not any clearer than when I arrived, I felt a strange sort of peace within me that perhaps things would work out. I just needed to keep my options open and think with my heart, not my head.

But six months? That would put me at April. Could I really find true love by April? It felt unlikely, but I was up for the challenge.

Chapter 17

"What's up with you and Jaime?" Marissa leaned forward, holding my gaze until I looked away. My face burned, and several responses ran through my head, but my mouth couldn't formulate the words.

"What do you mean?" Playing dumb, I analyzed the loose string hanging from the hem of my shirt.

"I don't know. It's weird. He used to stay out late and stroll in after we were asleep, but now he's home with us. He's from Ireland. Why would he be hanging out with a bunch of annoying Americans? And late at night, I hear you giggling in your room."

I blinked a few times, unable to meet her gaze. "Do you need a drink?" I cleared my throat and walked to the sink, filling two glasses with water. When I gave her the glass, she smirked at me.

"Your silence is telling." Her smile stretched across her face. "I can't believe you're sleeping with him!" She slapped me on the arm.

"No, no. I'm not. We're not. We're just friends." I held my breath, but her eyes told me she didn't believe me. "With benefits. We have an agreement." I fumbled with the cup and drank tiny sips. My parched mouth wanted water, but it was like I had forgotten how to swallow. I wanted to run to my room and hide under my bed, but my legs had stopped working.

Marissa leaned back. "You're not serious!" When I didn't reply, she leaned forward. "You are! Does Zoey know?"

I shook my head. "No one knows—except you. But now that you know, we have to tell Zoey. It's not fair to keep a secret from her." *What am I saying?* I sounded like a blubbering idiot. My mouth clamped shut, worried Jaime would be mad that the cat fell out of the bag and onto the kitchen table.

Marissa's eyes sparkled. "How long?"

I looked around the room, not wanting to share too many personal details. "Since Connemara."

She smacked her hand on the table. "Are you serious? That was almost a month ago! How did you not tell us?"

I shrugged. "Because it isn't anything except two people having fun. You have fun almost every weekend, meeting guys at the pub and dancing with them at the clubs. If I didn't see you with them, I probably wouldn't know."

Marissa sat back in her chair, and looked me up and down. "But I don't live with them, and it's one night of fun. Not four months as roommates. Your fun is way more complicated than mine."

She had me there. I knew Jaime sang in the shower, only did laundry once a week, and so far, he hadn't washed his sheets. It felt more personal than I wanted.

"I'm just having fun." Leaning forward and staring into Marissa's almond-shaped eyes, I whispered, "Please pretend you didn't figure it out. I don't want to make it any weirder between Jaime and me than it already is."

Marissa zipped her mouth, twisted the corner, and threw the invisible key onto the floor. "Mum's the word."

That Friday, I went to a football party on campus with Jaime and promised Marissa and Zoey I'd meet up with them later that night.

Marissa pulled her hair up in a bandana. "Eleven o'clock work for you? I'll make sure we're at The Pub on the Quay. I think it's new, so I heard it hasn't been inundated with tourists yet."

"Like us?" Zoey asked.

Marissa straightened her jacket. "Nah, we stopped being tourists weeks ago." The two girls fell into a conversation about all the pubs they wanted to visit and I continued getting ready.

Glancing at Jaime, I asked, "Can you walk me down after the party?"

He nodded and squeezed his feet into his sneakers.

"You know," I pointed to his shoes, "You're going to break the heel if you don't undo the laces first."

"Thanks, ma." He grinned and slid his other foot into the tightly laced shoe.

I reminded myself that he didn't need me to mother him. I needed to be his roommate, or friend, or whatever I was to him.

I hugged the girls. "See you tonight."

They winked at me. "Take care of her," Marissa called to Jaime.

"No monkey business," Zoey added.

"Be home by curfew, or you're both grounded," Marissa said.

"And don't do anything I wouldn't do," Zoey chimed.

I raced out of my bedroom to rush them out the door. Marissa and Zoey knew, but Jaime didn't know they knew. So now, when the four of us were together, Marissa and Zoey gave each other looks, giggled, and made jokes about my dilemma. Jaime often egged them on, thinking they were laughing at his jokes, but they were really laughing at our situation.

Both girls burst into giggles, and I shooed them out, slamming the door behind them and leaning my head against it. I inhaled and exhaled, waiting for my racing heart to slow.

I hurried into the bathroom and finished getting ready. Jaime watched me from behind, and my chest tightened. Smiling nervously at him through the reflection, I leaned forward to apply my deep red lipstick with shaking hands. Feeling his stare made my body heat from the inside and my stomach flutter.

"You look beautiful," he said.

He was gone when my eyes moved from my reflection to the door. It was almost like I had imagined it, but my ears heard him and my mind hung onto his words.

When I left our room, he was on the couch, with his leg crossed over his knee, flipping through the channels. "I'm ready whenever you are."

We walked into the city, traveling amid groups of college kids making the most of their weekend. The autumn night held a chill that felt like fire pits and s'mores. I had refused to wear a coat because although the temperature was cold, the pubs were hot, and walking home with pints in my belly always kept me warm.

"Where does Owen live?" This was my first time hanging out with Jaime and his buddies. I didn't know what to expect, and not having my female roommates there to protect me made me nervous. A bunch of football players and alcohol didn't mix well, so I decided to stay sober until I met Zoey and Marissa later that night.

Jaime nodded sideways. "The apartments behind the school along the River Corrib. We should be there in about ten minutes."

Listening to the chatter and seeing the groups of college kids walking in front and behind us, I hurried my step to stay with Jaime. "Popular place, huh?" A barrage of music traveled over the river to the street as we marched onward.

"Yeah, one of the biggest party places in town."

My pace slowed, and I took in the sounds, lights, and people. Jaime slowed his gait to match mine. "No worries," he said, "Just stay close to me. Let me know when you want to go, and I'll walk you into town."

I lifted my head high and embraced my badass self. I wanted to live life in Ireland, and Jaime could show me the way. *This is it, Rory. Your first Irish party.* My stomach somersaulted and I hooked my arm through his while he ushered me into the party.

The tiny apartment reeked of men and women wanting to have a good time. Beer, perfume, and cologne filled my nostrils. Squeezing behind Jaime through the throngs of sweaty bodies, we made our way to the cramped kitchen. Bottles of whiskey surrounded empty shot glasses along the crowded counter.

The layout of Owen's apartment was the same as ours; the standard dorm furniture, now covered in people and outerwear, looked similar, and the tile floors matched my own. I could have been throwing this party, and I would have been a better hostess. The counter would be clean and I would have draped the jackets across the beds. I wanted to remove all the shot glasses and place them in the sink, but I refrained.

"Hey," Owen called over the chatter. He raised his arm in a wave and handed Jaime a shot. "Whiskey?" Jaime tossed it in his mouth without a flinch or a gasp.

"Rory?" Owen held up a full glass.

I shook my head and held up my water bottle. Shoving it in my purse, I squeezed my hands and fiddled with my watch. My water bottle told everyone I was an outsider.

"How's the foot?" Owen asked.

"Better, thanks. Good as new." My mother's nagging voice sang in my head. *Be safe, Rory. And don't forget, moderation is key.*

A group of tall, strong-looking guys surrounded Owen and Jaime. They laughed about things I didn't understand, and I looked around the room, eavesdropping on their conversation. I desperately wanted to be part of the narrative.

There was only one other girl I could see, and my guard immediately rose. *Maybe this is a mistake.* It was the girl from the photograph smiling at me in Jaime's room. Watching her, she appeared overly familiar with the guys, bouncing to the fridge, leaning against Jaime, and throwing back shots.

Her striking eyes, perky breasts, and cute button nose accentuated her flirtatious ways, and the wall around my heart fortified.

Sitting on the couch, I continued to watch Jaime from the corner of my eye. He put his arm around her, and Owen handed her a beer. Jaime had never spoken about female friends, and I wondered how he knew this blonde woman. Based on my detective skills in Clifden, he knew her well. I assumed she was Irish, but so many accents floated in the air, I couldn't be sure.

She and Jaime chatted for a while, laughing, sharing drinks, and playfully leaning into each other. I clenched my teeth and squinted my eyes to get a better look. *Yep, definitely flirting.* I leaned forward and rubbed my hands up and down my chilly, bare arms. Waves of jealousy leaped at me like a tiger jumping through a fire-soaked ring. I questioned my reaction and bit my lip. *He's not your boyfriend. He's your friend. He can do whatever he wants.* No matter how much I tried to convince myself the emotion I was feeling wasn't jealousy, I couldn't shake it.

Giving into my jealousy, I asked the guy next to me for a shot. He rubbed his hand over his face and hoisted himself off the sunken couch. A few moments later, I threw the tiny glass back and gulped. The amber liquid burned my esophagus, traveled through my stomach, and down my limbs. My face twisted, and I gasped, feeling the heat race through my body. My muscles tingled, and my chest tightened before my entire body relaxed.

I moved toward Jaime with the woman's ear-piercing laughter cutting through the room, causing my head to throb. I didn't want to intrude or make a scene, but I wanted to be seen.

Jaime turned and smiled. "Hey! Where've you been?"

Like he couldn't see me. I half-smiled, pretending I hadn't taken offense to his question. "Just hanging out over there." I threw my hand backward, not aiming at anything in particular. "Who's this?" I looked at the woman beside him.

"Aoife. Owen's sister."

My hand jutted across the counter. "Ay-fa," I pronounced. "Nice to meet you. I'm Rory, Jaime's roommate. Your brother helped me when I hurt my foot, and he drove me home. It was nice of him. He's a nice guy." I fixed my mouth shut, aware of my intoxicated blabbing.

Jaime's eyebrows resembled a red unibrow. I stopped rambling and pulled myself together. "Damn, that whiskey's stronger than I thought." I leaned on the counter, my shoulder pressed against the wall.

"Yeah. Let's get some fresh air." Grabbing my elbow, Jaime led me out into the cold.

The night breeze hit me in the face, and scent of peat swirled through the air. I dropped into a chair, closed my eyes, and let the wind whip the alcohol out of me.

"You okay?" he asked.

"Grand." I didn't feel grand. I felt out of control, obsessive and possessive over a guy that was just my friend. I wrung my hand in my lap and shivered, imagining the next day with a hangover and pneumonia. This night was not going the way I had hoped.

"Are you okay with walking to the pubs? It'll take at least ten minutes." He turned and greeted three girls who walked out of the house and stood beside us.

I smiled, tight-lipped. "Yeah, it'll be good to walk."

I hugged my torso and ran my hands up and down my arms, trying to force the goosebumps down. From the corner of my eye, I watched him greet everyone with hugs, high-fives, and pats on the back. *Popular guy. It's like I'm out with the mayor.*

Jaime seemed perfectly fine, even though I had watched him swallow at least three shot glasses of whiskey. He reminded me of Hercules. A thinner Hercules with red hair.

He draped his sweatshirt over my shoulders and went into the house to say goodbye to Owen, Aoife, and whoever else he knew but hadn't introduced.

The walk into town was quiet. I concentrated on my steps, careful not to trip over the broken sidewalk, and hooked my arm through his. His sturdy body supported me as I stumbled into town. I didn't know how to get there, and I put all my trust in Jaime.

The light from the main drag beamed up at me as we made our way down the hill.

"What time is it?" I asked.

"Half-ten. Let's find the girls."

The dim pub was just as crowded as Owen's apartment and I held onto Jaime's hand as we pushed our way to the bar.

"What do you want?" he asked me.

I pressed my lips together, raised my eyebrows, and pulled my head back. "Water." My drinking tolerance wasn't up to Ireland's standards, and I wasn't legally allowed to drink at home, so my experience was minimal. I needed to keep my guard up, just in case something awful happened.

We stood against the back wall, facing the front of the pub so we'd see when Zoey and Marissa walked in. My legs hurt, and I knew they'd hurt more after climbing the hill home, when the fog around my brain had cleared.

"Holy shit."

I looked at Jaime, and he pointed toward the door.

In the corner, under a stained-glass overhead light, were Zoey and Marissa. Kissing.

Chapter 18

Hypocrite. I couldn't believe what I was seeing. *Marissa told me dating your roommate was a bad idea, and here she was, making out with her roommate.* I was too tipsy to get annoyed, and instead humor overtook my mouth. "Ha!" I nudged Jaime in the side. "Look at that!"

A sly grin spread across his face. "I wondered. They're both beautiful and they're always together." He raised his beer to his mouth and swallowed, and his eyes remained on the two women in the corner. Their heads bent close in conversation and as we watched, Zoey reached out and touched Marissa's hand.

"Let's hide." I pulled him back to the bar. "They need their privacy. Let's pretend we didn't see that." I pulled his face close so my voice wouldn't carry through the packed pub. "We're not even supposed to be here." Each word took its own final punctuation, like I was sharing the world's secrets that no one else could hear.

His glassy eyes pulled away from mine, and he greeted a couple also pushed up against the counter.

"Who's that?" Whispering into his ear and nodding at the couple, I squeezed my way into his world.

"Not sure." I focused on the lopsided smile hiding behind his beard, and admired his confidence. The crowded pub encouraged us to be close, and I took advantage of the rowdy drinkers occasionally bumping into me and pushing me closer to Jaime.

At eleven o'clock, I turned to face the door because that was the time we agreed to meet. Marissa and Zoey walked toward us. Marissa's rosy face and hunched posture reminded me of when I went to a frat party, spent the night, and walked back to my dorm in my crop top, short skirt, and heeled boots. At first, I had regretted that decision, but bad choices led to learning good judgment, so I gave myself a pass and told myself never to get that drunk again.

"Hi," Zoey shouted over the chatter. "I didn't expect to see you here."

Jaime leaned down so his mouth was next to her ear. "Yeah, we got here at half-ten."

Marissa's shoulders pulled back sharply, and she raised her head. Her smile vanished and creases appeared between her eyebrows as her eyes dated between us. I kept my expression carefully neutral, and as quickly as her posture had stiffened, it relaxed again.

"How was the party?" Zoey asked.

"It was fine," I said. "Lots of people I didn't know."

I exchanged curious glances with Jaime and noticed Marissa and Zoey did the same. I was dying to know what had transpired a few minutes before, or even days or weeks, but I couldn't bring myself to address the elephant in the room.

"Marissa, I'm gonna grab a beer. Do you want one?" Zoey nodded to the bar.

"Yeah, I'll come."

The two girls left Jaime and me alone, and I word-vomited all my thoughts. "Do you think they're together? It's so weird. Marissa told me the other day she would never date her roommate. Maybe they're not dating. Maybe they're just hanging out....like us? I don't know. I kind of want to say something, but I don't. It's none of my business."

I glanced at the bar, and Marissa and Zoey were still waiting. Jaime checked his phone. "Jaime." I widened my eyes at him and lurched my head forward.

He looked up. "Sorry. I wasn't listening. Are you okay if I head back to Owen's?"

"What?" I threw my hands up in the air. "You weren't even listening?" I took a sip of my water and gently placed it on the table.

"Sorry. Owen needs some help." He stood, shoved his phone into his pocket, and kissed me. "I'm crashing there. You'll be okay, right?"

I glanced at my two roommates standing inches apart near the high-top table behind the bar. "Sure." Grabbing my drink, I said, "Let me check and see what they're up to."

As I approached, Marissa and Zoey were speaking with their heads close together. I knew whatever they were discussing was special to them because they stopped and looked at me when I walked into their space. Zoey jumped up and hugged me. "I love you," she said. I smelled the alcohol on her breath and heard it in her slurred speech.

I was more alert than her, and dread consumed me as images of the long walk home galloped across my mind. "I love you too, Zoey. Is it cool if I hang with you? Jaime's going back to the party."

"Ooh! Jaime, can I come?" Zoey stumbled over to him.

He scanned her slanted body, pressed against the wall, and grinned. "I think the party's over. He needs help cleaning up."

Zoey pouted, exaggerating her bottom lip. "Okay, Jaime. Maybe next time." She returned to Marissa, staring at the musicians. Sounds of flute, fiddle, and accordion transformed the tiny pub into a rollicking party.

"I'd like to stay and listen to the music," I said.

Jaime said goodbye and made his way toward the door. His short stature, by American standards, bobbed away from us until he disappeared into the sea of people.

112

Always the responsible one, I sipped my water, praying my roommates would sober up before the pub closed. Someone needed to navigate through the twisty residential streets of Galway to the safety of our apartment, and I was the best choice.

Like waves in the ocean, people came and went, but we swayed like seagrass on the ocean floor. After the music ended, a bell rang and the lights clicked on, signaling closing time.

Zoey leaned her head against Marissa, and her eyes closed.

"Hey, Zoe?" I looked at her and then at Marissa. "I think we should get a cab or something. I don't think she'll make it home if we walk."

"Rough night, aye?" the bartender asked, collecting empty bottles littered around the pub.

Marissa tightened her lips, looking at Zoey. "You could say that. Do you know where we can get a cab or taxi?"

His warm eyes moved to Zoey and back to Marissa. "I have a car. I can drive you."

Marissa's face lit up, and she leaned toward me. "He can drive us."

Alarm bells rang in my ears, alerting me to stranger danger. "I don't know." I played with the empty beer bottle left in the middle of our table to distract my mind from moving toward a worst-case scenario. My watch read one-forty-five, and a sudden wave of mental and physical fatigue washed over me. *We couldn't sleep at the pub, could we?*

"That's okay," I interrupted, "Do you have the number for a taxi?"

He handed me a bent, sticky card from behind the bar, and I struggled to read the numbers.

"Can I use your phone? Sorry," I mumbled.

He passed me the phone and continued to wipe down the pub tables.

"How do I do this?" I felt like an idiot. I knew how to make an international call but hadn't dialed another person in Ireland before.

Irritation crossed his face and he took the card and dialed for me.

"Hello?" a sleepy, deep voice answered.

"Hi, yes, sorry to bother you. Are you a taxi service?"

"Aye. I'm a hackney service."

I scrunched my eyebrows together. "What's that?"

"Like a taxi."

"Oh, my roommates and I need a ride from the Pub on the Quay to Bealtaine. Can you pick us up?"

"Aye. Be there in ten. Pick you up near the Spanish Arch."

I hung up the phone and retrieved my roommates. "Thank you, again, but we got a ride," I said to the bartender. I turned to Marissa, whose giant eyes moved around the pub, while Zoey slept on her shoulder. "Taxi will be here in ten."

We waited at the edge of the pedestrian street near the Spanish Arch, the place where Spanish ships had docked during Medieval times. Unsure what our taxi looked like, I stayed on high alert while Marissa and Zoey plopped against the stone wall. The traditional music seeping out of the pubs had died down, and only a few tourists and college kids stumbled down the road.

As predicted, a black car from the 1950s zoomed around the corner and screeched to a halt. "You need a ride?" he called out his window. A yellow sign with lit numbers decorated the roof of the car. "Bealtaine, right?"

He flew up and down the streets of Galway, tires squealing as he took turns too wide. Zoey and Marissa ooh'd and ahh'd like they were riding a roller coaster while I gripped the handrail like this was my last ride on earth. He zipped down our street and slammed on the brakes in front of the main entrance.

Shoving money at him, I jumped out of the car and retrieved my roommates.

It was quiet and dark when we reached our apartment. I couldn't help but wonder how Jaime's night went, and fell asleep wishing I had gone with him back to Owen's.

A blazing headache greeted me in the morning, not from the alcohol, but from the stress of taking care of my drunk roommates. My calendar dictated a trip to Blarney Castle today, but I didn't have it in me. The constant pressure to hit all my weekend excursions took the fun out of traveling, so I remained in bed, staring at the wall.

Jaime's messy bed, with crumpled blankets on the floor and a balled-up sheet in the corner, hadn't been slept in. Thinking about where he slept the night before, I rolled over and covered my head with my pillow. Thoughts of Jaime and the blonde flashed at me.

So much had changed within the past few weeks, I almost didn't recognize myself. The apartment remained quiet, and I questioned whether Marissa and Zoey had left. When dishes rattled in the kitchen, I finally removed myself from my blanket cocoon and ventured out of hibernation.

"Morning," Marissa said. "Or, good afternoon." She sat at the counter eating a bowl of cereal. "Weren't you traveling today?"

She looked better than I had expected. She had showered and dressed, and there was no sign of alcohol on her face. "Maybe tomorrow. I need a day to recoup from last night."

She smiled. "Yeah, it was crazy."

"How did you sleep?" I grabbed an apple, and the crisp smack of my teeth breaking the skin echoed off the generic walls.

"Awesome. I fell asleep as soon as my head hit the pillow."

"Meet any cute guys?" I asked, breaking eye contact.

Her overflowing spoon crammed into her mouth, and she chewed noisily before responding. "A few, but Zoey got wasted, so she took up most of my attention."

"Yeah, no kidding! I don't think we would have made it home if we didn't get that taxi."

Marissa shrugged and drank the milk straight from the bowl.

"Where's Jaime?"

"Don't know. Probably still at Owen's."

"What are you doing today?"

"I think I might go to Eyre Square. It looks like a beautiful day, and I could use the sunshine."

"Want company?"

"Nah, I'm kind of moving slow today." I didn't think I'd be able to hold a conversation for the entire walk downtown, although I was curious if she would open up about her rendezvous last night.

I pulled myself out of my chair and forced myself to prepare for the day. I glanced at Jaime's empty bed again and frowned. I wanted to call him but didn't have his number.

The hike to Eyre Square was longer than I remembered and I picked up my pace until I marched into the mobile store. "I need a mobile phone," I said to the clerk behind the counter.

Thirty minutes later, I walked out with a smile and a flip phone smaller than the palm of my hand. I could now call my Irish friends, call home, and call a cab.

Sitting in an internet café, I emailed my family and Marty. **Greetings from Galway! I got a cell phone today, so anytime you need to talk, call me. Here's my number.** I flipped open my phone and typed in the ten-digit number. **–Rory**

I scanned through my email and pulled up the latest from Marty. **Hey Rory! I miss you so much. I can't wait for Thanksgiving! It's only four weeks away. Here is my plane info. You might have to help me get to you from the airport. I'm super nervous about traveling to a foreign country, but if you could do it, I can too. I invited my sister.** I scrunched my nose and exhaled. Marty's twin sister, Mandy, was fine, but she wasn't my favorite person. She always needed to be the center of attention. Whenever I hung out with her, my plans went to crap. **She's really excited to see you. Please** send me all the important stuff I need to remember...like your address, how to get to you, and what to pack. We'll be there from Wednesday to Saturday. Love you!

I replied to her email, outlining the steps to find me. She'd need to hop on a bus from the airport and then find a cab at Eyre Square. *She'll figure it out.*

The frequency of my parents' emails had dwindled over the past few weeks. I didn't want them to think I only emailed when I needed money, so I sent a quick hello. Over the past decade, my relationship with my parents had thinned. They forced their ideals of a perfect life onto me, yet they lived a fake life where no one really knew what went on behind the curtain of our home. A cheating dad and a pill-popping mom, both afraid to ruin me, actually did ruin me by their inaction.

I kept the email short and sweet, then scanned through the rest of my inbox.

Nothing from Scott. Even though I broke up with him, I still expected some sort of response, but his silence illustrated just how shallow our relationship was.

Alone with my thoughts, I left the internet café and wandered out to the enormous park to people-watch. It seemed half of Galway had taken advantage of this beautiful day. The hot weather reminded me of late August, and the radiant blue sky scared all the rain clouds away. Looking around, the changing leaves reminded me of home.

Far in the distance, I saw a group of guys playing football. My stomach dropped when I recognized the red hair. Stepping closer to get a better view, I watched Jaime kick the ball high in the sky and a group of guys chase after it. Following the ball, the image disintegrated with the sun's rays. Shielding my eyes to get a better view, a blow to my shoulder rocked me back, and I spun and fell on my knees in the hard, grassy dirt.

"Oomph!" escaped from my lips. Someone ran over and grabbed

my hand. The sun shone directly above me, and the image remained in shadow.

"You grand?" he asked.

I moved my head to the side to block the sun and saw Jaime's lovely, tender eyes.

"Never better."

"Funny meeting you like this. Again." He reached out his hand and pulled me up.

I brushed off my pants and waved at Owen.

"Want to play football?" Jaime asked. "We need another player."

I dropped my bag at my feet and leaned into him. "I was the soccer team star when I was five." I didn't break his gaze and felt my nose grow with deceit. "Am I on your team?"

He looked past me at the guys standing around, waiting to play. "Nah, other team."

"You're on. You're still coming to Dublin with us next weekend, right?"

He cocked his head back. "Aye."

"Winner gets to pick out the Halloween costume of the loser for next weekend."

He stuck out his hand. "Deal." I stayed in step with him as he jogged back to his friends.

Turning on my biggest smile and confident stature, I joined the group but stayed close to Owen. Wiping my sweaty palms on the back of my jeans, I introduced myself to the guys, hoping my confidence made me competent. *I can't play sports. What am I doing? Just go with it.* Images of Jaime dressed like a cowboy in tight jeans that squeezed his round, muscular butt, passed through my mind, and I shivered with anticipation. *I must win.*

Chapter 19

Americans obsessed over soccer when their kids were little and needed to learn how to play a sport. We had a national soccer team, but they never dominated cable as they did in Europe. I knew the basics but didn't know the official rules. *You run and try to get the ball in the net, right? No hands allowed. It can't be that hard.*

Owen motioned for everyone to join the huddle and I found myself wedged between a short, skinny guy covered in freckles and a tall, wide guy with chiseled arms. I recognized some guys from the party, but didn't know anyone's name except for Owen. Aoife sat on the sidelines near the dropped backpacks, and I half-waved in her direction before leaning into the huddle.

"We're tied. The next team to score wins," Owen recapped. "Paddy, you're fast; I need you to take the ball. Rory, I need you to block Jaime. Everyone else, you'll have to switch between attacking and defending." I nodded at the fellows like I could do this with my eyes closed.

Stay with Jaime. I zeroed in on him and lunged forward to prepare myself for kick off. Before I could process what was happening, the guys moved like a blob, racing back and forth from side to side. I tried to stay out of their way, avoiding contact, but remained focused on my main target.

I waved my arms around his head like I was playing basketball and blocking a shot at the hoop.

He squinted and tipped his head before sidestepping past me. I spun in a semi-circle and raced after him. I didn't know where our goal was, but if I didn't have the ball, it didn't matter.

My heart threatened to bust my chest open, and I could feel it beating through my fingertips. Desperate for water, I leaned over, clutching my side. Sweat droplets formed at my hairline, and I cursed global warming for stopping the rain from falling today. My jeans hung at my hips, and the hem of my pants dragged along the grass. I yanked them up and ran toward Jaime at full speed.

The ball traveled up and down the field, and a small crowd of people huddled near the goalpost cheered. Eventually, my parched throat hurt to swallow, and I stopped running. Clammy streams of sweat ran down my face, and I regretted not wearing deodorant that day. I couldn't show weakness, so I fought through, pretending I was a superhero with healing powers. *Almost over, Rory. Keep running.*

Jaime had the ball, and he was coming close to a goal. I didn't know if it was my goal, but I assumed he knew where he was running. Cutting in front of him, I kicked for the ball, but my foot smashed into his shin. He tumbled to the ground, rolling with his knee pressed to his chest. His face pulled into a grimace, and his eyes squinted shut as he hollered through clenched teeth.

"Jaime!" I knelt at his side. "Are you okay?" The rest of the guys swarmed around us.

"Yeah, lovely."

I pulled back at his harsh voice, knowing I had gone too far. I held my hand to pull him up, but he pushed against the ground and limped to the sideline.

Aoife jogged to us and handed Jaime a water bottle. "Need a drink, aye?"

He unscrewed the cap and guzzled four gulps before wiping his mustache with the back of his filthy arm. "Thanks, Aoife." He handed it back to her, and she finished the bottle.

I cocked my head, and shielded my eyes from the bright sun.

"Rory, you coming back?" Owen yelled over the grassy field.

I turned to him, then back to Jaime. "Are you okay?"

"I'm injured, but fine. Go play."

Aoife sat beside him on the grass and smirked up at me. "No worries. I'll take care of him."

I narrowed my eyes and turned my lips upward. "Sure thing."

The rest of the game was a blur. I didn't know who I needed to be blocking or even who was on my team. Every time I ran up and down the field, my eyes darted to where Jaime and Aoife were talking, and my heart pounded from jealousy or exertion; I wasn't sure which. This unfamiliar feeling prickled my skin, and I didn't know what to do with it, so I ran with the group, trying to disappear into the crowd. Occasionally the ball whizzed past my head, taking me by surprise. My eyes traveled with it as it flew between two sticks, acting as the goal. I spun to see Jaime's reaction, but he was deep in conversation with Aoife, handing her his phone.

Half the team cheered, and half the team groaned. I looked at Owen instead, and he huffed his way to the sideline. Jaime stood and high-fived a group of guys.

Damn, we lost. I jogged to the sideline and grabbed my water out of my purse. I didn't want to see Jaime. I hated losing, and I didn't know what he'd have in store for me next weekend or if he'd hold me to it.

"Good game," I said to the guys. Most of them ignored me.

I gathered my belongings and sat beside Jaime.

"Good game," I said.

121

"Good match," he replied.

"Good match, Rory. Nice try," Aoife added.

I ignored her and faced Jaime. "Sorry about your leg." My eyes scanned down his body to his grass-stained knees.

"No worries, it's fine." He turned to me, with a glint in his eyes. "So, next weekend, we're dressing up for Halloween, huh?"

I pulled my legs into my chest and rocked backward. "I guess we are." I smirked at Aoife and readjusted my sweaty ponytail. She smiled back with kind eyes this time, but I wasn't quite ready to trust her.

As I spun my head to face him, my smirk turned into a smile. *We are definitely hanging out again.* My stomach flip-flopped, and my chest got hot. The excitement rose to my cheeks and I prayed he wouldn't notice.

"We gotta go see my ma and da and get some costumes," he said.

A nervous laugh escaped my mouth. "I can't wait to see what you come up with."

Not only were we going out next weekend, but we were heading back to Clifden. I spent the rest of the week imagining what costume I'd be destined to wear. Back in the states, Halloween was an excuse for women to disguise their costume with sex appeal, like a cat wearing fishnets or a bunny in heels. I would never wear something like that back home, but I would challenge myself for Jaime.

A few days later, I followed Jaime up the bus stairs and down the aisle, feeling the engine rumble through the floor and against my feet. He slid against the window a third of the way back, and I plopped beside him, dropping my bag on my lap, and watching the rest of the bus fill.

"You know," I said to him, "I've never skipped class before, so this is a first." Just the thought of throwing away money or jeopardizing my final grade point average was enough to make my heart race and nervous firecrackers explode in my stomach. Jaime had purchased bus tickets to Clifden with a return ticket the next day, which meant I wouldn't attend four classes. My seat would remain empty in the large auditorium, and the professor would continue, unaware that I wasn't there.

"Living on the wild side, eh?" He threw back his head and laughed, and the firecrackers in my belly turned to butterflies.

"When in Ireland, do as the Irish do, and you get to be my tour guide today." I shimmied out of my raincoat and stretched my arms before settling into him.

The bus pulled out of the station and crawled along the narrow, hilly roads. The urban homes and apartments in Galway gave way to remote towns, leading into the vibrant green mountains of Connemara. This was my third time traveling these roads, and they were beginning to feel like home.

"Who's picking us up at the station?" I asked, handing Jaime my opened bag of candy.

His hand disappeared in the bag. "My ma. She's been talking about this all week. Said she pulled out the Halloween trunk. She's been collecting things since I was a young lad."

"What was Halloween like for you, growing up? Did you get a lot of candy?" I brushed my hair back with my fingers.

"My mom cooked colcannon. Ever hear of it?" He shifted toward me, and I couldn't help but fully attend to his golden-brown eyes.

"No, what's that?"

"Mashed potatoes."

I laughed. "Why not call them mashed potatoes?"

"Because they're Irish."

My lips turned up, and I leaned across him to observe a flock of sheep grazing on the hillside.

"My ma would hide little toys for me to find in my colcannon. Usually, it was a gift from the fairies. After dinner, I'd walk around

123

trick or treating, throwing dust at people's feet to release any souls held captive by the fairies." He smiled at me, and I couldn't tell if he was joking.

I bit my lip and bobbed my head. "Interesting. Sounds fun."

Falling into easy conversation, a warmth filled me from the inside. Outside, a quaint town presented itself and rainbow colors painted against the different shops jumped out at me. "Are we here?"

Jaime looked around the town. "Ehm, not yet."

The bus meandered through the small streets and pulled to a stop. "Now we're here," Jaime said, gathering his things. The engine cut, and the front door swung open.

A heavy feeling in my pelvis rose through my abdomen. My heart beat like an African drum, and I suddenly felt nauseous. I wanted to grab Jaime's arm for support, but held back. *What is wrong with me?* My body was betraying me, and I didn't understand why.

"Jaime, are you sure your mom and dad are cool with me staying the night?" I whispered.

"Aye."

I ran my hand through my hair, but my fingers caught in the knots. My bag rested over my shoulder, and I imitated Jaime's relaxed strides down the street. Deirdre's wild hair bobbed near their car. She held a sign that read, "Seamus and Rory" in black and orange bubble paint.

I burst out laughing, the restlessness in my body dissipating through my feet and onto the pavement like a rain puddle.

Crisp, clean air welcomed me, and scents of rain, and possibly snow, lingered on the air molecules as they pushed against my body. I filled my lungs with Connemara air, and slowly exhaled before approaching Deirdre.

Standing behind Jaime, I noticed Deirdre's grin as Jaime wrapped his arms around her in a tight hug. Little champagne bubbles popped in my abdomen as I recognized their strong love for each other, and my heart ached, knowing that I didn't have that intimate level of connection with my parents. I rocked back on my heels, unsure if I should wave or give Deirdre a hug.

Before I could commit to one greeting or the other, Deirdre wrapped me in an equally tight hug. My breath squeezed out of my lungs, and I dropped my bag on the hard, cold sidewalk. I embraced the warmth of her soul and inhaled the sweet fragrance of tea. "I'm so glad you're here." She squeezed my shoulders and turned to Jaime. "Ready?"

He picked up my bag in one hand and carried his bag in the other, and I followed close behind.

When we arrived at the house, Deirdre pulled us into the living room and gestured at the plastic boxes stack on the floor. "Rory, dear. I've been looking through the house and have quite a few ideas. I hope you're ready for a brilliant night."

I smiled and glanced at Jaime. He returned the grin and his eyes crinkled with mischief. *Brilliant night, huh?* I hadn't a clue what she meant.

"This bucket is filled with treasure," she said before removing the lid.

Peering inside, I saw the piled fabric, sequins, and hats.

"I already have an idea; I just hope it's in here," Jaime said. He ravenously dug under the top items, pulling out a pirate sword. "Ah-ha! Good as new." The thin blade bent cock-eyed in the middle, and a significant dent permanently imprinted into the hard plastic. When Jaime swung, it shook.

"A pirate?" I asked.

"Not just any pirate, but a pirate from the 1990s, when I was a kid. Back then, we wore black bin bags and let our imagination soar."

I squinted at him and laughed with uncertainty. "A what?"

"A bin bag. Everyone did it. Hottest Halloween costume of the decade." He moved to the kitchen and rummaged under the sink.

"Do you mean a trash bag?"

"Yes, dear, it was what we did," Deirdre said. "We didn't have money for fancy costumes, so we got creative. The kids didn't know the difference." She readjusted the Halloween props, pressing down on the lid. A tattered photo album rested at my feet and Deirdre flipped through the weathered pages. When she got to the back of the book, she struggled with the sticky plastic sleeve and handed me a yellowed photo. "Would you like some tea, dear?"

"Yes, please." I watched her move to the kitchen before turning my gaze to the old photo. Four kids, about ten years old, sat on a couch. Face makeup covered the children, and each wore a hat and a black belted trash bag. I identified them as witches, pirates, and wizards.

"Oh, wow. This is great." I waved the photo at Jaime.

"Do you know which one I am?" he asked, leaning over my shoulder. Jaime's warm breath stroked my neck, and I shivered.

"Uh, this one." I pointed to the pirate wearing a bandana covering his head and an eye patch over his eye.

Jaime's wide smile practically touched his ears. "Nah."

"This one." A wizard wearing a tall, pointed hat with tassels sat beside the pirate.

"No." He shook his head. He was so close, I could smell his musky soap, so I breathed in deeper.

"This one?" I held the picture closer to my eyes, examining the blurry shot.

"No." Leaning closer, his hair brushed my cheek and my breath hitched.

"Let me guess…you aren't even in the picture." I turned my head and held his gaze, the force of his eyes drawing me closer to him.

Breaking the moment, he snatched the picture out of my hand and sat beside me, his hip and thigh pressed against mine. "I am. I'm the one hiding under the blanket."

I grabbed the picture back from him and scrutinized the yellowed photograph. Two eyes popped out at me. "Very cute."

He placed his hand on my arm. "It's tradition. Here." He handed me the bag, the pirate sword, and a hat. "We have your costume."

I took the items and rubbed my finger over the smooth plastic. *He cannot be real right now.* My face froze with a tilted smile, and I looked past his shoulder into the kitchen. I didn't want to make a scene in front of Deirdre, so I accepted the items with gratitude.

"What are you going to be?" Deirdre asked Jaime, setting a tray with a serving set on the table in front of us.

"Dunno yet."

I pictured myself out in Dublin, celebrating Halloween in Ireland for the first time, dressed in a trash bag. My pride was wounded, but I pushed it aside, and glanced at Jaime and Deirdre. "I'm sure we'll find something," I said.

Deirdre packed away the tote, and Jaime and I settled in his room. I dropped my bag on the sofa bed and walked up to him in three steps. A smile ran across my face, and I grabbed his shoulders. Heat grew inside me, and the tension I felt earlier evaporated.

"I can't believe you're making me wear a trash bag!" I slapped him on the arm.

"What?" His eyes sparkled and I kissed his lips.

"We came back here for a broken sword and a trash bag," I said. "I'm missing classes for this!"

"Eh, you gotta live a little, Rory. Have a little fun." He kissed me again, deeper this time.

After I pulled away, insecurity swept in and I crossed my arms over my chest. "I have fun."

"Sure," he said.

"Why don't you think I have any fun? Seriously." I brushed my hair behind my ears.

He looked around the room and hesitated before he replied. "For starters, you don't drink."

"Yes I do. I had a drink the night we went out, but I'm careful when I drink." I pressed my hand across my chest. "Why does alcohol equal fun? Haven't you heard of moderation? Plus, I'm only nineteen. I can't drink in my country."

He smirked. "But you're in Ireland now. Alcohol is our beverage of choice."

I dropped my eyes to my hands. "I don't drink excessively because I don't trust being in a vulnerable state around people I don't know in places I've never been. You can never be too careful."

He looked at me with closed lips. "I'm sorry."

I waved my hands, trying to lighten the mood. "No, no, it's fine. I drink, Jaime, but only when I'm with people I trust. And I do have fun." We locked eyes, and my heart rate sped in my chest. His head leaned toward mine, and my limbs turned to jello. "What else?"

His lips touched my nose. "You never skip class."

"My parents are paying good money for me to be here. I have to take it seriously...and that's not even true. I'm missing four classes to be here with you right now."

He tilted his head back and forth, thinking. He rubbed the top of my hand, and sparklers lit up inside me. "Your calendar. You never stray from what's on the calendar."

"I'll probably never be back here, so I have to make the most of it. Time is not on my side."

"What if making the most of it means dropping all the touristy things and seeing the country for its beauty? You'll find more genuine people, places, and food if you venture off the paved road that every other tourist follows. I can show you the country and it'll be a million times better than the bus tours and breweries that everyone sees."

I tried to reply, but I didn't have time. His lips pressed against mine, and fireworks in red, blue, and yellow lit up behind my eyes. My stomach somersaulted and flipped and, like a hungry lion, my hands were on his head, pulling him closer to me. I explored his lips with my tongue, drawing myself into every nook and cranny and feeling his desire match my own.

He was a gentle kisser, not too rough or demanding. Just like his personality, he was comfortable, making me want him more. I pulled away and gazed into his eyes. I wanted to say thank you, but felt strange thanking him for permission to let go of my structured life and encouraging me to let life unfold naturally.

"Will you trust me to show you what Ireland is all about?" he asked.

I kissed him again and nuzzled against him. "If it means wearing a trash bag out in the streets of Dublin, then so be it. It'll be a Halloween I'll never forget." I leaned back on my arm and jabbed him in the chest. "You better not leave me like you did last time."

He kissed me again. "Promise."

Willie Daly's words echoed in my head. *It's someone you least expect.*

Chapter 20

That night at dinner, I sat beside Jaime and across from Connor and Deirdre. A large bowl of mashed potatoes sat in the center of the table. Green specks poked out of the ivory puree, and in the center sat a puddle of butter.

"Cead mile failte," she said, sticking a spoon in the bowl. "That means welcome. Rory, I wanted to share our Halloween traditions with you. This, here, is colcannon."

I licked my lips. "Looks delicious. What is it, exactly?"

Jaime's lopsided smile stirred my belly. "I told you already. Mashed potatoes."

"Why is it green?" I asked.

"Kale," Connor said.

Deirdre held out her hands and Connor took one in his. "Potatoes, onion, kale, butter, and milk. That's all. Before we eat, I'd like to say grace. Seamus?" Her right eye looked at Jaime, and her left eye remained closed. I immediately closed my eyes and grabbed Jaime and Connor's hands, creating a ring around the table.

"Slainte. To friends, family, and food. Amen." He squeezed my hand before releasing it, and I looked away to hide my reddening face.

"So." Deirdre clapped her hands. "Colcannon is a traditional Halloween meal. Usually, there's a ring inside, and the person who gets it will get married in a year, but I left it out tonight. I have a surprise for later. Would you like some?" She held her hand toward me, palm up, requesting my plate. I passed it to her, motioning her to stop after she dropped two heaping spoonfuls in the middle.

"Halloween originated in Ireland. Did'ja know that?"

I shook my head, blowing on the steaming hot potatoes to avoid another burn on my tongue, like last time.

"It originated two thousand years ago at a pagan festival. We've always been about fun."

"I never knew that. This is delicious, by the way." I wasn't crazy about kale or the bitter aftertaste, but the salty butter enhanced the earthy greens.

"Also, what you call jack-o'-lanterns originated here, too. Except instead of pumpkins, we used turnips."

I imagined a white turnip with a carved face and pictured a mummy head. "Carving pumpkins is one of my favorite things to do for Halloween," I said.

Deirdre snapped her fingers. "Drats. I almost bought some turnips today, but didn't think we'd have time to carve." She placed another dish on the table. "This here is barmbrack, another Halloween tradition, originally used as a fortune-telling device at the Celtic festival, Samhain."

Connor cleared his throat. "Barmbrack is something my mammy made and was my favorite Halloween food when I was a kid."

Looking at the brown bread with light and dark raisins almost reminded me of a fruitcake my grandmother made for Christmas. I had never liked it, and used to dissect the insides until a mountain of jelly candies sat on my napkin before throwing it away.

Deirdre placed her hand on Connor's. "I rarely bake this, but tonight's a special night. Barm comes from a brewery, and we use it as yeast. We bake it with raisins and little surprises. Little trinkets. Each trinket symbolizes something for the coming year."

Jaime cut a thin slice and spread butter across the side. "Ma, what's in the bread?"

I expected a list of ingredients; instead, Deirdre rattled off objects. "A stick, a ring, a coin, a rag, a pea, and a thimble."

I widened my eyes and then looked at the slice of bread Jaime had placed in front of me. "That's in here?" I pointed to the flat slice on my plate.

"Yes and no. I hid charms representing all those items and wrapped them in parchment paper so the cake is still safe to eat. I think we all should dig through and see what we find."

The four of us ripped our barmbrack into tiny pieces, searching for parchment paper and charms. More than half the bread remained uncut.

"I got one," Jaime said, revealing a coin.

I leaned over to get a better look. "What does that mean?"

"Good fortune," Connor said. He held up a tiny metal thimble pendant. "Looks like I'll be a spinster for life." Leaning across the table, he kissed his wife, and Deirdre chuckled.

"You aren't so lucky," she said, and I smiled at their cuteness.

I continued digging. "Ooh!" I pulled out a bag and removed the charm. "A ring."

Deirdre's eyes widened, and her eyebrows rose to the top of her head. "Ooh, that means you will find love." Willie Daly's prediction of finding love within the next six months poked me in the heart. She winked at Jaime and smiled at me. "That's a great one to have." After a moment of silence, she said, "It appears the others are still in the loaf. Guess my life won't be changing this year, aye?"

After dinner, Jaime and I cozied on the couch in front of the telly.

My belly was full of comfort food, and my soul was full of love. With the help of Jaime, Deirdre, and Connor, I was falling in love with Ireland. I had never imagined being so welcomed into a family and couldn't imagine my own parents treating Jaime with the same level of hospitality.

"Jaime," I whispered.

He looked down at me and stroked my hair.

"Thank you. For showing me what it's like to be from Ireland. As much as I don't want to be a trash bag for Halloween, I'm happy I'll get to spend the night with you." I gazed into his eyes and counted the freckles sprinkled across his cheeks.

"No, no, if you hate it, you don't have to wear it." My body tingled with every touch and I closed my eyes, memorizing the way he made me feel.

"A bet is a bet, and I lost fair and square."

He smiled and gazed at my face. "Would it make you feel better if I wore a bin bag, too?"

A grin erupted at the thought of Jaime wearing a trash bag with nothing underneath, and I nodded quickly. "Yeah."

"We'll both be pirates. It'll be grand."

Chapter 21

"I look ridiculous." The tiny bathroom of the youth hostel closed in on me and I struggled to breathe. My reflection illuminated my shoulders and face, and I jumped up and down to see my body. The *swish-swish* of the plastic trash bag ricocheted off the bare walls and I tightened the belt around my waist. Black eyeliner highlighted my pirate persona, and I almost didn't recognize myself.

The door thundered behind me. "Ya'lmost done in there?" I didn't recognize the high-pitched voice, and I flung my makeup into my small cosmetic bag.

Pasting on my most poised smile, I pulled my shoulders back and opened the door. *Whatever. It's Halloween.* I passed a woman dressed as one of the Spice Girls, and sneaked back to our room for the night. Zoey, Marissa, Owen, Aoife, and Jaime lounged around the room; small, empty liquor bottles, Halloween accessories, and the clothing we wore on the train to Dublin splattered the top and bottom bunks like a Jackson Pollock painting.

"How do I look?" I asked, spinning in a circle holding out the skirt of my plastic dress.

"Like a pirate," Zoey said, "Kind of. I think you need something else, like a telescope or a parrot."

I looked around the tiny hostel, searching for something I could borrow for the night. "I know!" I ran to the bathroom, ripping off the remaining toilet paper from the cardboard cylinder.

"Argh!" I hollered, as I entered our makeshift bedroom. Holding the used toilet paper roll as a spyglass, I zoomed in on Zoey. "Now do I look like a pirate, matey?" I said, in my best pirate accent.

"Argh, aye-aye, matey." Marissa grabbed my spyglass and colored it with the gray eyeshadow I had used to create my eye patch. "Perfect." Her feather headband created animal-shadows against the dim light.

"Where'd you find that?" Jaime asked.

"Bathroom, my pirate pal. Would you like one?"

I rushed to the bathroom and found an almost empty paper towel roll and ripped off the extra sheets of paper, leaving them on the sink. "Jaime, I found you a spyglass, too!" The dark eye shadow created a matching glittery smoky telescope that Jaime shoved in his back pants pocket. "Now we're twins." I eyed his costume and hugged him. "Thank you for dressing up with me. I feel less foolish."

He kissed me on the cheek. "I said I would."

"How do we look?" Marissa asked. She linked arms through Zoey's and jutted her hip. Her fishnet stockings traveled under the tassels of her skirt and the flowing, glittery strings swished with each movement. Zoey and Marissa's tight, sparkly dresses, headband, and elegant makeup contradicted the rough and tumble look Jaime and I wore.

"Like Nicole Kidman, but shorter," I said.

Owen walked behind them. "Who are you again?"

Marissa spun in a circle and extended her arms before taking a bow. "Moulin Rouge."

"Looking brilliant," he said.

"As do you. But what are you?" Marissa readjusted her sparkly headband, pushing her curls away from her face, and scanned him from head to toe.

"I'm a warlock. Can't ye tell?" He wore a blue bathrobe and triangular dunce cap, and carried a walking stick that he probably found in the woods that day.

I covered my mouth to stifle my giggle. "You look amazing. Almost as good as me." I wiggled my eyebrows at him.

Owen pulled me into a side hug. "We'll stick together if we need to." I fell into the warmth of Owen's bathrobe and hugged him back.

"What time is the celebration?" Jaime asked.

"Half-nine," Aoife replied. "Every pub in Temple Bar is celebrating. Jaime, do you remember last Halloween? What were we again? I can't remember." She batted her eyes at him and my eyes remained on her a moment too long. When our eyes connected, I quickly busied myself with tying my shoes.

"Jaime was an American football player and you were a cheerleader." Owen gathered his wallet and shoved it into his pants pocket underneath his wrapped bathrobe.

"Oh right. We looked great that night." She looked me up and down and I glanced at Jaime, daring him to compliment our costume.

When he didn't, I sputtered, "Right. Well, I'm sure we'll be the talk of the town, too." I turned away and sucked it as much air as I could, holding it in my belly until I couldn't hold it any longer.

"Sure. Perhaps for the hokiest costume." Aoife walked toward Jaime and brushed his hair back, her long red fingernails disappearing in his red beard. Wearing black chunky heels, she hovered at least three inches over him, and I felt my breath catch in my throat. Her tight, yellow plaid miniskirt and blazer barely covered her butt and boobs. She screamed sexy school-girl, and all I could see was the Britney Spears video flying through my head.

His eyes rested on her pouty lips and I saw the redness creep up his neck. "Thanks, Cher. You look great."

She flipped her bouncy hair over her shoulder. "As if!" and she handed him a small bottle of whiskey. He took a sip before passing it to Owen and it traveled around the room. I shook my head no, and it continued to Marissa. She swallowed, and her face scrunched and tightened in disgust.

"Blech." Her mouth contorted into a snarl and her nostrils flared.

"Let me show you how to do it," Zoey said, and she took two baby sips. Her face fought the urge to scrunch, and her mouth twitched. She pursed her lips and then pulled them up in a slight smile. "Here you go." She handed the bottle back to Aoife, who finished the rest.

Unease settled over me as I looked at my friends and frenemies. The biggest threat I felt was with the blonde in the corner, but I deflected my emotions and focused on our room. Three sets of bunk beds sat against three of the four walls. "Are you sure this is safe?" I asked, imagining the hostel owner breaking in and stealing our stuff.

"Dublin's been celebrating for thousands of years," Jaime said.

I sat down on the thin, squeaky mattress. "No, not that. I mean this place." *My parents would freak out if they saw me here.* "It cost sixteen euro for a bed for the night…there isn't even a lock on the door. Is it safe?"

Zoey walked over to the door and slid the chain lock above the door handle. "It locks. We'll be safe sleeping."

"It's grand," Owen said. "Sleep with your items in your pillowcase, just in case. And don't drink too much."

I shoved my wallet, phone, and apartment keys into the crossbody under my trash bag and zipped it closed. I silently prayed tonight would be a success.

We followed our Irish friends through the capital city of Ireland toward the Temple Bar area. The damp air traveled through my black trash bag, and I shivered when the raindrops hit my head. The random drops led to a steady stream, and then a deluge.

My hair dripped with water and when I wiped the raindrops from my upper lip, the black eye makeup streaking down my cheeks went with it. Glancing at Owen, I noticed his carefully hand-drawn mustache now resembled a squiggle my toddler cousin could have drawn.

"How do I look now?" I asked Jaime, wiping at my eyes.

"Like you walked the plank."

I threw my head back and embraced the raindrops hitting my face. I didn't care that my bones ached with cold or my saturated costume now resembled someone shipwrecked. It was Halloween. In Ireland.

We pushed through the crowds of people filling the sidewalk and entered a pub pulsing with traditional music. The heat from a peat-burning stove blasted against my skin, and I watched the black plastic morph into a shiny wave.

"Wanna pint?" Jaime asked. "You may not want to stand so close to the stove."

I ran my hands over the smooth plastic and stepped back. "Just water for now."

The five of them wrestled to the bar and left me in front of the fire to burn.

Seeing an empty table in the back, I hurried and sat, waiting for my friends. Jaime, Aoife, and Owen sidled next to me while Marissa and Zoey went to the bathroom.

"Here, Rory." Jaime passed me a water bottle and I guzzled the cool liquid.

The three of them clinked glasses and drank their pints. I took Jaime's Guinness and took a large sip, appreciating the coffee-chocolate flavor. When I looked up, Jaime rubbed at his upper lip with a quiet chuckle.

"What?" I pawed at my face and hair.

He leaned into me, and I smelled the bittersweet malt travel across my cheek. "You have a mustache," he whispered.

"Yeah, I know. That one-euro eyeshadow wasn't waterproof."

"No, not that." Jaime's husky voice made the skin on my neck tingle. My hand rose to my face but he beat me to it. With the backside of his thumb, he gently stroked the skin under my nose. Without thinking, I puckered my lips and kissed his thumb, and his hand stopped. I raised my eyes, encouraged by the desire hiding behind his pupils, and kissed him again. Redness crawled up his neck and face, matching the color of his hair, and I grinned.

"Thank you." I look another large sip of his beer, feeling frisky. Our friends leaned into each other, unaware that Jaime and I had just shared an intimate moment, and I was pleased with our little secret.

Being an inexperienced drinker, the two gulps of Guinness shot bravery up and down my body, and I took another gulp before shifting my weight toward Aoife. "Aoife." I interrupted her conversation with Zoey, and clinked glasses to break up the awkward glare coming from her beautiful blue eyes. "I've noticed a chemistry between you and Jaime. What's your story?"

Zoey leaned toward us as Aoife explained. "He was my boyfriend. Owen set us up on a blind date. We had our fun, but it wasn't a match made in heaven. He was one, but not *the* one. Now we're best friends." Her explanation made it sound so simple.

I blinked and scrunched my brows. *He never told me they dated. Or that they were best friends.* "When did you date?"

"Second year of college."

I blinked again, and I detected a smirk pulling at her lips. "Second year, like last year?"

"That's the one."

Jaime sat on the other side of Aoife, but he was deep in conversation with Owen and oblivious to our discussion. I glanced around the table and excused myself to the bathroom. A sudden tightness formed in my chest, and I bit my cheeks. My vision blurred from the tears threatening to fall. *How did I miss this?* My walls rose around me, and the protection around my heart turned to stone.

Later that night, I stood in a line about ten deep for the loo and used the extended time to clear my head. I raised my eyes to Marissa and Zoey as they passed and gave a little wave.

I needed to play it cool. Aoife knew I was jealous. I could see her confidence grow in the crinkle of her eyes, the carefree touch on Jaime's arm, and how she leaned into him to get his attention. I couldn't tell if she liked him or was trying to make me jealous.

Owen. That's my ticket to get Jaime interested. A plan unfolded in my mind as I crept closer to the loo door. Rage burned behind my eyes, determined to show Aoife that she couldn't push me around.

I didn't notice the line moving until the girl behind me tapped me on the shoulder. Stepping forward, and lost in my thoughts, I had lost track of time and didn't know how long I was away from the table.

A semi-solid plan formed in my head by the time I was in and out of the bathroom. I marched to the bar and ordered a whiskey, tossing it down my throat in one gulp. I threw an extra coin on the counter out of habit and left before the bartender could return my tip. I wasn't feeling drunk, but I knew I would once the alcohol circulated throughout my limbs.

Sliding into Aoife, she shimmied closer to Jaime, and I immediately regretted my seat choice. Owen sat across from me, looking out at the crowd, and Marissa and Zoey giggled in their private bubble.

In my distorted mind, I saw our party of six as a party of two pairs, and Owen and I on the outskirts.

"Hey, Owen," I said. "Need another drink? My treat."

He and I pushed through a mob of Halloween characters, squeezing between zombies, witches, and leprechauns, before we ended at the pub bar. "Two pints, please," I said to the bartender who was dressed in an American Flag t-shirt and cowboy hat.

"Harp," Owen added.

After handing us our pints, I said to the bartender, "I see you're an American. Nice costume."

"Toby Keith. My American cousin sent me his CD and I can't get enough."

"You look great!" A sudden flush traveled up my cheeks, remembering the wet trash bag. "I, on the other hand, look ridiculous." I looked around the bar, admiring all the costumes.

"Black bin bag?" Toby Keith asked.

Pleased with his recognition, I clinked my pint glass into his.

"Cheers," Owen said, raising his glass. "To new friends." We all clinked again, and I took a sip. The alcohol zipped around my body and the movement around me started to slow. "Tell me about you," I screamed to him. The loud music and jumbled conversation reverberating against the wooden beams drowned out my regular speaking voice.

"What do you want to know?" he asked, eying me curiously.

"Tell me about you and your family." This was my round-about-way of getting to know Aoife. "You and your sister seem close."

"Aye. We're twins."

I nearly fell out of my chair. They looked nothing like twins with Owen's shorter stature and her mile long legs. They reminded me of Arnold Schwarzenegger and Danny DeVito. Really?"

"Aye. We've been inseparable since birth." He chuckled at his pun. "We're at the same college but study different courses, and we live in different flats but in the same building." He shrugged. "It's a twin thing."

I couldn't believe Jaime hadn't told me this. Things started to click.

"And how long have you known Jaime?" I thumbed the pint glass, feeling the golden harp emblem against my skin.

"Since our first year of college. He's a good bloke. A good friend."

I nodded. There was zero attraction between Owen and I, despite the shot of whiskey clouding my judgment. I couldn't get Jaime and Aoife out of my mind. "I heard that he and your sister were dating."

Owen snickered and took a gulp. "I guess you can call it that. I think it was more of an instant attraction than anything else."

I pictured her silky blonde hair, clear skin, and long legs—*an instant attraction.* Comparing her body to mine, I understood why Jaime would like her. I shook my head, wiping the image of them as a couple out of my mind. "Yeah?"

"Aoife and I are so close, I can feel her pain when she's hurt. It's a twin thing," he said again. "She likes him, but she bounces around." He took another deep sip. "She doesn't get serious with anyone."

I nodded, confused. The alcohol affected my thinking, and I couldn't figure out what Owen was saying. *Were they using each other? Were they friends with benefits? Were they actually dating? Are they still kind of seeing each other? Or using each other?* He wasn't making any sense. I leaned into his chest, and his hand pulled my shoulder closer.

"So, how'd it end?" I asked.

"I don't know that it has."

My heart dropped to my feet. I didn't know Owen well, but he had no reason to lie. Maybe I didn't know Jaime as well as I had convinced myself, and I promised to be more watchful, intentional, and cautious.

I pulled back from him and ripped the trash bag over my head, tossing it in the bin.

"What are you doing?" Owen asked.

My black sweatshirt and jeans stuck to my slender frame. "I don't want to be a pirate anymore. Call me a thief instead. It'll be grand."

I motioned Owen to follow me and led him back to the table.

Various costumes pushed up against me, and I stepped back into Owen, feeling my body press against his leg and arm. He put his hands on my shoulders, directing me through the crowd. When we got back to the table, Marissa and Zoey were gone. I scanned the pub and found them in front of the band. Emotionally weak, I didn't want to talk to Aoife or Jaime.

Instead, I excused myself and approached my two roommates at the private table away from our other friends. "Hey, girls." I glanced at Marissa's hand, resting on Zoey's leg. "Tell me, what's going on with you two?"

Marissa pulled her hand away and bunched her sequined skirt in her fist. "Nothing."

"Nothing? I've been watching you guys for a few weeks now. I saw you. The night of Owen's party. We saw you." I pointed to Jaime across the room and returned my finger to me. I lowered my voice and hissed, "Kissing."

Blushing under the dim light, Zoey stared at her pint glass. Her pursed lips and shaky hands waited for Marissa to say something.

Marissa grabbed Zoey's hand. "We're just having fun." She looked at Zoey from the corner of her eye, and Zoey nodded.

"Just having fun," Zoey repeated.

I hugged them, feeling the whiskey lighten my mood, and squeezed. "Whatever you want is fine with me, but don't ever feel like you need to hide anything. I'm your friend and I love you, and would never judge you. Besides, you know what's going on with Jaime and me."

Marissa pulled away. "What is going on? You never really told us."

I felt my body warm as I replayed all the kisses just a few days ago. His sweetness and kindness dripped over me like sugary syrup. I knew the liquor highlighted my memory, but I clung to it like a winning lottery ticket. "Honestly, I don't know."

Both girls looked at me and waited.

Taking a deep breath, I sank into the wooden table. "Whenever we're alone, I feel alive. Like he's showing me what it's like to be free. But then, when we're not alone, I feel like one of the guys. Like he's afraid to show how he feels about me. And then there's Aoife, his ex-girlfriend over there. Ex-girlfriend or something." I shook my head in disappointment. "Whatever they are, they have a history. And I don't know if I can trust him with my heart, you know?" The words spilled out of me before I could process their meaning. A string of letters, syllables, and words slung together like a love song I'd heard a million times before.

Marissa squeezed my hand. "I'll keep my eyes open. I can tell a shady guy a hundred miles away, but from what I've seen so far, he's sincere and respectful. I think he has a lot of good qualities."

Zoey nodded. "Remember that weekend when I got really wasted? You guys weren't around, but he went to the hotel next door and ordered a take-away Irish breakfast. He delivered it to my room with tea. It was a surprise, and I think that was the first time I saw him for him…you know, beyond the funny, goofy roommate vibe."

I tapped my fingers on the table, thinking. "I didn't know he did that."

I looked over at the table we had all been inhabiting and saw him, Owen, and Aoife, comfortably chatting and laughing. *I don't know their story, but do I need to know? I can protect my heart.* I pulled my shoulders back, shocked that I considered myself his girlfriend, even if I hadn't spoken the words. *Do I want to be his girlfriend?*

The room rocked, and the music bounced through the soles of my boots. My beer had disappeared, yet I didn't know where it went. I must have drunk it without thinking. My stomach felt heavy and bubbly, and my toes tingled. "You guys wanna go?" I asked.

We pushed our way to the table and flopped into the booth. "Wanna go?" Marissa asked the others. "I've never been to Dublin. You locals need to show us how you party."

I smiled at her for taking control of the night.

Owen and Jaime downed the rest of their pints, and Aoife left her half-empty glass on the table. She stood beside me, towering over me in her clunky heels. Her skirt almost covered her butt, and I admired the muscular tone of her thighs.

Her toned arms grabbed me, and I stumbled into the wall, cornered. She kissed me on the cheek. "I love your costume."

I narrowed my eyes and let the negative energy roll off my shoulders, not in the mood to be nice to her until I knew her intentions with Jaime. "Thanks. I thought it might be better than a hoochie mama."

She grinned at me, but I saw the wheels spinning behind her eyes, and I basked in the way I flipped the script. I turned toward the guys, fighting a smile from spreading across my lips.

I grabbed Jaime's hand, and let him lead me out of the overcrowded pub. The rain had stopped, and the moon peeked behind the cirrus clouds, illuminated by the bright streetlights. Feeling buzzed, a warmth spread throughout my chest and cheeks, and my muscles relaxed. In my head, I gave myself a high-five for not allowing Aoife to ruin my night.

For the rest of the night, I allowed my insecurities and reservations to die on the dance floor. We crawled through a strip of pubs, drinking in each one. I kept up with Aoife, downing Guinness, whiskey, and cider until my belly stretched beyond capacity. With each drink, my mood lifted, and I inferred that every word, touch, and kindness Jaime exhibited toward me was due to his growing attraction.

I found myself beside Jaime most of the night, and then things got blurry. The lights hurt my eyes, the noises in the bar became one big white noise machine, and my body rocked like we were cruising on a boat. Aoife became a shadow in the background, and all I could focus on was Jaime and my growing desire to feel his skin against mine. My stomach flipped, my chest tightened, and an urge to kiss him overpowered me.

Then the night washed away and all I saw was darkness.

Chapter 22

I woke up the following day in Owen's bed, pressed between him and the wall. My head throbbed, and my stomach churned. *How did I get here?* Laying on our backs, our shoulders didn't fit on the small twin-sized mattress, and I shifted to my side. The blurry room became focused, and a mixture of blonde and red filled my vision from across the room. There lay Jaime and Aoife. In the same bed.

Overcome by nausea, I climbed over Owen to get to the bathroom down the hall, careful not to stumble on the clothes and shoes strewn across the floor.

Falling between the toilet and the wall, my stomach knotted like a pretzel, and I wasn't sure if it was the alcohol, stupidity, or embarrassment. Whatever it was, I needed to purge all the bad feelings eating me from the inside. *Why was my love life influenced by this unhealthy need to be accommodating to others?*

Despite my silent protests, Scott always cancelled our plans, flirted with other girls and borrowed money to blow on poker games. According to my father, I wasn't worthy of his love unless I was successful at school, and my mother and I got along best when I ignored her overdependence on pills. My entire life, I tried my hardest to prevent the boat in our house from capsizing, and I had been taught that other people's problems were more important than my own, so I minimized my needs and focused on keeping them happy.

Afraid my baggage would prevent me from standing up for myself, I needed to learn the truth about Jaime and Aoife. *Think, Rory, think.* My head pounded, and the small room continued to spin, so I laid my face on my folded arms over the filthy toilet seat and closed my eyes. *Tomorrow. I'll figure it out tomorrow.*

Stumbling back to the room, my eyes moved to Aoife and Jaime, watching her lips curl gently against his cheek and his arm drape over her waist. I didn't want to be in there, imagining mistakes and hypotheses that may or may not have happened.

I grabbed my items, stuffed them into my bag, and slipped back to the dirty bathroom. Peeling out of my beer-scented clothes and dropping them in the trash can, I pulled on the same outfit I wore on the train ride into Dublin, trying to erase the entire night from my memory. Perhaps these clothes could turn back time—to a time before Dublin, when Jaime hadn't stomped on my fragile heart.

Creeping down the wooden staircase, I greeted the young man working behind the counter. He looked about fifteen, with scrawny arms, pimply cheeks, and the same smattering of freckles Jaime carried. I dropped into an old, ripped leather armchair that looked like something my grandparents would own.

"Excuse me, do you have any water?" I asked the kid. Based upon his complacent reaction, he'd seen worse in this establishment.

He pulled out a plastic cup and advised me to fill it from the bathroom. Under normal circumstances, I would have thrown him a disgusted glare, imagining the grime coated sink, but I was frantic for liquid and too confused to care. *Think, Rory. What the hell happened last night?*

I walked to the bathroom, filled the tiny plastic cup, and helped myself to refills until my stomach shuddered like a stormy sea. The cold water raced down my esophagus and landed in my sour belly with a splash.

Visions from the night before zipped past me, creating a blur of music and color. The pub crawl was something I remembered. I tried bringing up the aesthetic of each pub to count on my fingers how many drinks I'd had, but my recollection was murky. I remembered telling myself that I would flirt with Owen, but that was short-lived and I had decided to kick back and have fun with Jaime instead. Images of myself dancing the Irish jig in the center of a circle formed, and I cringed at my sloppiness. I saw myself fall into a guy's arms but didn't know who. My lips crashed into someone's lips, and my breath caught in my chest. *Who was that?* I didn't remember coming home.

Returning to the worn armchair, I stared into the city street, and watched the people of Dublin go on with their busy lives. I wanted to be out there, mixed in with the crowd like a Where's Waldo picture, so no one could find me.

"Excuse me," I heard a voice croak. "Do you want some tea? It looks like you can use it."

I closed my eyes, willing my body to morph into the pillow I was holding on my lap, and turned my head. The boy behind the counter had pulled his chair next to mine and stared at me with curious eyes.

"Sure, thank you."

"Rough night?" He handed me a delicate tea cup with blue and purple flowers next to a small ceramic teapot filled with steamy water. A tea bag sat inside, and I hurried to get the tea brewed so I could boil my throat with the bittersweet drink.

One side of my face tensed, and I threw my head back against the chair cushions. "It was a doozy." *I can still feel Owen's body next to me.*

"Ah, Halloween can be wild, ya know. Lots of alcohol leads to lots of choices, and maybe some mistakes. But like me mammy says, there's nothing so bad it couldn't be worse." He rose from the chair across from me and disappeared behind the wooden door.

I squinted after him, confused by his extrovertish advice despite his young age. Blinking a few times to wipe away my headache, I scrunched my forehead. Returning to the window and holding my steamy cup, I watched the lives of Dubliners move past me. *I would give anything to be any one of them right now.*

Dragged away from my daydream, Marissa's cheery voice interrupted my solo pity party. "Rory, there you are!" Her disheveled hair resembled Frankenstein's wife, and Zoey stood beside her with sour skin and bloodshot eyes.

"Did you have fun last night?" I asked my teacup. The spoon swirled the liquid like a whirlpool. Marissa nodded. "Where'd you get that tea?"

"Ah, the guy at the counter." I nodded to my right.

"I'll be right back."

Marissa returned with two steaming cups and handed one to Zoey.

"How was last night?" I asked again, hating that my question sounded like I hadn't been there. In a way, I hadn't. The entire night had disappeared from my mind, and I was hoping she could provide some insight into what happened.

"It was wild. How much do you remember?"

I pulled my lips back and felt tears form behind my eyes, promising to never drink that much again. "Um," my voice quivered, "I think I remember getting food, a little step dancing, and coming up with the brilliant idea of crawling through the pubs." My stomach turned again, and I hugged my abdomen.

Zoey sat on the edge of her seat, blowing on the teacup. "Do you remember dancing at the bar?"

My eyes widened, and I placed my forehead in my hand. So that flash of memory was true. "Not really."

"Yeah, you and Aoife were dancing queens. The two of you had a dance-off at the end of the night."

Marissa added, "You were pretty wasted by then."

Zoey continued. "You both were dancing to trad music. Obviously, Aoife won. Why wouldn't she? She's Irish."

Marissa threw a warning glance at Zoey, but I caught it.

"Wait. Why the look?" I asked.

"No look," Marissa said, glaring at Zoey.

"No look," Zoey echoed.

I pushed myself forward, my head feeling heavy. "Yes, look. I saw it. Tell me."

Zoey paused and wrung her hands in her lap. "Well, you had a bet that you could dance better than her. The people in the pub voted, and Aoife won."

I rolled my hands in my lap. "And? What did she win?"

Marissa took a sip and leaned back in the chair. "A kiss and a date with Jaime."

Chapter 23

T his is bad. This is so bad. My plan to make Aoife jealous completely backfired. I didn't want to know any more. I'm sure I ran my mouth and said something stupid and did something stupid and made everyone realize what an idiot I am.

The room spun and closed in on me. My teacup shook in my hand, and I slammed it down on the end table to stop the shaking. "Excuse me." I jumped and ran to the bathroom, and for the last time that day, I emptied whatever remained in my stomach. I needed to go home. And maybe by home, I meant America.

When I emerged from the bathroom, the rest of my bunkmates lounged in the lobby, looking like we had lived through an insane night, but I was the only one who truly felt insane. My mind raced with clarifying questions about the night before, but I was too afraid to verify my humiliation.

I walked to the group like I was in a death march, refusing to make eye contact with anyone. Leaning against the far counter, I kept my eyes on the clock, hoping the minutes would pass at super-speed.

On the long walk to the train station, I told my inner voice to shut up. The last thing I needed was to show any weakness by crying.

The next few hours tortured my soul. Nauseous from the jockeying of the train, the noise of side conversations pounded my brain, and the glances I caught between Jaime and Aoife made it difficult to breathe. *What was I thinking last night?*

Closing my eyes, I pretended I was in my bed at home, with Marty beside me watching a Real World marathon. A sudden desire to see Marty overcame me, desperate for my best friend to tell me to get my head out of my ass and march forward. I heard her chipper voice in my mind, "Rory, there's no sense in dwelling on mistakes. You can't change them. Just accept the lesson and move on."

The rolling hills whipped passed my window, blurring into one green masterpiece, and a small black bird soared below the clouds. I checked my watch—one more hour. Closing my eyes, I leaned against the window, and my head slammed into the glass with every acceleration and brake. Embracing the pain, a single tear dripped down my cheek and I wiped it away.

I didn't talk to anyone because I couldn't. Sentences had organized in my brain, but my mouth wasn't cooperating. All I could do was listen to those around me and avoid any attention. My backpack sat in the chair next to me, and I leaned across, using it as a pillow.

When we finally pulled into the station, my mind had disconnected from my body. I waved to Owen and Aoife, trying my hardest to act normal but not having enough drive to really pull it off. Jaime and Aoife said goodbye away from the group, and I couldn't help but see him place his hand on her lower back. I blinked back the tears that threatened to fall.

The taxi ride to our apartment was silent. We all needed to sleep it off and reconnect later. I wasn't ready to have a conversation with anyone, so I walked into my bedroom and closed the door behind me.

I was stuck with Jaime. He crawled under his covers, and pushed the plaid blanket under his chin. "I'm taking a nap. Wake me in an hour?" he asked.

Pretending to read a book, I watched him sleep over the top of the page. I still didn't know what had transpired the night before, and I hadn't quite figured out how to get the truth without sounding needy or vulnerable.

Succumbing to a hot shower, the scalding water burned my skin, and I fully submerged myself below the pelting drops, zapping my face. The water washed away my shame and embarrassment, and when I emerged, I almost felt like a new woman.

Jaime was still sleeping. "Jaime," I whispered. "Time to get up."

Once his eyes opened, I grabbed my raincoat and left the apartment to walk off my negative energy.

Over the next few days I watched his every move, questioning his motives and intentions and refusing to address our weekend. I disengaged eye contact every time I accidentally found myself staring into his kind, loving eyes. He tried to make jokes, but I didn't react to his humor, halting his funny personality from penetrating my heart again. I tried my best to only be in our room when he wasn't home, and if he was home, I slept on the couch, blaming insomnia for the change in my behavior.

I pulled open my email and wrote to Marty. **Hey Marty! I can't wait to see you in a few weeks! You're still coming, right? So much has happened, it's insane, but I'm still loving it over here. Missing you, of course, but still loving it. I meant to tell you, I met someone, but he might be interested in someone else. What should I do? I really like him, and I'd hate to ruin what we have, but I can't seem to shake this feeling that he still cares for another girl.** *Bitch.* Visions of him and Aoife danced through my head to the tune of a sad country song. I watched them explode in my mind and returned to my email. **What do I do? Tell him how I feel?**

Confront the girl? Ignore it and pretend it's nothing? I mean, it's not like we can have an actual relationship thousands of miles away. Love you, Marty! I hope you're having fun, but not too much fun without me! I can't wait to see you. -R

A few minutes later, my email dinged. **Rory, you only live once. If you like him, tell him. If he rejects you, move on.** *If you only knew he was my roommate.* **There are other fish in the sea. But if you are together, you better not be planning on spending all your time with him when I come to visit. There's so much I want to see and do in Ireland. Oh, I wanted to tell you, I'm dating someone too. It's not serious, but it's been fun. I used to think of him as a brother, or a best friend (besides you, of course), and somehow my feelings changed for him.**

Who could that be? The male friends we hung out with were few and far between. *Maybe it's a friend from home?* I searched my brain for guys she talked about, but no one came to mind. *Huh.* Her email continued. **I'm so happy to hear you've moved on from Scott. He wasn't the right guy for you. Love you! See you in a few weeks! –Marty**

Reading Marty's advice, I knew what I had to do. I had to talk to him. The idea of sitting down with him and baring my soul made my stomach churn and my head spin, but like my mom always said, 'Go big, or go home,' and I needed to blow up this living situation.

Chapter 24

I t had been six mortifying days since Halloween, and with every day that passed, I felt more like myself. I still hadn't spoken to him, but I pretended nothing had happened between us. The giant elephant grew beyond our small bedroom, but it hadn't stomped on me yet. Despite my burst of confidence after speaking to Marty, I couldn't seem to get up enough nerve to speak my mind.

Jaime sat on his bed, drawing in his notebook, and I lay in mine, scanning the newest Victoria's Secret catalog Marty had sent me in my care package.

"Rory?" He put his notebook down, and I glanced at him. "Can you turn a little to the left?"

I didn't respond, but turned toward the window.

"How've you been?" he asked.

"Fine." I rustled the magazine pages in my hand, staring at the sexy lingerie I would never wear.

"I haven't seen you all week."

"I've been busy, Jaime." It was a lie, but I couldn't shed my skin for him. Not when I didn't understand what we were or what his intentions were.

His pencil grazed across the paper like water flowing down a waterfall. I felt his eyes on my legs and pulled my blanket up to my waist.

"Can we talk? It's been weird lately."

I rolled my eyes and twisted my thin frame against the corner of my bed.

He ripped out the drawing sheet from his spiral pad and tossed it across the room like a frisbee. "Here, this is for you."

I flipped the paper over and smiled. Patting the space next to me, he joined me on my bed, but not so close that our hips and thighs touched.

An image of a woman with a similar likeness to me rested between us. I stared at the silky hair, slender legs, and almond-shaped eyes. "Is this me?"

"Yes."

I looked at Jaime, and a fire burning behind his eyes caused my heart to smolder. "Why'd you draw it?" I asked.

"You've looked so sad this week. In a beautifully weird way, it hurts to look at you."

Shameful memories from my past dropped on me like bombs, splattering my self-respect. Tears burned behind my eyes, and a rock formed in my throat, splitting my vocal cords open. I heard my father tell me I would never amount to anything because I wore a crop top in middle school. I felt my creepy neighbor look me up and down and comment on my tight jeans in high school. Then, I heard Scott tell me I would be nothing without him.

At the realization of that last memory, my heart stopped and the room spun.

This is not okay, Rory. Protect your heart. I leaned back and closed my eyes to force the tears back into my body. Falling in love with Jaime in nine weeks when he didn't love me back was the worst thing I could have allowed.

"No, no, I don't mean it in a bad way. You're beautiful. Stunning. But I like you, and it upsets me to see you so sad." His hand hovered over mine, and then he retracted it, seeming to realize that he was moving too fast for my vulnerable state. "What happened?"

Could I tell him?

"Nothing happened. Homesick is all. My best friend is coming for Thanksgiving, and I guess I'm sad that Thanksgiving is so far away," I lied.

We locked eyes, and like a string holding us together tightened and pulled, the tips of our noses brushed against each other. My body screamed yes, but the voice in my head cried no.

"No-no-no," I stuttered. Backed into the corner of the room, and trapped between Jaime and my bolted nightstand, I couldn't escape this excruciating confrontation. My heart raced like I had just run with a bull in Pamplona and I teetered on wanting to know the truth or disappearing like a snowman in April.

He leaned back and analyzed my face. His loving eyes trapped me again, and I hated him for being so damn kind.

"Jaime." My voice shook, and I didn't know if I could continue. *So much for my plan. I'm losing control again.* I inhaled, refusing to let his presence knock me down. "What happened last weekend? Between you and Aoife. Owen told me you dated, and he didn't know if you were still seeing each other." I didn't feel bad in the slightest calling out Owen or sharing who gave me my information. Chewing on my lip until I tasted blood, I waited.

He chuckled, causing my blood to boil and feelings of idiocy grow. *This is a mistake.* I turned away and gathered my magazines, frantic to escape his presence.

He grabbed my arm and pulled me toward him. "Wait." His eyes pleaded for me to stay. "Listen. Don't go." His body stiffened, and so did mine. "This past weekend, I didn't drink a lot. Well, at least not as much as you."

I dropped my eyes, and my face burned.

"No, look at me."

Looking up, a single tear rolled down my cheek. I couldn't stay here and listen to him tell me he wasn't interested.

"You seemed like you were having a great time. You drank a lot, which surprised me since, you know, you said you never drink around people you don't know, but you seemed like you were having fun. You and Aoife hung out all night."

I recalled my idea to make her jealous and couldn't bring myself to ask if Jaime had picked up that vibe.

"When the last pub cleared out, you and Aoife danced in the middle of the pub."

I held up my hand to stop him. "Wait, did we dance on the bar?"

He laughed, and shame grew inside me for not remembering. "No, you tried, but the bartender stopped you."

Relief coursed through me for not disrespecting Ireland.

"It was your idea to have a dance-off. In the end, Aoife won. She's been dancing since she was three, so no one was surprised."

I covered my eyes with my clammy hand. *Of course.* I must have looked like a fool.

"She said she won a shift and a date with me. I don't know if you'd decided on that beforehand or if you even knew, but everyone cheered. So I leaned over and shifted her. As for the date, I don't plan on dating her. We've already done that."

I tried to conjure up the memory of them kissing, but nothing came. "So, what happened after that?"

He leaned against the wall. "We walked back to the hostel, and you passed out on the bottom bunk."

"With Owen?" I interrupted.

"Yeah, you passed out, but that hostel had no blankets, so we all bunked together to stay warm."

"But why Owen?" I asked again. "Why not you?" The desperation in my voice pulled me back to when I was a little girl, and all I wanted was for my dad to like me. Searching for his approval, I would do anything to prove that I was worthy of his attention. I would do handstands and cartwheels around him if that meant he would love me the way I needed. Looking at Jaime, I dropped my frantic tone and tried again. "Why didn't you want to bunk with me?"

He smiled, probably remembering the night I couldn't. "Because you didn't want me."

My eyes creased in confusion, and I shook my head. "I don't understand."

"I asked you if I could crash with you, and you mumbled no. You said you couldn't trust yourself around me." His smile spread across his face. "You told me you loved me."

I recoiled and covered my face with the blanket. Too shocked to cry, I needed him to disappear. "Nooo," I exhaled. "Did anyone else hear?" I imagined Aoife's smug, beautiful face sweeping Jaime into her arms, declaring him hers.

"No, just me," he whispered. "I didn't want to say anything because I knew you didn't remember, but I couldn't stand to see you so upset this week."

"What did you say?" I whispered back. I couldn't look him in the eyes, so I stared at his collarbone instead. His skin was fair and smooth and I counted the freckles to distract myself and fill the silent void.

"I said nothing. I said good night and left you to sleep."

Thankful he hadn't taken advantage of me in my less-than-conscious state, I said nothing.

"And I needed to think about what you said."

I challenged him with my eyes, begging him to be honest but gentle.

"And?"

"And I like you, Rory. Like, a lot. You get me, and you get my family. You're beautiful and thoughtful and excited for life."

Damn it. Another tear seeped out of the corner of my eye, and I wiped it with my thumb. I swallowed the egg in my throat. "What about Aoife? Are you and she a thing?"

Jaime looked away and then returned his gaze to me. "We were. We were a thing for about six months, but it didn't work out. She's a good friend, mostly because she's Owen's sister, and Owen's my best buddy. I like her as a person, but I'm not attracted to her like I am to you. We have a loose relationship. She likes to flirt, and I like to be flirted with, but we aren't together, no."

"Did you break up with her, or did she break up with you?"

"I broke up with her. It was too weird. She wanted more, but it didn't feel right. I'll always protect her and care for her, but I don't want to be with her." His eyes reflected honesty, and his body communicated sincerity.

I played with my fingers, picking at my cuticles. "So, what does that mean for us?"

Jaime leaned closer, and his intense eyes filled my vision. "Can we see what happens? Let's hang out and see how things unfold. You're leaving in six weeks, and I'm afraid to fall too hard because I don't know what will happen to us once you've gone." I closed my eyes and felt his soft lips gently brush against mine.

I understood why he was afraid. "I'm scared too."

Jaime stood and browsed my calendar. "Would you like to go on a date today?"

"Where to?"

"Ah, it appears you have a trip to the Aran Islands booked."

"Not really, I never got my tickets."

"No problem, we can get them now. Shall we go, m'lady? It's a beautiful day to explore an island."

I jumped from my bed and hugged him. "I would love to."

I scribbled a quick note to Zoey and Marissa informing them we'd be back tomorrow and taped it to their bathroom mirror. Jaime made reservations at the hostel on Inis Mór, and my nerves sprinted around my body like a racetrack. My hips swayed to a song sung in my head as I threw the last of my toiletries in my backpack. The past twenty-four hours had been an emotional rollercoaster, and I felt like my train car was approaching the hill's peak. The exciting part of the ride was yet to come.

I didn't fully trust Jaime, but the chains around my heart slowly cracked, allowing space to grow. I welcomed the chemistry between us, and tried my hardest not to think about my life back home. Ireland had thrown me a curveball and I swung and missed with full confidence. Just like with American soccer, I was never good at baseball.

Jaime stepped out of the bathroom wearing a pair of loose-fitting jeans and a hooded sweatshirt. My heart skipped a beat, seeing his freshly shaved face and baby-smooth skin. Instead of looking thirty, he looked twenty, and I couldn't help but slide my hand down his smooth cheek. I traced his lips with my finger, noting for the first time a cleft in his chin and dimples in his cheeks.

I analyzed every square inch of his face. "You look great." A tugging in my pelvis alerted me to the magnetic attraction, and I pressed my lips against his. "You have no idea how much I want you."

"Just you wait." His eyes sparkled, and I stared at his full lips. He tossed me my crossbody bag and we locked up the apartment. I was ready for a do-over and a remote island seemed like the perfect place to rewrite our story.

Thirty minutes later, Jaime and I climbed the bus to Rossaveel, and then the ferry for the second leg of our trip. Settling into seats on the lower deck, I looked out the round window and noticed the rise and fall of the sea. Leaning my head against the wall, I closed my eyes while my stomach tumbled with the waves.

"Not too busy today," Jaime said.

He was right; about half the seats on the lower deck remained empty. "It's a good thing it's almost winter. I don't think we would have gotten a room otherwise."

The boat engine kicked on, and the waves outside my window moved backward. My stomach lurched, and I took a sip of water to calm myself. Focusing on my breathing, I tried to eliminate the noise and movement around me.

"How long's the boat ride?" I asked.

"Eh, don't know. Less than an hour, I think."

"I need to close my eyes. I'm not a fan of boats." My mouth felt like sandpaper, and a set of trapeze artists flipped and swung in my stomach.

We were out on the open water, and the aroma of diesel fuel filled the cabin, intensifying my little performers. My wet, icy fingers grabbed onto each other. "Jaime, talk to me. I need a distraction, and I feel kind of sick." My head pushed against the seat, and I closed my eyes again. "Tell me a story. Please. Something."

"A story? Let's see." He moved closer to me and put his arm around my shoulders. I leaned into him and hugged his torso. My eyes pressed together to avoid any visuals from messing with my stomach. "A story," he repeated. "Once upon a time, there was a princess who didn't know what she wanted. She enjoyed being a part of the kingdom, but felt like maybe there were more fun and exciting things beyond the castle walls. The king and queen picked a husband for her, and she knew she should marry him because that was what princesses did."

"Wait." I adjusted my face toward him, but kept my eyes closed. "Did she get along with the king and queen?" I leaned against him again.

"Eh, no. She wanted their approval, but never felt like she was good

162

enough. She tried everything to make them proud and did what they wanted and expected, but felt like there was some level of disconnect. So, the man they picked out was not a good man. He seemed nice, but he didn't treat her well when no one was looking. On her wedding day, she broke free to start over, but was afraid of leaving behind everything she knew."

I sat up again. "Wait. Did she know how to live outside the castle walls?"

"Ehm, no, she didn't. But she didn't care. She knew she would be okay even if she didn't have their approval. She walked deep into the forest, lost, hungry, cold, and scared. Stumbling upon an abandoned cottage, she found a leprechaun."

A giggle escaped from my chattering lips.

"No, no, he was like a fairy. A good fairy," he revised. "He told her he could grant her one wish, and she said with a rather bad American accent, 'I wish I were happy for the rest of my days.'"

I laughed again and swatted him on the stomach.

"And the fairy jumped three times, and a swirl of fairy dust wrapped around her. When the dust settled, she was standing in front of a man. A real man. The fairy was gone, and he welcomed her into his home, and they lived happily ever after. The end." He stroked my hair. "Feeling better?"

I sat up and groaned, "I was until you reminded me!"

Lost in our thoughts, the ferry pulled into port. I let his story settle around me, as I pondered his thinly-veiled interpretation of my life. I wanted to ask if he was the fairy, but it almost felt like the decision was mine to make.

I stood up and stepped, but the floor below me rocked and swayed on a rogue wave, so I grabbed onto the handrail to steady myself. "Hey, Jaime? Can you grab my stuff for me?" I gestured at my backpack and purse on the seat.

"Got it." He hurried to gather our things and returned, holding onto my arm. We filed one by one down the plank to firm ground, but I wasn't steady. With every step, the planet tilted and wobbled with the waves and I grasped onto Jaime's sweatshirt to steady myself.

"I need to sit." We settled on a boulder at the port, and I focused on the people passing, the waves hitting the rocks, and the sounds of the birds chittering. "Is it cool if we check in at the hostel before venturing out? I need some food."

A stone's throw away stood our hostel, an old brick building facing the water. We checked in and dropped our belongings on two of the four beds. So far, no one else had claimed the other beds.

"I'll take the bottom bunk."

Jaime threw my backpack on the bed.

"Hey, Jaime?" I searched through my bag, dumping the contents beside me. "My purse. It was that small crossbody, and it had my passport and bank card. It was on the seat next to my bag." I couldn't look at him, searching meticulously to make it appear like magic. "Jaime?"

He didn't answer, but came over and sat beside me. "Your purse?" He said it like he had never heard that word before.

"Yes, my purse. I took it off because it was heavy on my shoulders and was making my anxiety about the boat worse. I put it next to my backpack on the seat beside me." The clothes I had ripped out of my bag fell to the floor, and I looked at him. "Did you get it?"

His wide eyes and long face told me everything. "No, I didn't." I watched his Adam's apple bob and heard him swallow.

"What am I going to do?"

His body sprang into action. "I'll be right back." He dashed out of the room.

Alone, I cried giant tears of frustration. I knew I should have left my passport in Galway. My parents would kill me if I got stuck in Ireland.

164

To pass the time, I lay on the bottom bunk, staring at the springs above me, and rummaged through my backpack for an already-opened bag of chips. *I'm trapped, and Jaime's gone. I have no ID, money, or way to get home.* I couldn't decide which home I desired more.

The door swung open and hit the wall with a bang. "Got it!"

I sat up quickly, hitting my head on the bedpost as my small black bag soared through the air towards me. I unzipped the main compartment, running my fingers over my personal items. Jumping up, I hugged him, but he didn't hug me back. When I disengaged and stepped back, he pulled a bouquet from behind his back. "This is me saying sorry. And that," he pointed at my purse, "is me saving the day. You're welcome."

"Saving the day? The day needed to be saved because of you!"

"Nah-ah." He waved his finger at me. "The day needed to be saved because you got seasick and didn't tell me I needed to get your purse."

I tried not to laugh, but a chuckle escaped. "Nah-ah," I mimicked, waving my finger in front of his eyes. "The day needed to be saved because you invited me to the Aran Islands."

He stepped closer to me, and the air between us intensified.

I wanted to say something witty, but my brain turned to mush. Instead, I mumbled, "It doesn't matter. You saved the day." I leaned into him and kissed his chilled, soft lips. When I tried to pull away, he grabbed the back of my head and pulled me closer. I felt his tongue roam the perimeter of my lips, and my stomach fluttered and flipped.

My little leprechaun saved the day. Maybe if I let him, he could save the princess, too.

Chapter 25

That afternoon, Jaime and I rented bikes and wandered the narrow, paved roads surrounded by towering limestone walls. My calves ached and I calculated how far we had ridden, expecting to fall off the other end of the island at any moment. Jaime dropped his bike on the side of the road and waved me to follow him.

He moved faster than me, and I hustled to keep up, careful not to trip over the craggy rocks. At the top of the hill, a flat clearing opened up overlooking the Atlantic. Jaime stopped and scanned the horizon. "Here we are."

"Wow." Breathless and speechless, all I could do was place my hand over my heart and creep toward the edge. To our left stretched miles and miles of flat ground hundreds or thousands of feet above the ocean floor. To our right stood a stone fortress with openings interspersed around the perimeter. "Where are we?"

"Dun Aengus. Isn't it spectacular?" He walked to the fortress and through an open doorway. We were the only people up there, and the sound of the ocean waves crashing into the vertical cliffs grew as we stepped closer to the edge.

"What is it?"

"It's a prehistoric site over three thousand years old. It's amazing how people could survive back then. Especially here." He settled on the hard ground away from the edge and I sat behind him.

"I'm afraid of heights, so I'll just stay back a little." My toes tingled, signifying my increasing anxiety, and my breaths shortened.

Jaime slid back until he sat beside me and I felt the ocean breeze blow through my hair. I watched a flock of white birds fly below us along the cliffs. "Do you ever wish you were a bird?" I asked.

"All the time."

"Why?"

"So I could be free to go wherever I wanted whenever I wanted. So I didn't feel trapped on this tiny island."

"You can be a bird, and I'll be a dolphin. Dolphins have fun, they're carefree, and they make people happy."

Jaime stared at the vast ocean.

"If I were a dolphin down there, and you were one of those white birds, I would never eat you. You're too special to me." I laughed at my cheesy attempt at flirting and leaned into him.

"You know," he said, pointing into the horizon, "Way over there you'll find America. Boston, even."

Looking out over the blue sky and water, I couldn't help but wonder what my friends were doing back home. I had been in Ireland for almost three months and I had yet to feel homesick, beyond a fleeting moment of time. Sitting on that cliff, knowing my life was so far from where I was, I realized that for the first time in a long time, I was happy being away from the influence and expectations of my family and friends.

"Maybe one day you can visit me," I said. "I would love that."

Jaime didn't reply, but kissed my forehead and pulled me closer. "The sun's going to set soon, and we have a hike and a bike ride. We should probably go."

I reluctantly followed, sad to leave this private oasis, but excited for the rest of our night. We watched the sun set behind the ocean as we cycled into town. *This is so romantic.* I raced the orange fireball, as it disappeared behind the water. *How did I get so lucky?* Jaime's head glowed in front of the setting sun, and his smoldering hair had set my heart on fire. Despite the empty road and imminent end to our day, anticipation for the evening enveloped me.

We dropped our bikes at the hostel entrance and settled at the water's edge, sitting against the rocks with my body pressed against his chest, watching the careless roll of waves lapping the shore. We didn't return to our room until the stars dotted the slate-gray sky. A single raindrop dabbed my skin, and I pulled my hood over my head.

"Rain," Jaime said.

I turned toward him, and he kissed me. "Are you hungry?" I asked.

"Aye. Let's get some food." He stood and reached out his hand, pulling me beside him.

"I'd like to get out of these sweaty clothes." We walked to our room, the view of the ocean peeking through the hallway window.

"Is there or isn't there?" Jaime asked, referring to our bunkmates and holding the door handle to our room closed. "Shall I open?"

I nodded, my body tightening at the thought of being alone with him.

He swung open the door and flipped the light. A dim bulb buzzed above us and illuminated our luggage. Scanning the room, it looked the same as we had left it. I jumped up and down and hugged him.

"Does this mean we are alone tonight?" I raised my eyebrows and tried my hardest to look sexy. Shimmying my shoulders and batting my eyelashes, I knew I looked silly, but I didn't care. This weekend felt like a date. It was our first official date, and I couldn't wait to spend the night with him.

Jaime squeezed my shoulders. "Looks that way, but they could show up at any time."

At the thought of being alone and possibly getting caught, my hormones exploded. Attraction grew in places I hadn't recognized before, and my hunger for him both terrified and electrified me. I pushed him onto the single bed and lay beside him, kissing his face and focusing on his fiery eyes.

I wanted to remember everything—the slope of his nose, his plump lips, and the shape of his ears. I explored him with my tongue and lips, paying attention to his body.

A small moan escaped me as his tongue ran up my neck to my earlobe. Tiny sparklers danced inside me, and bursts of light flickered behind my eyes.

"Jaime," I whispered. "Is there any way to lock the door?"

He jogged to the door, slid the lock, and nudged our luggage against it.

I placed my finger over my lips and shushed him. "We need to be quiet."

He crept back into bed and pulled my shirt over my head. I retreated into myself, exposed and aware. My hands pressed against his shoulders to prevent him from leaning on me, and I stared into his eyes. "I have to talk to you first."

He didn't break my gaze and froze above me.

"I'm afraid you're going to hurt me."

He shook his head from side to side. "I would never hurt you."

I dropped my eyes to my perky breasts, held back by my black silky bra. Looking up at him again, I said, "I don't mean physically, but emotionally. How do I know that?"

He rolled off me and lay on his bent arm, staring down at me. "Rory, if you don't want to do this, we don't have to. I like you. I want to get to know you, but I don't want you to do anything you aren't comfortable with. I care about you."

I didn't respond and looked beyond him at the wall across the room. My brain tripped over itself, and all the voices in my head screamed competing thoughts. *He's using you. You don't deserve him, and you don't need him. He's not interested.*

He grabbed my chin and tilted it toward him. "You're smart and funny. And kind and thoughtful. You're beautiful. I've learned so much from you and your perspective on life. Don't you ever wonder why we ended up together? It seems random, doesn't it?"

I nodded. Willie's words from the Matchmaking Festival floated through my brain. His deep voice and heavy Irish brogue awakened my eyes to Jaime. *You must open your heart to new possibilities, or love will not find you. When you find yourself falling, you must not doubt yourself. Open your heart and follow it. Love is right around the corner.*

I nodded in agreement, realizing Willie had been talking about Jaime all along. The negativity in my head subsided, and I focused on his words that echoed around my mind. "Do you believe in fate?" I asked.

"I do. We had no control over who the office put together in each apartment. It was completely random, yet the opportunity fell onto us. We tried to fight it, but no one fixed it. That's how I think about our situation. It was meant to happen, and we shouldn't fight it."

I smiled beside him and played with his hair. My fingers glided up and down his hairline, barely touching his skin. He smiled, closed his eyes, and shivered.

I leaned into him, melting my lips against his. He pressed his hand against the back of my neck, pulling me closer. As his body smashed into mine, desire infiltrated every cell. I wanted him, and I knew he wanted me, too.

I let go and became the princess from his fairy tale.

Chapter 26

I flipped open my computer, overwhelmed by the final projects I hadn't yet started. I had spent all my time with Jaime since returning from our trip a few days earlier, walking around the city, exploring new pubs, and watching movies. Even though we lived with two other people, Zoey and Marissa were always together, shopping, drinking, and traveling. They gave us our space, and we gave them theirs.

I needed to get started on my Irish Women's History final, but my motivation waned. I couldn't stop thinking about Jaime. His goofy smile, intense but loving eyes, and witty remarks sprung at me like Cupid's arrows flying from his bow. I tried to focus on my work, but images of his hands on my body distracted me. When we weren't together, all I could think about was him. When we were together, I couldn't keep my hands off him.

Procrastinating, I opened my email and checked in with my parents. Thanksgiving was ten days away, and my flight home was in a month. It made me sad to think about leaving Jaime, so I didn't.

Hi Rory, it's mom here. *Obviously.* **I miss you. I've missed so many holidays with you. You missed the annual Labor**

Day picnic, Halloween, and now Thanksgiving. We're going to Grandma's for dinner. She's having about forty people, so it'll be crazy, as usual. You will be missed. I hope you're having a great time. I can't wait to see you! Love, Mom.

I quickly responded with a summary of my month, omitting the part about getting wasted on Halloween, sleeping with my roommate, and skipping class. Scanning my inbox, I noticed all the correspondence was with my mom. Maybe she'd finally kicked him out of the house. The idea of a true broken home caused sadness to embed itself into my tough skin, but I'd rather their honesty over lying about a perfect home and a perfect family.

The next email I opened was from Marty. **Hi Rory! You won't believe this, but my sister bailed! She's not coming anymore. Something stupid about going to Thanksgiving with her new boyfriend or something. I think it's more like she doesn't want to pay for her ticket, and there is no way I'm paying for her airfare. So here I am, with an extra ticket. Do you mind if I ask around and invite whoever can come? I can't get my money back. I promise it won't be someone you don't know. I mean, it's only a few days, right? Let me know. Marty.**

I felt terrible for Marty because I knew those tickets cost a bundle and she was afraid to fly alone, but I couldn't help but feel relief that I wouldn't have to listen to her sister babble on about how her life was better than mine.

I hit reply and started typing. **Marty, no worries. I would hate for you to lose all that money, so invite whoever you can. It'll be a party. The more the merrier, right? I already talked to my roommates, and we're going to cook a traditional Thanksgiving. Turkey and stuffing and pumpkin pie. My roommate's parents sent pumpkin puree through the mail because they don't sell it here. Isn't that crazy? It'll be the best pie you can imagine. I can't**

wait to see you, and no stress. If you can swap the tickets with someone else, do it. Love, R.

Marissa, Zoey, and I had planned on cooking dinner for Jaime, Owen, and Aoife on Thanksgiving. I wasn't wild about having Aoife around, but I didn't want to be rude. Owen was a nice guy, and Aoife was his twin, so I bit my tongue and encouraged her to come. It was one meal, and would be fine.

I closed my email, opened my final paper, and spread out my textbook. Staring into space, I pulled out a scrap piece of paper, and jotted down Thanksgiving sides and desserts. Our freezer and refrigerator paled compared to what we had in the States, and I knew Thanksgiving morning would be a mad dash to buy ingredients and start cooking. I was up for the challenge.

I knocked on Zoey's door and found her and Marissa lounging in her bed, watching television. "Hey, you guys want to plan Thanksgiving dinner? It's coming up, and we'll have a full house."

I told them Marty was bringing a friend, and I probably wouldn't know who it was until closer to the flight. "So we're going to have at least seven, maybe eight, people here. Two pies, stuffing, mashed potatoes, turkey, and green bean casserole."

"And rolls," Marissa said and I jotted it down.

We worked out who was cooking what dish, and considered the translation of standard American measurement to the metric system. "I think the hardest part will be measuring grams and milliliters."

I loved Thanksgiving and couldn't wait to share it with Jaime. My stomach turned as I thought about Marty meeting him for the first time. His physical look wasn't what typically caught my eye, and Marty knew that better than anyone. Jaime's shorter frame and red hair contrasted with Scott's tall, broad build and dark complexion. Physically, they were complete opposites. *Maybe I won't tell her.* I didn't want to share my secret with her just yet. I was leaving in a month, and my journey with him felt like a fairy tale that just began. I didn't want anyone's opinions hampering my daydream.

I knew nothing would happen beyond December because we lived an ocean apart, so I continuously prepared myself for goodbye. I reminded myself that life was too short to dwell on the past or anticipate the future, and for right now, Jaime was mine. He'd forever hold a piece of my heart, even when it took a plane ride across the vast ocean to see each other. I didn't know what I wanted come December, but I knew for November, he made me happier than I had ever been.

I didn't think anything could destroy my euphoria for Jaime O'Sullivan.

Chapter 27

⚬⚬⚬

The days leading up to Thanksgiving were a glorious blur. I attended classes learning about Irish history, the Conflict, and Irish culture, and spent time with Jaime at night. We knew we had only a few weeks left, so we opted for quiet nights at home or traveling throughout the country together to make memories before he disappeared like a dream.

I hummed cheerful tunes as I walked to and from town, eating scones and other Irish sugary desserts. Jaime listened to me talk about nothing in particular, giving me his undivided attention. He treated me like a princess, which turned me into a new woman: confident, sexy, and laid-back.

Marissa and Zoey commented on how annoying Jaime and I were to hang out with because we acted like little puppy dogs in love, but I reassured them it was only because I knew I was leaving. It was like we each had a timer clicking above our heads, and one false move would blow up our perfectly curated existence.

Marissa and Zoey became one duo, while Jaime and I became another, and our apartment contained an invisible dividing line.

Since our trip to the Aran Islands, I'd only seen Aoife briefly at the pub. She inserted herself into a new group of football players, and Owen rotated between Jaime and Aoife, keeping the connection between his old group of friends secure. They were still coming for Thanksgiving, and I was looking forward to it, but I felt pleased that Jaime prioritized little ole' me over Aoife's long legs and ample bosom.

Things finally felt right, like I was in the right place at the right time. I knew deep down I was living a fantasy, which wasn't sustainable or going to last, but I couldn't protect my heart any longer. The beauty and mystique of Ireland had grabbed hold of me and encapsulated me in a joyous bubble. I knew when it popped, I would be alone but more beautiful because of the magic I had endured.

My heavy blankets rested on my lap and I doodled in my journal, excitement bubbling inside me at the thought of Marty coming to visit. I tapped my foot against the wall as I debated if I should share Jaime with her.

I had crawled out of his bed about an hour before. Wide awake and slightly uncomfortable, I couldn't sleep with excitement for the upcoming holiday. Kissing him on the cheek, I crawled over to my bed and let him rest while I snuggled under my blankets with my notebook.

I looked at Jaime, and one eye stared back. "Morning, sunshine."

"Morning, how'd you sleep?" His froggy voice broke in three places, and I admired his wild hair and reassuring eyes.

"Pretty good. Woke up about an hour ago. I'm thinking about Thanksgiving. I have to meet Marty at the bus station around lunch. Is it okay if I go alone? I'm not quite ready to share you with her just yet." I looked away, unsure if he would feel offended.

"No worries. I told Owen I'd meet up with him for a rugby match in the park. I'll catch up with you tonight. Enjoy your friend."

He's so understanding. I swallowed and sat straighter. "Hey Jaime." My serious tone alerted him to sit up and give me his full attention.

"I know this will sound weird, but I'm not ready to tell Marty about you. Yes, she's my best friend, but she has a way of sticking her nose in other people's business, and I don't want to let her meddle in our personal lives."

He looked down, and I recognized the hurt that flashed across his face and then disappeared. "Ah, I see. You're ashamed of me, aye?" His fun-loving eyes taunted me, and I threw my pillow at him.

"Never." I climbed out of bed and sat beside him. "I think we're perfect, and I don't want anyone to mess it up."

Marty's flirty personality attracted men, even when she wasn't trying. The flick of her hair, the jut of her hip, and her damsel-in-distress stories turned guys on, and their reactions gave her power, which encouraged her to continue. Eventually she required rescuing, and I was always there to bring her back to safety. There were too many moments over the past year when I had exclaimed, "What were you thinking?" as we rehashed the night before.

"Marty and I have our roles. She's the irresponsible one who pushes me to have fun, and I'm the responsible one who reels her in when things get out of control."

Jaime scrunched his lips and cocked his head. "She doesn't really seem like that great of a friend, if you don't mind me saying."

I shrugged and sighed. "I've only known her for less than two years, but she was the first friend I made at college. She pushed me out of my shell. If I hadn't met her, I might still be hiding in the library on Friday and Saturday nights, afraid to get out and meet people. She's a handful, so be aware. I love her and would do anything for her, but she doesn't always have the filters or manners you'd expect. Guys love her, and girls hate her but pretend to like her. I think I'm the only real friend she has." I leaned down and kissed him again. "I'm going to shower and get ready."

"Is she bringing a friend?" Jaime called through the bathroom door.

"Yeah, she never told me who, though. I guess I'll find out later. Prepare yourself. Tonight might be wild."

Chapter 28

I hustled to Eyre Square wearing the cutest outfit I owned. My new flare jeans squeezed my thighs, and my belly button peeked just below the hem of my black crop top. It wasn't warm enough for this November day, so I threw on my jean jacket before I hurried downtown.

It was a beautiful day for a walk, but there was no way Marty could walk up the hills while juggling a suitcase. She was only coming for a few days, but I imagined she had packed her entire closet. I had told her it rained every day, and the weather often changed on a dime, so she probably packed double in case she had to change out of wet clothes.

Busses pulled in and out of the station as I arrived, exchanging riders coming and going, and I saw Marty standing alone on the street corner. *Huh, maybe she came alone.* She looked up and down, observing the Irish architecture and possibly judging European fashion. I wasn't close enough to yell to her so I picked up my pace and speed-walked. She gripped her luggage and scanned the hundreds of people walking by.

"Marty!" I waved my arms over my head, but she couldn't hear me.

"Marty!" I called again as I hurried across the busy street. "Marty!"

When she saw me, she jumped up and down, waving her arms over her head like an S.O.S call before running toward me. Her luggage trailed behind her, thudding over each crack in the sidewalk. She threw her arms around me and spun me in a circle. "Rory! I can't believe I'm here. I'm exhausted, but so excited."

It was lunchtime, but Marty had pulled an all-nighter. Jet lag would hit her in a few hours, allowing me time to prepare for Thanksgiving tomorrow. I narrowed my eyebrows at her. "Are you alone?"

"No, no, bathroom." She tipped her head toward the bus station entrance, and I nodded. "How have you been? You look great!" She eyed me up and down, and I spun in a circle.

"So do you. I love what you did to your hair." The ginger strips of hair framing her face used to be blonde.

"Yeah, I did it for Ireland." She leaned closer to me and her voice dropped so no one around could hear. "Do you think it looks cheesy?"

I shook my head. "No, no. You look great."

We stood in silence, smiling like a couple in love. "I can't believe I made it." Marty flipped her hair over her shoulder, and we stepped to the side to allow pedestrians to pass. "It's so beautiful, and I love the accent. Have you fallen in love with an Irish man?"

I nervously giggled and turned my head away to hide the redness I could feel traveling up my cheeks.

"Are you staying here forever?" she asked.

"I wish. I love it here." Looking behind her, I couldn't help but wonder who was in the bathroom. "We'll get a cab to my apartment. My Irish roommate has an air mattress, so you'll be sleeping in the living room for a few nights. I hope you don't mind. You can either crash there or on the couch. We don't have a lot of room, but everyone is cool with you coming. Tomorrow, a few Irish friends are coming over for dinner, so we'll have to pack up your stuff and set it up again when they leave." I ran down the outline for the day.

"Rory, whatever works. We don't care where we sleep. We're excited to see you and want to have fun. Maybe go to pubs, drink beer, and listen to music."

I smiled at her. "Speaking of we, who got your other ticket?"

"Speak of the devil," Marty said, waving behind me. Her wide smile crinkled her eyes and her newly bleached teeth lit up the street.

Turning, my chest constricted, my lungs tightened, and a golf ball grew in my throat. My voice caught, and I couldn't do anything beyond wave. Instead of smiling, I sneered. I shot Marty a death glare, my mind reeling at how this could happen or why Marty thought it would be a good idea.

"Hi, Rory." His deep voice brought back a wave of memories, and the joy I had felt earlier sizzled with disdain and disappointment.

I cleared my throat. "Scott. What are you doing here?"

The street tilted and spun, my eyes struggling to believe who was standing next to me in Ireland. Unable to trust her, I recoiled from Marty. "I—I—uh, I don't understand." My eyes raced between them, searching for a reasonable explanation, but their eyes reflected eagerness and adventure.

"Rory, I told you my sister couldn't come." She dropped her voice below a whisper and stuck her head toward me. "There was no one else."

"Excuse us," I said to Scott, grabbing her elbow and dragging her to the corner of the building. I glanced behind me, and Scott stood where I left him, pretending to be interested in the window display of the souvenir shop.

"Ow!" Marty rubbed her upper arm, where my fingers had dug into her precious, delicate skin.

"What are you doing?" I half-whispered, half-yelled. "Why would you think bringing Scott would be a good idea?" Furious, my nostrils flared, and spittle flung out of my mouth.

Marty ran her hand down her face, removing the wetness. She stepped back and gripped her luggage. "So what? It's three nights, Rory. You'll be fine. I didn't want to travel alone, and he missed you—I don't see the problem."

I threw my head back and stared at the rolling clouds. My right hand gripped and squeezed my forehead while I tried to compose myself. "If you didn't think it was a problem, you wouldn't have kept it from me. There were so many times you could have told me who was coming."

Marty shrugged with one shoulder. "You said you didn't care." That was true, but that didn't make it right.

My eyes narrowed, and I took in her confident posture, arms wrapped around her chest, and jutted chin sticking out at me.

My mouth hung open at her nonchalance. "Marty! He's my ex-boyfriend. Why the hell would I want him here?"

The familiar gaze of Marty's manipulative eyes scanned my face. "You're right. I should have told you. Can you let it go? I'll keep him away from you so you don't have to deal with him, and we'll be out of your hair in a few days." Her soft lips brushed against my cheek and she squeezed my hand. "I promise."

I sighed and checked my watch. "Fine. What time is it at home?"

"I don't know, like, eight-thirty?"

"Did you sleep on the plane?"

"No, I couldn't. I'm delirious right now."

I inhaled and exhaled, counting the rush of air entering and exiting my body until I got to 'three-Mississippi'. "Fine." I picked up her luggage and stepped closer to her, my eyes inches from hers. "It's just three nights, but if he does anything to ruin my weekend, he's gone. I don't know where, but I won't have him bringing up bad memories or disrespecting me in my house."

I didn't wait for Marty's response, but marched back to Scott. "Hi,

Scott. Welcome to Ireland. Are you ready?" Before he could reply, I walked away and hailed a taxi.

Marty tried to converse in the car, but I wasn't in the mood. She asked questions about the city and the country, and the taxi driver volunteered after the awkward silence forced someone to engage. I sat in the front, pressed against the door, willing myself to open it, jump out, and escape this nightmare.

"Here ya are." I paid the cab driver and exited the car, stomping toward my apartment. Marty and Scott fumbled with their luggage and hurried behind me, running to catch up.

We filed into my quiet apartment, and I pointed to the couches. "That's where you'll be staying." In the corner sat a deflated air mattress and a pile of blankets and sheets. "My roommates are out, but should be home in a few hours." I couldn't believe I skipped class for this.

Marty dropped her things. "This looks great, Rory!"

I smirked at her overly enthusiastic compliment. "Let me show you around." We walked through the tiny apartment, and I showed them the kitchen and the bathroom. "I know you're tired, so I'm going to leave you. Maybe we can figure out what we're doing tonight in a few hours. Shower if you need one. The towels are in the closet. I have some schoolwork to do, so make yourself comfortable." I closed my bedroom door and flopped on my bed.

I wasn't tired, but needed to get away from them. Thanksgiving was my favorite holiday, and I refused to let one ex-boyfriend dampen my mood.

I pulled out a notebook and pen, doodling as I thought. *When life gets too complicated, I do what I always do. I make lists. How do I handle this?* I had Jaime to consider, Thanksgiving weekend to host, and a variety of relationships and personalities to manage. My emotional strength had stabilized with Jaime, but it now teetered precariously with Scott's arrival. I jotted down a few avenues: **ignore him, talk**

to him, talk to Marty. The only option that seemed halfway decent was to ignore him and deal with it when I got back to America, but I wasn't in America, and I didn't want to be that person anymore.

I sneaked out of my room around three-thirty and peeked into the living room. They both napped soundly on the tiny, uncomfortable couches, and I crept back into my room, feeling trapped like a lion in a cage unable to explore my homeland. I wanted to be out there prepping Thanksgiving dinner, or at least getting myself organized, but I needed to minimize the amount of time spent with them.

I pulled out Jaime's notepad and drew him a picture. A small hill with one tree, a leprechaun, and a princess decorated the page. I drew a heart in the tree trunk and wrote **R. + J. 4-EVA** within it. I didn't know if he'd ever see it, but I needed to lean into something, and right now, his support calmed me.

I heard the front door squeak open, and the familiar stomping of boots traveling across the floor echo throughout the apartment.

"Hi," I heard. "I'm Marty, and this is Scott."

I put my ear against the door, sure it was Jaime with the heavy footsteps, but hoped Marissa and Zoey had brought home a random friend with a similar gait.

"Jaime. I live here."

The door to our bedroom swung open and pressed me against the wall. "Ugh," I groaned, feeling the door slam against my nose.

He stepped into our room, and I pushed the door closed. "Ow." My fingers turned red as I rubbed my nose, and my heart dropped to my feet. "I'm bleeding. I'm bleeding. I'm bleeding." I sounded like a broken record but my brain wasn't processing the impact of his arrival. I raced into our bathroom and spun the toilet paper roll until a yard of paper bunched into a messy ball. Gripping the toilet seat, I tipped my head back, and squeezed the bridge of my nose, breathing through my mouth.

"I'm sorry. I didn't expect you to be behind the door." He didn't smile, and watched me struggle with the bloody mess. "I met your friends."

I dropped my head to look into his golden eyes. "Yeah, about that, Jaime. I didn't know. I had no idea he was coming." I shook my head in disgust and looked at the ceiling to slow the bleeding.

"It's grand. But if anything happens that makes you feel uncomfortable, you tell me, and I'll take care of it."

My heart swelled and grew three sizes. I smiled behind the ball of toilet paper, but he didn't return the expression. "Thanks, Jaime."

"He doesn't know about us, right?"

I shook my head. "No, neither of them."

"Perfect. Let's keep it that way."

Jaime turned and exited the bathroom, and my stomach dropped. I heard his shoes stomp into the living room. "Hi, I'm Jaime. Scott, aren't you the guy who's ignored Rory since she got here?"

My heart fell to my stomach, and my eyes widened. Heat rose within me and my neck and shoulders tensed. I wanted to disappear, but I had to go out there. I forced my body to stand and tiptoed to the door before gaining enough courage to smooth the altercation. Peeking around the corner of the door, I watched Jaime hover over Scott and Marty.

"I didn't mean to ignore her. College is busy, you know?"

"Yeah, I know." Jaime agreed. "But what you don't know is that disrespect is something I won't tolerate under my roof."

Scott stood up, puffing his chest. "Your roof?"

"Yeah, my roof, my house, my country. If you show her or any of us disrespect, you'll have to find yourself another place to sleep."

I stood behind the door and threw my fisted arm up, pumping the air. *You go, Jaime!*

Scott placed his hands in front of him to show surrender. "No disrespect, man. I'm here to have fun and see an old friend. That's all."

"I'm glad we understand each other." Jaime turned away and winked at me. "Want a beer?" he called over his shoulder.

"Sure," Scott said.

"Okay," Marty squeaked.

"Rory?" Jaime called through the apartment. "You want a beer?"

That was my cue to enter. I dropped the ball of toilet paper in the trash and smoothed out my shirt. "Sure, thanks, Jaime." I stepped out of our bedroom and saw Scott's crumpled face and tense body cowering on the couch. "I see you met Jaime. He's my roommate."

Chapter 29

The tense afternoon rolled into a tense evening. Either Marty didn't sense the strain or it made her uncomfortable, because every now and then she threw out random topics to lighten the mood. "I got a new job waitressing at that bar," she had said, or "my sister's new boyfriend is the quarterback of the football team." But I wasn't interested, and no one else knew who she was talking about, so the conversation quickly fell flat.

I sneaked into Marissa and Zoey's room to grab an extra blanket for my guests, and the two of them sat on the bed whispering. "Psst, Rory," Marissa hissed, curling her index finger. "Come here."

Squeezing myself onto their bed, I rested my head on Zoey's shoulder. "Happy Thanksgiving," I whispered.

"How did this even happen?" Zoey asked. "That's your ex-boyfriend, right?"

I nodded before responding, my voice flat. "Yep."

"Is he so close with Marty that she'd invite him on vacation?" Marissa probed.

I leaned back. "I don't know. I didn't think so, but I have no idea. He hasn't responded to any of my emails since I arrived. He didn't even respond when I broke it off, but Marty told me it was over."

Marissa leaned over Zoey's body and stared at me. Her eyes dared me to connect the dots, but I wasn't ready.

"Were they friends before you left?" Zoey asked.

"Yeah, Marty and I were always together, so if I was with Scott, so was she." I hopped off the bed. "Do you guys have an extra blanket? They need another one."

Marissa dug through her wardrobe and pulled a bagged throw from the top shelf. "Here."

I carried it to the living room and placed it on the air mattress. "You should be warm enough tonight."

I returned to my room and lay on my bed, staring at the ceiling. Jaime sat at his desk, drawing.

A few minutes later, a knock on the door jolted me upright. "Come in," I called.

Marty squeezed through the door. "Hi. I wanted to say I'm sorry, again, for upsetting you. I didn't mean to. I honestly thought the three of us would have fun, like old times." She sat delicately at the edge of my bed, careful not to ruffle the comforter. I watched her eyes scan the room and inferred the judgment hiding behind her stiff posture.

"Marty, he's my ex. I wanted to see you and show you Ireland, but now I have to worry about that idiot. It was a shock, is all. I wish you had given me notice."

Her blonde hair shook as her head turned left and right. "Looking at it now, I should have. I promise I won't do that again. Can you move on for the next few days?"

"Yeah, I guess there are worse things in life. Thank you." I leaned over and pulled her into a brisk hug.

"We only have a few days, and I would love to see the country, hang out with you, and have fun. Will you do that for me?"

It's just three days and day one is almost over. It'll be fine. But why don't

I feel fine? "Of course. What do you want to do tonight?" My previous learned response to acquiesce during conflict reared its ugly head.

Marty fell onto my bed, and she flipped her hair. "Let's go out to a pub. We can grab food, listen to music, and drink."

It was a Wednesday night, so they'd get a toned-down version of the nightlife in Ireland. "Sure. I can't stay out too late, though. I have a lot of cooking to do tomorrow."

She hugged me, but my arms hung rigid at my sides. Still simmering, I couldn't seem to forget that she had deceived me. "Great! I'll tell Scott." She dashed out of my room, and Jaime threw me a questioning glance.

"What?" I snapped.

"Nothing. So that's Scott, eh?" he asked.

My face fell, curious about Jaime's feelings toward Scott, but I was afraid to hear his answer. Instead of responding, I nodded.

"He seems okay. Like a harmless bloke."

"You're too polite. I'd like to hear what you really think on Sunday." I looked at the picture on his desk. "What are you drawing?"

"Oh, it's for my drawing class, the only class I like this semester."

I recognized the shading along the craggy cliffs and the reflection of the sun on the ocean horizon. "It's beautiful. Is that from the Aran Islands?"

"Yeah, it was a moment I don't want to forget."

"What do you want to do when you graduate in the spring?"

He took his notepad out of my hand and placed it on the table. "Well, art is just for fun. Finance is boring but necessary, so I hope to have a job to pay the bills and somehow make money off my art. Maybe next time you visit, you'll find me along the Spanish Arch selling my paintings to tourists."

Draping my arms across his shoulders, I said, "I'll buy every painting you create. Your drawings are exquisite."

"Thanks. Yeah, I don't know. I'll probably start applying for jobs in April and start in the summer. Maybe I'll even work for my dad, running the books on his landscape company. I have options." He kissed my neck, and I melted into him. "Just so we're on the same page, what's the story with us, again?"

"Between us? Just roommates. Especially with Scott here. I don't want him to know anything about my personal life. And Marty clearly can't be trusted."

Jaime kissed me again. "With that, my darling, we're entering the friend zone." He pushed me off his lap and stood beside me before leaving me alone in our bedroom.

"Hey, Scott!" I heard Jaime call. "Are you ready for a night out? I know all the places you'll want to go."

I heard them bro-hug, and when I entered the room, I saw Jaime snug between Scott and Marty on the loveseat. I hid my laughter and disguised my pursed lips by drinking from a can of soda. Facing the sink, I heard Jaime say, "Yeah, man, it'll be grand. I'll take care of you."

My eyes bugged and I fought back a smile. *My boyfriend is taking care of my ex-boyfriend? This should be interesting...*

Chapter 30

⁓ ≈❀≈ ⁓

We usually walked into town, but the damp November night was too much for Marty's hair. She had packed an outfit for every occasion but had forgotten an essential item: a raincoat. Owen and Aoife met us at our apartment and we took three cabs into the city center. I pointed out all the landmarks as we flew past, but Marty was too preoccupied with checking her makeup in a small, compact mirror to look up and admire the location.

Walking up and down the quiet, pedestrian streets, Jaime pointed at a small pub wedged between two restaurants. "This pub is famous for Irish set dancing. If you want to experience dance, music, and beer, this is the place to go. Have you done this yet?"

Marissa, Zoey, and I shook our heads. "Set dancing?" I asked. "Never heard of it."

"It's kind of like what you guys know as line dancing," Owen explained.

We walked into the dark pub and settled at a round table. "Let me buy the first round," Jaime said. His acting skills and generosity impressed me.

He made two trips from the bar, carrying stacked pyramids of

Guinness pints. The white heads of the pint glasses contrasted with the dark stout below, reminding me of a developing storm.

"Thanks, Jaime." Marty flashed him her most confident smile and flipped her hair over her shoulder. I took a sip to avoid speaking.

We chatted cordially, and Marty took over the conversation, always bringing it back to her. I rolled my eyes in the shadows as she told us about their flight and their first impressions of Ireland. The pub filled more than I expected for a Wednesday night, and soon it was full. Being the courteous hostess I was, I grabbed the next round after the first set of beers emptied.

As the alcohol flowed, the tension in my body loosened, and I laughed, joked, and danced to the traditional Irish music playing a few feet away. I wanted to keep my walls up to show Marty she couldn't barrel in and destroy my weekend, but the Irish magic tore down the barricade, and I found myself giggling and reminiscing with her. It was my only Thanksgiving in Ireland, and I wanted to make it exciting—but not as memorable as Halloween. I pushed my beer to the center of the table, making it last.

The fiddle and bodhran filled the small room, dampening the patrons' chatter. People of all ages jumped to the middle of the dance floor and formed facing lines. "Set dancing," Jaime confirmed.

Zoey jumped up. "Can anyone do it?"

"Yeah, but you don't want to mess it up. Those people mean business."

I kicked Jaime under the table and giggled.

"Oh, we won't. Does anyone want to dance with me? What do I do?" Zoey looked around, and Marissa stood. "Anyone else? Jaime? Aoife? C'mon, you're the Irish dancing queen."

I crouched down in my seat, embarrassed by the memory I couldn't recall.

Jaime took a sip of his beer. "Only if we all do it."

"Oh no, I'm a terrible dancer," I said.

Marty leaned forward so we could hear her over the loud music. "Rory, you are a brilliant dancer!"

I cringed at her forced use of Irish adjectives.

"Come on. Let's do it," Zoey agreed. "You're only in Ireland once. Scott? Marissa? Owen?" She was

already up, pulling people beside her.

The group filed toward the empty space in front of the band. "How do I do this?" I asked Jaime.

"It's a repeated dance, so you'll get it after a few tries." The eight of us lined up facing each other at the group's tail to not mess up the veterans and watched the crowd dance two complete sets before joining in.

Kicking, sashaying, spinning, and sidestepping my partner, I danced beside Owen. Jaime stood beside Aoife across from us, Marissa and Zoey stood to my left, and Marty and Scott stood opposite. The four pairs faced each other to create two squares. Exhausted and elated by the end of the first set, I spun in a circle, falling into Owen's arms.

I tripped my way to Jaime, hooking arms with Scott and spinning out of control with Marty, and I blamed my enjoyment on the magic of Ireland.

We danced for hours, the pints flowed, and Jaime and I sat back, watching the others take lessons from Aoife.

"Does anyone need to use the bathroom?" Marty asked a few hours later. Scott sat beside me, watching Aoife teach Marissa how to sequence the steps.

"Me." Zoey handed her drink to Marissa and followed Marty out of the main room.

Jaime ran his hands through his sweaty, spiky hair. "Scott, want another drink? I'll buy another round," He walked to the bar, leaving me alone with Scott for the first time since he arrived.

"Welcome to Ireland," I said. I felt good, with just enough alcohol flowing through my veins to eliminate the hurt he caused by avoiding me. I pushed that emotion down and focused on the cheerful music and dance, trying to let the allure of Ireland sweep me away to a life without worries.

"Thanks for having us. It's been awesome."

After a moment of silence, I swallowed the lump in my throat and leaned forward. "Scott, did you get any of my emails these past few months?" His face flinched and his shoulders tightened.

"Yeah, sorry about that. I was busy with school, and every time I went to email you back, I got busy and forgot."

Liar. The manipulation evaporated off his sleezy skin and I could almost see it in the air. I continued smiling and closed my eyes, pretending I didn't hear him. *I will not let him ruin my last weeks in Ireland.*

Zoey and Marty returned from the bathroom and Zoey cuddled next to me and gripped her arm through mine. Her hands fluttered, shredding a napkin into tiny pieces. "You okay?" I asked.

"Yeah, yeah. I think I'm done drinking for tonight."

"Too much?"

"Yeah, I'm not feeling well."

"You don't look well," I said, noticing her pale face and sunken eyes. "Let me know if you want to go home. I'll go with you."

She squeezed my arm with her free hand. "I want to go home."

Frowning with concern, I grabbed my bag and slung it over my shoulder. "Uh, sure thing. Let me tell Jaime."

I maneuvered to the bar and told him Zoey wasn't feeling well. "Have fun tonight, and if they get annoying, make an excuse and send them home."

"No worries," he said.

"I want to kiss you, but I can't. Just know that I miss you." I slid my hand down his torso and patted him on the butt. He jumped, grinned, and raised his eyebrows at me. "I'll see you later." He squeezed my hand, and I returned to the table.

"Marty? Scott? I'm taking Zoey home. She's not feeling well."

Marty threw Zoey a concerned look, and the fine lines around her lips deepened. "Okay."

"Don't worry. Marissa and Jaime are staying. I'm not sure what Owen and Aoife are doing, but I'm sure they'll make sure you have fun tonight."

Marty jumped up and hugged me, and I stiffly tapped her on her shoulders. Scott stood, and I waved before turning on my heel and escaping from the pub before he got any ideas.

Zoey and I rode home in silence. She rested her head against the window with her eyes closed. Once we got home, I tucked her into bed and got her a glass of water. As I got up, she grabbed my wrist. "Wait." Her eyes reflected fear. "I have to tell you something."

I froze, not sure what she could have to say.

"Marty and Scott. They're dating. She told me in the bathroom. After you sent that email to break up with him, they hooked up. And they've been together ever since."

The room spun, and nausea bubbled inside me. Heat rose from my gut to my head, and I felt my heart beat in my fingers. Everything turned black, and then I saw red.

Chapter 31

Lying in bed the following day, I couldn't rise. My bones hurt, my muscles ached, and my lips, chapped from crying, stuck together like dried glue. Peeling my eyes open, I crawled to the bathroom and examined the red, puffy rings above my cheek bones.

Slogging back to my bed, I burrowed under the heavy covers, and allowed the sounds of Jaime's breathing to swallow me whole. Memories from the night before crashed against me like a hurricane. My little dinghy couldn't sustain the constant hits of rage, frustration, and disappointment, and I cowered in a ball until the waves of emotions stopped.

Last night, I needed to be alone. When I heard the door to our apartment open, I froze. My eyes squeezed shut, my heart raced, and I slowed my breathing, pretending to be asleep. I wasn't ready to see anyone, and I needed more time.

Jaime climbed under my blankets, but the smell of smoke and alcohol made my stomach turn. I told him I wasn't feeling well and needed space. He reluctantly crossed the room into his bed, and I pulled my body into a tight ball, gripping my abdomen. My body shook as the tears raced down my face, but it was dark, and Jaime was sleeping. I tried my hardest to be quiet, but if the moonlight hit me just right, he would see me sobbing.

I dozed in and out of consciousness, the nightmare of Marty and Scott crossing into my dreams. Tossing and turning all night, I felt like a monster, unsure if I could pretend nothing had happened. My best friend snatched my ex-boyfriend the moment we broke up. I knew Scott wasn't 'the one', but friends didn't do that to friends. What she did was sleezy and manipulative, and I wondered what secrets of mine she had shared, knowing the issues I had with him and the feelings I had confessed to her over the past year.

Wake up, wake up. You have to wake up. It's Thanksgiving, your favorite holiday. Do NOT let her ruin it. The room slowly came into focus, and I stumbled out of bed to face the consequences of the night before. I needed to get in the kitchen, but the open concept floor plan would wake Marty and Scott, and I didn't want them in my view.

Procrastinating, I showered. The hot water cleared my cloudy head, and I stayed under there for who-knows-how-long, with the hot, foggy haze suffocating me. The warm air stung my lungs and made my head dizzy.

I waited until nine-thirty before convincing myself it was time to go out there. "Jaime." I rocked his shoulders and knelt beside him. "Jaime," I said louder.

He hmm'd and opened one eye. "I'm going to the grocery store to get some last-minute items, and my backpack isn't big enough for everything. Can you come?" I needed him to come so I could refresh myself on his night and prepare myself for the day. "Please?"

Jaime rolled toward me and stretched his long limbs, hitting the wall behind his head. "Sure."

He stood, stumbling to the piles of laundry on the floor, and I saw his boxers hang just below his belly button. I looked away quickly, not wanting anything to happen right now, but I couldn't resist watching him. His confidence and swagger quietly stood out to me. He pulled on a pair of pants and a sweatshirt, and we walked the mile to the store.

Our conversation was dismal. My brain fired questions, but I couldn't pull up enough nerve to ask. Instead, I kept it polite. "Did you have fun last night?"

"Yeah. Was Zoey okay?"

"Yeah, she needed to go to bed, but she was fine. I think she's getting homesick." I didn't know if that was true, but it sounded legit, seeing that Thanksgiving was a significant holiday away from home.

The rain pelted my face, and I pulled the hood of my raincoat over my forehead. I'd gotten used to the gloomy weather, embracing the gray before the beauty could come out. It reminded me of my life.

Jaime popped open his umbrella and half-heartedly held it over my head. I waved him away, pointing to my hood.

"What'd you guys end up doing last night?" I couldn't look at him. My pink eyes were ready to turn red and watery again.

"Hung out at the pub, went to the chippy, and then to the club. I think they got a full taste of nightlife here."

I smiled and shoved my hands in my pockets. "Great. Thanks for staying with them. I know it wasn't ideal. I swear, Jaime, I had no idea he was coming." I stopped and grabbed his arm, staring into his eyes, begging him to believe me. "I don't want him here."

The cars raced by us, and we stepped aside to avoid the splash-over. "No worries. It's just two more days."

We walked the rest of the way in silence. I filled my backpack with potatoes, green beans, turnips, sweet potatoes, and stuffing. I carried the turkey breast in my arms, and Jaime carried the milk. His backpack held pie crust, sugar, flour, butter, and apples. He placed a bag of rolls on top so they wouldn't get squished. We had everything we needed for a great American dinner.

"I don't know what I was thinking, having a Thanksgiving dinner." I looked at my turkey-baby, saturated in rainwater from the walk home. "This is a disaster."

"Eh, insanity makes life interesting. I'll help you cook, but you have to show me how."

"You'll have to help me with the measurements. I don't know what a milliliter is," I confessed.

"I'll do my best. I'm not too good in the kitchen."

My mood had lifted, and I felt half-normal. "How can you not be too good in the kitchen? Your ma is an excellent cook."

Jaime passed the milk to his other hand. "She is, but I never paid attention. I just enjoyed eating it."

"Typical male." I threw him a side smile and he grinned in return. "Well, I'm not a great cook, but I try to put love into it. My mom emailed me all the family recipes but they're in cups and teaspoons. It might be a little wonky. Consider yourself warned."

Jaime laughed. "Hey, it'll make the day even more interesting."

By the time we opened the door to our apartment, it was close to eleven. The entire house was awake, but they looked like something out of the Night of the Living Dead. Bags under their eyes, pale, dehydrated skin, and Medusa's hair greeted us, not to mention the stale scent of beer and body odor.

"Phew!" I said. "I'm opening windows." I ran around the living room, cranking the top windows open to get the air circulating.

"Morning." Marty yawned and stretched. Her tank top rose above her belly button and her hoop piercing sparkled in the light. I sneered and clenched my teeth. *I wonder what Scott thinks of that sexy piercing.* Her big, blue eyes made her look innocent, but I knew how she operated now. She didn't care who she hurt as long as she got what she wanted, and I couldn't believe it had taken me this long to realize.

I ignored her and made my way to the kitchen.

"Need any help?" Scott asked Jaime.

Jaime and I dumped our food on the small kitchen island. "You'll have to ask Rory. She's the chef today."

I shook my head, afraid to face him. Instead, I stuck my head in the refrigerator, searching for an invisible item. "No. All set." I pulled the sweetest smile from somewhere deep inside and mustered, "You're the guest. Sit, relax, and enjoy your day."

Scott leaned into the couch and turned on the television. British accents filled the room.

"Dinner will be served at five," I announced. "Marissa, if you and Zoey can chop the potatoes and apples, that would be awesome. I'll get the turkey in straight away, and we'll start the sides around two. Jaime, what time are Aoife and Owen coming over?"

"Around three, I think."

"Okay, at three o'clock we'll have the table set." I looked around the kitchen, counting the chairs. We had a table for four and three stools at the island. *We'll slide in a desk chair from one of our bedrooms. It'll be lovely.* "Questions?"

I refused to let the betrayal of my supposed best friend ruin my favorite holiday.

Chapter 32

A fter a quick tap on the wooden door, Owen and Aoife barreled into our living room like they lived there. "Happy Thanksgiving!" I called from the oven. "Owen, Aoife. You remember Marty and Scott." I gestured at the couch, and they looked up from the vegetable platter and waved. My upbeat voice hid the surrounding tension, and my carefully composed face hid the confusion that followed me like a trail of cigarette smoke.

Owen and Aoife dropped their coats on the arm of the couch and grabbed a drink. "Five o'clock somewhere, right?" Aoife held her can up in the air. "Slainte." She and Jaime clinked beers, and I stuck my head in the oven again, rearranging sides.

Zoey sat beside Marty, and her knee rocked rhythmically. She cleared her throat, and quickly told Marty about the weekly farmer's market in the center of Galway. "It's open on Saturday if you want to go, but we'd need to get there early because it's busy. Local cheese, scones, vintage clothes, and music," she listed. "It's a fun time."

Marissa leaned across the island. "Need any help?"

"Dinner should be ready in forty-five minutes. Want to get the table set?" I asked.

She set three plates on the island and squeezed five more on our square table. It was tight, but it would do. I wanted to sit Marty and Scott up at the counter away from the group, but I didn't know which of my friends should be the sacrificial lamb and sit beside them.

After setting the timer on the oven, I sat beside Zoey and a gracious smile drifted across my face. I hadn't made eye contact with Scott or Marty since Zoey spilled the beans. Marty's betrayal stabbed me, and my heart was bleeding all over the kitchen. *Survive the day* repeated like a daily mantra.

"So, Marty," Aoife said, "How was your flight?"

She flipped her hair back and smiled. "It was fine. We watched a few movies and tried to sleep." She glanced at Scott, and I imagined her nuzzled into his shoulder with a shared blanket over them.

"Scott, how do you know Rory?" Owen asked.

I choked on my water and excused myself to check the pies. I hadn't said Scott's name around Owen, and I guess Jaime hadn't mentioned him before. Owen looked at me with pressed eyebrows and returned to Scott.

Scott hesitated before responding. "Rory and I dated for a little over a year."

"Oh, shite." Owen stood up and walked into our tiny kitchen. "Need help?" he asked me.

"It's fine. We're fine, right Rory?" Scott said.

My lips pulled into a slight smile. "Mm-hmm." I turned to Owen. "No thanks, I'm all set." I busied myself in the fridge, my fingers shaking.

"It lasted through the summer, but we grew apart and parted ways." Scott approached the counter and watched me work.

Liar. My face burned with contempt because I was not part of that conversation. I excused myself from the room and splashed water on my face from our pedestal bathroom sink. My vacant eyes stared back at me. *Two more days.*

Rubbing a rough towel across my face, Jaime appeared in the mirror's reflection. "You okay?" he asked.

I nodded and sat on the closed toilet seat, making room for him to come in and close the door. "I'm okay. I can get through this. I don't know if Zoey told you, but he and Marty are dating. Marty told Zoey last night at the pub. That's why Zoey asked me to take her home."

The tears fell down my cheeks, but I didn't understand why. I didn't love Scott. He treated me like garbage, and I believed it was normal... until I met Jaime.

Jaime wrapped his arms around me and held me while I let it all out. "Why are you crying?" he asked.

I chuckled and pulled away. "Because I'm so stupid for trusting her. I never thought she would do that to me, you know? You don't do that to your best friend." I waved my hand in the air. "I don't care about him. He can drop dead for all I care, but she hurt me. It's like she was a puppeteer controlling my life, and when I came here, I broke free of the strings. And now she's back, pretending nothing happened so she can control me again."

"Do you want me to ask them to leave?" Jaime asked.

I shook my head, wiping my eyes. "No, it's fine. I'll get through it. They deserve each other."

The timer in the kitchen dinged. "I'll take care of that." He walked away from me, and I wanted to call him back so he could protect me, but I knew I had to handle this on my own.

As I wiped my eyes one last time, an ear-piercing screech screamed at me. I covered my ears and raced out of the bathroom. Black smoke filled the kitchen, and Marissa waved a towel under the smoke alarm. Zoey stood at the open front door waving her arms, and the others stood on the balcony looking in.

"The yams," Jaime yelled over the beeping. "They're blackened." He tossed the glass dish on the stove and poured water over the black marshmallows, which should have been a golden brown. Smoke erupted from the pan, and everything sizzled.

Jaime pulled out the cookie sheet with the black balls, which used to be rolls, and removed one, knocking it on the counter. He threw it into the trash can, and it landed with a thud. My apple and pumpkin pies, which rested on the rack below the sweet potatoes, dripped with black marshmallow goo.

Once the beeping stopped, our guests stepped inside, still covering their ears with their hands. Our kitchen could only handle two people moving simultaneously, so the rest of our friends huddled in the corner of the living room.

Trapped between my boyfriend, my ex-boyfriend, and my former best friend, I struggled to keep it together. The delicate dam behind my eyes broke, and tears of frustration slid down my face for the second time in ten minutes. I wanted to run away but couldn't leave Jaime to clean up my mess. Instead, my legs carried me to the counter, and I raced the burning dishes to the cold outside. Once alone, I squatted behind the door and sobbed into my arms.

It's ruined. Not just my dinner, but my sanity. So many missed opportunities to prevent this moment, but it's too late. I let Marty walk all over me, and now my favorite day of the year is just another day thrown into the dumpster fire that is my life.

A firm hand gripped my shoulder. "No worries." Jaime's deep voice brought me back to him, and I peeled myself off the wet, frozen concrete slab. "I got this." I followed him inside and excused myself to change into dry clothes.

When I returned, he had removed the black topping and transported the yams into a bowl and mashed them into a chunky puree. "Now we have mashed potatoes or mashed yams. It's okay."

I shivered and wiped my nose. "Thank you."

Jaime addressed the group like a mayor standing on a podium after winning an election. "Lads and lasses, dinner is a tad delayed, but it will be ready in a few minutes. Grab your drinks and take a seat."

He took out a loaf of bread and threw it on the table, placing the bowl of mashed and sweet potatoes beside it. Sawing through the turkey with a steak knife, he put the moistest pieces on a dinner plate. Next to the turkey went the gravy, sitting in a coffee mug. After tearing through the cabinets, Jaime poured a package of chocolate-coated biscuits into a bowl. "Dessert," he said, winking at me, "Also known as digestives."

I breathed a sigh of relief. *He saved me again.* I didn't know why he picked me, but I knew I needed to remain by his side for the rest of Marty and Scott's visit.

"Dinner is served."

We arranged our plates and gathered around the table and counter. Jaime, Zoey, and I sat at the island, facing the kitchen, while Owen, Aoife, Marissa, Scott, and Marty squeezed around the tiny table behind us.

"Thanks, Rory. This looks great," Owen said. He buttered a piece of bread and placed it next to the mountain of potatoes on his plate.

Swiveling on my stool, I turned toward the group behind me. "You're welcome. Before we eat, I'd like to go around and say what we are all thankful for. It's a holiday tradition, so I'll go first. I'm thankful for this experience in Ireland. I've learned more about myself than I ever expected." Jaime reached under the counter and rubbed my knee. "Jaime?"

He cleared his throat. "I'm thankful for new friends. I wasn't thrilled about being thrown into an all-girls flat, especially with all Americans, but it's been a great experience."

I played with my fork and felt his eyes on my fingers. Beside him, my body relaxed for the first time since Marty and Scott had arrived.

"I'm thankful for new roommates and new relationships." Zoey looked at Jaime and then Marissa before tucking her head in her chest. A smile crept across her lips.

The five people at the table looked at each other, waiting for someone else to go next.

"I'll go," Marissa began. "Pumpkin pie is something I'm thankful for. I still can't believe we shipped our pumpkin puree from the States."

Jaime grimaced. "Uh, Marissa, sorry, but there won't be any pumpkin pie today. It burned under the marshmallow lava."

Her head dropped, and she scanned the kitchen for dessert. "Okay, I'm thankful for digestives, the cookie I thought would make me poop." Everyone chuckled. "They're delicious and a close second to pie." She looked at Owen to continue.

"I'm thankful for football. It was how I met Jaime. Aoife?"

She cleared her throat and took a sip before continuing. "I'm thankful for my brother. It was how I met Jaime." She looked at me and our eyes locked. I refused to break her gaze until I felt Marty's eyes on me. Aoife smirked at me and smiled at Marty, sensing the audience.

"I'm thankful for Rory. She's the best friend I've ever had." A smile traveled across Marty's lips, and I distracted myself with my fork. I leaned forward to deny her eye contact and reached for a napkin, keeping myself busy.

Scott chuckled. "I'm thankful for Rory's cooking. It appears the magic of Ireland hasn't quite helped her in the kitchen, but at least she's moved beyond hotdogs and cereal."

I whipped my head around and cackled, anger brewing like a tea kettle. *Jerk. Who invited you, anyway?*

I pulled my emotions in and smiled. "Happy Thanksgiving. It may not be how I imagined it, but it will still be a memorable day."

I ate my dinner in silence, tuning out the surrounding conversation.

Zoey appeared just as uncomfortable as I felt, probably because of the secret she had shared with me the night before. She rushed through her meal and excused herself, grabbing a digestive on the way out of the kitchen. "I'll help you clean up dinner," she whispered.

"So, what's the deal with you two?" Aoife asked Scott. I didn't know if she was referring to Marty or me, so I turned for clarification.

She looked back and forth between Scott and Marty. Marty took a sip of her beer and adjusted herself in her chair, facing Scott. "We're just friends."

My blood ran cold, and my veins turned to ice.

"How'd you guys meet?" Aoife asked. I assumed her questions were innocent, but they twisted the knife in my back. I tapped my fingers on the counter, staring at the clock on the microwave.

Scott cleared his throat. "Actually, through Rory."

I kept my mouth sealed, afraid to say something I would regret. Adrenaline traveled through my body at dangerous speeds and my eye twitched.

"Oh, were you friends before you dated?"

"Yeah, we dated for quite a while. Like a year, right Rory?"

Scott's convenient lack of memory regarding our relationship made it difficult to breathe. "The worst year of my life," I mumbled.

Zoey walked into the kitchen to grab another biscuit.

"What was that?" Aoife asked.

I tapped my foot on the rung at the bottom of the stool. "Eh, nothing. Yes, we dated last year. We, um, just broke up. When I came here. Well, we didn't break up. He stopped returning my emails, so I assumed we had broken up. Right, Scott?"

His back straightened, and his rigid posture held up his bobblehead. "Right."

Waiting for him to confess his betrayal, I tapped my fork on my plate.

Zoey's mousy voice cut through the room. "Well, since we're being honest here, when did you and Marty hook up?" Zoey shoved the digestive in her mouth.

Marty widened her eyes at Zoey, and Aoife covered her mouth to hide her laugh. I narrowed my eyes at Marty. "What? Marty, you're dating Scott?" I played dumb to save Zoey's confidentiality. Owen and Jaime continued eating, awkwardly shoveling food into their mouths and staring at their plates.

"Uh, not dating."

"Just screwing?" Zoey's voice carried a flame and I sensed a forest fire building.

Marty looked at Scott for guidance, but he stared at his beer can.

"That's none of your business," she said. She stood from the table and tried to walk away, but our apartment didn't provide privacy. She awkwardly paced the room, gathering her sweatshirt and throwing it over her top. "At least I'm not sleeping with my roommate." She looked from Zoey to Jaime, and Jaime covered his eyes.

"What's it matter to you? I'm in love and not afraid to show it." Zoey crossed her arms over her chest, daring Marty to question her further.

I looked at Marissa, whose pale face and stiff movements told me this was news to her.

Scott looked at Marty, throwing her a quizzical look. "Zoey's sleeping with Jaime," Marty summarized.

I slammed my glass down and looked at Zoey. Her face turned white, and she dropped her biscuit, racing down the long hallway.

Jaime shook his head before marching over to Marty. "This is fecking shite," he yelled. Marty's steely eyes didn't break.

Marissa stood from the table and dashed down the hall to her bedroom. I stumbled from my stool and followed her. "Marissa, wait," I called.

We found Zoey in their bedroom, out of breath and struggling to form her words. "Marissa, it's not true. Rory, I swear. It was a misunderstanding."

Marissa pulled her legs into her chest and held them close like a protective bubble. She raised her eyes, and wetness coated her cheeks.

"I swear, Marissa, I was talking about you. I love you. I told Marty last night in the pub that I hooked up with my roommate because she confided that she was sleeping with Scott. I had to build her trust, so I told her about us. She assumed it was Jaime, I swear!" She looked at both of us, her face honest but concerned.

Something inside me snapped and I couldn't allow them to ruin our Thanksgiving. I marched back into the living room and found Marty and Scott huddled in the corner with Jaime cleaning the kitchen, watching them like a hawk. Owen and Aoife sat at the table speaking quietly to themselves. Jaime's eyes reminded me to be careful, and I nodded my head in strength. Marty and Scott's invisible bubble was no longer protected from the wrath of Rory.

"What the fuck, Marty. I knew he was a loser, but I didn't expect that from you." She stood from the couch and my eyes focused on the bridge of her nose.

"You broke up with him."

"Why'd you invite him here? You're a manipulative, calculating bitch. I can't believe I called you my best friend."

"You needed me and I needed you. It was a mutually beneficial friendship. Sure, Scott and I are dating, but it's not like we're getting married. We're just having fun. You two never had a real relationship, anyway."

Shocked at her dismissal of the previous year, I picked up her coat and threw it at her. "Because he never returned any of my emails!" Surprised, the sleeve hit her in the face and fell to the floor. "Get out, you crazy bitch. You're not welcome here. And you, you piece of shit, were never welcome in the first place."

I stormed out of the room and attended to Zoey, whose tears had dried. "Zoey," I huffed. "You're beautiful, and brave, and amazing. Seeing your honesty inspired me. I refuse to let people walk all over me, anymore. It's bullshit, and I'm sick of it." I pulled her against me and whispered, "Thank you."

The front door slammed shut, and heavy footsteps traveled down the hall. A gentle knock sounded on the other side of the door before it opened. "Everyone's gone." Jaime sat on the edge of Zoey's bed. "Are you guys okay?"

I nodded. "Where'd they go?"

"Owen and Aoife went home. They said they'd check in with us later. They didn't know what they were walking into today."

A giggle erupted out of me and transitioned into a laugh, and then a belly guffaw. "What a ridiculous day." A small smile spread across my lips, and I leaned against his shoulder. "Where did Scott and Marty go?"

"They left. I told them the main office could call them a cab, and there was a youth hostel in the city center."

Guilt mixed with satisfaction. "Jaime, I don't know how you do it, but you saved me again."

His soft lips met mine and I blushed under the public display in front of our roommates. "You did it Rory. I was just following your lead."

Chapter 33

Thanksgiving was a bust, but at least it was over. I hadn't heard from Marty or Scott in the forty-eight hours since Jaime had banished them from our apartment. Even if they wanted to get in touch, there was no way for them to, unless they called my parents for my phone number or emailed me from an internet café. They were due to leave tomorrow, so I didn't expect to hear from them.

My emotions were a jumbled mess. Until now, my entire college existence had revolved around Marty and Scott. Marty and I still shared an apartment and every time I thought of moving back in with her, my stomach turned sour. It was too late to move out, but I couldn't fall back into my pre-Ireland life. Not that I would want to when she was sleeping with my ex-boyfriend. Deep down, I wasn't surprised; Marty always did what she wanted regardless of other people's feelings.

Marissa stuck her head through the door. "Rory? Your dad's on the phone."

I rose from my desk and picked up the phone, curious as to why he had called. "Hi, Dad. Happy belated Thanksgiving."

"Hi, honey. How was your day?"

"Oh, one for the memory book. Sorry I didn't call. With the time change and everything, the day got away from me." I tried to speak with varied intonation but my dismal mood carried on my voice. "How was yesterday? Did you go to Auntie's?"

"Yes, just like last year. It was fine. Everyone missed you."

I swallowed the lump in my throat. "Was Debbie there?" Debbie was his girlfriend when I left for Ireland, but his girlfriends never lasted long.

"No, actually your mom came."

I twirled the phone cord around my index finger. "Huh. I thought mom was going to Grandma's."

"She did, but she came to Auntie's for dessert."

"Is mom there? I'd like to talk to her."

"No, she's at work."

"Oh, so what's up?" I didn't try to sound rude, but my dad and I weren't exactly close, and I couldn't imagine him calling international just to check in.

"I just wanted to say hello," he quickly said, "And also to tell you that December first I'll be depositing the rest of your money into your account. That's the last of it, so make it last."

Relieved by his generosity, but still confused by my mother's presence at his Thanksgiving, I stumbled over my words. "Thanks, Dad. I'll be sure to get you something."

"Nah, just have a beer for me."

I rolled my eyes. "Tell Mom I said hi. Love you."

"Okay, honey, bye."

I hung up the phone, empty from my dad's lack of words. *Would he ever say he loved me?* I reentered our bedroom and dropped on my bed, hugging a pillow to my chest.

"Are you okay?" Jaime watched me from the corner of his bed. "You look sad."

I looked up and hesitated, not sure if I was ready to share all the layers of my dysfunction. "I'm okay. Just thinking."

A flashback of my parents zipped through my mind like a car on the Autobahn. It was so fast I didn't recognize the scene, but the triggered feelings brought me back to that day. At eight years old, I came home from school with a stomach bug. The nurse called my mom at work, and not only did she have to deal with my sickness, but also my emotional dysregulation from throwing up in front of my classmates. She drove me home from school, and told me she'd cook me chicken noodle soup. I went upstairs to change, and I heard moans and groans coming from my parents' bedroom. Scared, I ran back to my mom. "Mama," I had asked, "Is the TV on? I think someone's up there."

She dropped her purse and bolted up the stairs. I slowly followed, unsure why she raced up the stairs like a sprinter at a track meet. She slammed open the door, and through the crack in the doorjamb, I saw a woman wrestling with my dad under the blankets. My heart caught in my chest, and I crept to my bedroom. I turned on my music to drown out the screaming that ensued.

My eyes shot to Jaime, and my throat tightened. My face contorted into shattered glass. Jaime gently placed his hand on my knee. "Are you okay?" he asked.

"When I was eight, I saw my dad cheating on my mom. That moment has stayed with me, and I promised myself I'd never get so close to a man that I'd miss the signs. And I did."

"I'm sorry." His voice hushed and I sat up straighter, refusing to allow my parents' marriage to stop me from finding love. Willie's prediction of finding love within six months gave me hope that my future would be better than their past, but time was ticking.

"It's okay. My mother pretended nothing happened. My dad moved into the basement, living his life, while my mom and I lived upstairs. It was confusing, being a child and seeing women and men come and go in a home where both parents lived but hated each other. To ignore my confusion, I buried myself in school, proving my worth to my dad. My mom had a mental breakdown and I was the one who picked up the pieces. She still hasn't fully recovered." I wiped my tears and smiled to reassure Jaime that I really was okay. "And now my mom is going to holidays with my dad and I don't understand. Are they together? Are they not? He didn't bring his girlfriend, but brought my mom. I don't ask questions because the answers only complicate things. Instead, I watch them destroy each other and myself in the process." I sighed and stood up. "Now you know why I'm fucked up."

He pulled me into him and the armor around my heart chipped away one piece at a time. "We're all fecked up somehow. You're not that special." Raising my eyes to his, I saw the laughter on his lips. "Just kidding, you're more than special. You're spectacular."

My ears heard him, but my brain had already moved on. "And then there's Scott and Marty. I still don't know how I missed the signs. I remember, one night after an all-nighter in the library, I walked into our apartment and the two of them were eating breakfast on our couch. They both wore the same clothes from the day before, which I found odd, but they told me that Scott got locked out of his dorm after a frat party and needed a place to crash. It didn't make a lot of sense, but I let it slide."

"Eh, you're better off without them."

"I ignored all the signs."

"Can I cheer you up? My parents and I decorate for Christmas every December eighth, and I'd love you to come to my house and be a part of it."

I kissed his soft lips and draped my arms around his neck. "Thank you. I would love that." Eagerness brewed at the thought of seeing Connor and Deirdre one last time before I left for America. I wanted them to know how special they made me feel by including me in all their traditions.

"And then, Rory Stanley, I want to whisk you away for a romantic night in a castle."

My eyes widened, and I pulled back to see his face. "Are you sure? That's way too much money." In all my time with Scott, he never took me away for a romantic weekend, let alone to a castle. My heart throbbed, hoping he didn't back out at my hesitancy.

"Consider it a Christmas gift from me. I hope you never forget this semester." He picked up my hand and kissed each finger. "You may not realize this, but I am completely smitten with you."

I wanted to tell him I was smitten too, but the words wouldn't form. Scott and Marty's betrayal, my father's infidelity, and my mother's indifference iced my heart. My vulnerability so soon after Marty's confession held me captive. Instead, I kissed his neck, and he sighed. "I can't wait! Next weekend?"

He nodded, and I jumped up clapping my hands. "I've always dreamed of sleeping in a castle," I said.

He pushed my hair out of my eyes and kissed my nose. "Princess Rory, you deserve it."

A haunting question from that seasick day dripped out of my mouth. "Jaime, are you my leprechaun? Or, uh, my fairy? Are you saving me from my evil parents and arranged marriage?" I chuckled, knowing how ridiculous I sounded.

"Our story isn't over yet. We'll have to wait and see."

Chapter 34

⁓⁂⁓

"Rory, dear, today is the Feast of the Immaculate Conception," Deirdre explained, "And to celebrate, we set up our Christmas tree."

"Do you do this every December eighth?" I asked.

"Yes, and the tree goes down on January sixth. That's Twelfth Night, the night the three wise men showed up with their gifts for the baby Jesus. If you take down your decorations before or after Twelfth Night, you'll bring your baggage into the new year. No one wants that, right?"

"No, not at all." I thought about the baggage I would carry into the new year: Scott, Marty, school, and my parents. I carried baggage like a prized possession and wished my family had some tradition of leaving it at the door.

She sat before me, and I gulped when I saw an ax gently swinging from her gloved fingers. I'd never seen one in person before, and this was the length of a newborn baby, hanging to her knees.

"When I was a wee one, we spent the day shopping in Galway before returning home for dinner and setting up the tree."

"That must have been really nice." I glanced at Jaime through the small window, standing outside with Connor hooking up the trailer to the truck. "So, are we cutting down a tree or going shopping?"

"It's a splendid day to cut down a tree. We have trees growing in the back acres. Not too many, not enough to sell and turn a profit, but enough to decorate our home year after year."

"I hope you don't mind, but I'd rather not do the cutting." I widened my eyes at the sharp, shiny ax.

"No worries, dear. I'm the one who usually picks out the tree while the boys chop it down."

Deirdre placed the ax against the coffee table and walked to the kitchen to stir the mulled apple cider simmering on the stove. Hints of cinnamon, cloves, and apples rose from the pot when she removed the lid.

"Thank you for having me today. I know it's an important day for you and your family, and I'm happy to be here."

"Aye, I should be the one thanking you." She scooped cider into a mug and passed it to me. The hot cup immediately warmed my hands, and I inhaled the sweet aroma.

"Why?"

"Well, you make my son happy. I once met his girlfriend." She air-quoted the relationship. "In fifth class, and I haven't met anyone since. Not even during secondary school."

"What's fifth class? How old was he then?" The vocabulary around education confused me.

"Oh, about ten. It was nothing serious, just the girl down the street. Cute thing. They always played together. He'd bring her over, and they'd play outside. One day, I made them sandwiches, and he handed her a flower, announcing her as his girlfriend. It was sweet. It meant nothing, but still sweet. I knew then that he'd make a great husband when he found the right lass."

I took a sip, hearing the word *husband* roll around in my brain. *Did she think we could get married?* Puzzled, I smiled and sipped my cider.

The screen door swung open and slammed shut, surprising me and causing my drink to spill on the table. I rushed to the sink to clean it up.

Connor stood in an oversized jacket, black cap, and ski gloves. "Trailers ready and the truck's warming up. You ready to find a tree?"

The four of us squeezed into the bed of the small truck. Deirdre pressed against Connor, the stick shift in between her legs, and Jaime beside her with me on his lap. Two axes rested at my feet, and I stiffened, just in case a divot on the trail caused the ax to nick my legs. We bounded down the dirt path into the woods behind the house and stopped beside a cluster of trees. Climbing out, I scanned the field.

"What do you think of this one, Deerdj?" *Deerdj.* Deirdre's nickname sounded too intimate for me to hear on Connor's lips, so I slowed my steps behind her.

"Aye, that's a good one, but do you think it should grow for one more year?"

Jaime hung his arm around my shoulder and pulled me into him. "Every time we take a tree, we plant another one, so we'll never run out. It takes years for the trees to grow to the size we need."

"I've never had a real tree," I admitted. "My mom hates the mess pine trees make, so we decorate the same fake one every year. We set it up the day after Thanksgiving and take it down the day after the New Year."

"A fake tree...blasphemy," Connor grunted.

"Don't you miss the smell of pine?" Deirdre asked.

"We used candles. It wasn't the same, but it's all I know."

"Well, Rory, I'd like you to have the honor of picking out our tree," Deirdre said.

I leaned into Jaime and inhaled his cologne. Moving away from him, I walked beside Deirdre. "Are you sure?"

"Aye. It's your first Christmas in Ireland. Wouldn't you like to pick out the tree?"

I never imagined meeting such kind people. "I would love to."

I walked in and out of the trees, examining the height, width, and circumference of each one. Jaime's house was tiny for American standards, and I didn't want to insult them by picking out a tree too small or overwhelm them by picking out a tree too big.

"This one," I said, pointing to a tree about four inches taller than Jaime and twice as wide. "This one is perfect." Deirdre nodded her head in approval and called Connor and Jaime over.

Connor hacked at the tree trunk with the heavy steel-tipped ax. Deirdre pulled me toward the truck and supervised from a distance. "Connor, dear, go to the other side! It's tipping."

Connor stepped back and motioned for Jaime to finish the job. Jaime removed his jacket and his arm muscles rippled with every smack. He pulled the ax back, fully rotating his shoulders and hips like he was hitting a baseball for a home run. His face scrunched, and grunts escaped his lips as the blade kissed the bark.

The men pushed the tree, burying their arms in the branches, and it fell to the ground. The sounds of leaves crunching, branches breaking, and the ground shaking stopped as quickly as it started.

"Come on, Rory," Deirdre called. The four of us grabbed the trunk and hoisted it out of the woods toward the truck. I browsed the branches for bugs but dove right in when I saw my three lumberjacks grasp the tree with their bare hands.

It was heavier than I expected, and sweat poured out of my armpits and forehead. "Hold on, hold on," I gasped. I ripped my jacket, scarf, and hat off and threw them on the forest floor. "Okay."

Jaime's eyes traveled up and down my body, and lust lingered on my skin. I felt his eyes on me from across the tree, and I licked my lips and pressed my top teeth against my bottom lip. This man turned me into a puddle with his eyes. Desire zapped through me at the wonderment of what he could do with his hands.

As we heaved the tree toward the truck, I couldn't help but focus on Jaime's backside as he manhandled that tree. My body tingled and I blushed behind my already red cheeks. *Behind castle walls, he would be mine.*

Chapter 35

The peat fire had smoldered, but the woodsy scent loitered throughout the air. I sniffed deeply, breathing in the remnants of soil, pine, and rain with the occasional hint of apple emanating from the kitchen. "It smells like Ireland," I said to Jaime as we walked into the house. I wanted to remember that comforting scent for the rest of my days.

I removed my coat and placed it on the chair's arm, hugging myself while Connor poked the fire to bring it back to life.

"Da, let me know when you're ready for the tree," Jaime said, rubbing his hands together.

Deirdre ran into the kitchen, carrying a tray of white and wheat triangle sandwiches. "Hang sandwich? Is anyone hungry?" A round floral plate waved under my nose.

I didn't know what a hang sandwich was, but I took one and peered at the insides.

"Ham, like you Americans say," Jaime explained with a terrible Southern accent.

A smile crossed my lips and I took a bite. "I love hang and cheese sandwiches." The intimate living room, now crowded with boxes of

Christmas decor, felt like home.

"Jaime, let's get the tree." The two men disappeared outside and emerged with the pine tree I had hand-selected. They shimmied it into the tree stand, and the top branch scraped the ceiling.

"Oh, perfect!" Deirdre clapped her hands in approval. "It's brilliant." She smiled at me, and I couldn't help but return her enthusiasm. "My favorite part. Time to decorate." She dragged a crooked box from under the coffee table and ripped open the seams. Pulling out a tangled mess of multicolored lights, we unraveled the previous year's kinks and wrapped it around the tree.

I admired Jaime's backside as he reached high and bent low to weave the lights in and out of the branches, and I noticed my breath quicken and the hair raise on the back of my neck. Warmth flooded me and I could feel my heart beating in my ears. I glanced away from him, begging my body to return to normal before anybody noticed.

When my desire subsided, I scooted next to Deirdre and focused on each ornament she removed from the box. She told the origin stories for each item, but I sensed Jaime's eyes on me and my brain became flustered.

Deirdre continued walking down memory lane. "This one was my ma's grandma. She made this ornament as a little girl. Gee, Connor, it must be close to a hundred years old, you say?" She showed me the crocheted angel, weathered and discolored from the years. "Oh, here is a reindeer Jaime made when he was a wee one." Googly eyes attached to a cardboard reindeer head wiggled at me. This commentary continued for the next thirty minutes, and I leaned forward, trying to get a better look. I focused on every word, learning about Jaime's past through this box that only came out once a year.

Once the ornaments hung on the branches in the 'most splendid spots', Deirdre pulled out a delicate angel to sit on top of the tree. "Rory, dear, you picked out the tree. I think it's time you place the angel on top."

Honor raised me to my feet, and I grasped the angel in both hands to protect it from any accidental drops. "Are you sure?" I asked, looking from Deirdre to Connor to Jaime.

They nodded, and I stepped on the dining room chair to get more height. The top branch pushed sideways against the ceiling, and I folded it down to better fill the angel's base.

We stepped back to appreciate the tree, and Connor plugged the lights into the outlet. Like angels singing, the faint glow of red, blue, and green blended into the burning fire of red, orange, and yellow hues. Music wasn't playing, but I heard 'Silent Night' faintly in my mind. Jaime grabbed my hand and squeezed, and tears blurred my vision. I wasn't missing my family, but missing what my family could have been.

Sadness washed over me and disappeared as quickly as it came. I couldn't remember the last time my mother, father, and I decorated our tree together. Usually, my mother dragged the artificial tree from the basement and set it up while I was at school. When I got home, the lights and ornaments were already in place. She always saved me a handful of ornaments to set throughout her perfectly decorated tree. My dad's job was to buy the gifts or at least provide the money to fill the space below the lowest branches.

"You okay?" Jaime looked into my eyes, and I forced my lips to rise in a wide grin.

I waved my arms in front of me. "It's gorgeous." Feeling his warm, soft shirt against my cheek, I leaned into his chest, and he pulled his arms around my body, drawing me closer. Deirdre leaned across the tree and kissed Connor on the lips. My smile wavered as I recognized another difference between Jaime's home and my own.

Connor and Deirdre left Jaime and me alone while they relaxed on the couch in front of the fire and we snuck upstairs until dinner. The sofa bed was pulled out and made precisely the same as last time. "I see we're roommates again tonight." I pointed at the two beds, and Jaime nodded.

"Not tomorrow though," Jaime said, biting his lip.

I lay face down on his bed with my bent legs kicking above me. "Thanks for having me over today."

He sat beside me and rubbed my back. "I loved having you here. And my parents love you."

Fiddling with my fingers, I felt that familiar lump form in my throat. "I love your parents, too." I readjusted and wrapped my legs under me. "My parents aren't like yours. They're still married but should have divorced years ago. Instead, we live in a fake house full of fake love." I felt my voice crack, and Jaime touched my hand, encouraging me to continue.

"My dad still openly cheats on my mom, and she turns a blind eye. Eventually, I stopped caring. I did my best never to be home because it was too weird. When I was home, I'd lock myself in my room and do homework. The busier I was, the less I had to see my mom's empty eyes or my dad's arrogance." I looked up from my lap into his concerned eyes. "They hate each other. And your parents love each other. They have so much love for you, for each other, for their life…it's hard for me to see, but at the same time, I'm so grateful to have witnessed it. It gives me hope that true love is out there."

I leaned against Jaime's chest, and silent tears dripped onto his sweatshirt. He wiped my eyes with his thumbs and kissed my eyelids. "I hate to see you sad."

Pulling away, I smiled. "I'm not sad, Jaime. I'm grateful. You're lucky you live in a family that loves you and loves each other."

He pulled his chin toward his chest and looked at me over the top of his eyes.

"Honestly, it gives me hope," I whispered.

His lips drifted onto mine, and a few more tears fell from my eyes. I felt his tongue glide along my top lip, and I welcomed him, embracing the love pouring from his heart, trying to fill my emptiness.

He pressed his forehead into mine, and I stared into his open eyes. I hooked my arms around his neck and searched his eyes.

He licked his lips and pulled the bottom one inward, biting down. "Rory, I'm falling in love with you. I love you." He closed his eyes when I looked at him and leaned forward. My stomach flipped, and I froze. I was leaving in two weeks, never to return. I was still in school, and so was he. *It wouldn't work. It couldn't.*

I dropped my arms from his neck and scooted off the bed. I couldn't stay here, but there was nowhere to go. Anger at myself traveled through my stiff spine, and irritation toward Jaime for putting me in an awkward situation settled in my clenched fists as I rushed out of the bedroom.

I tiptoed down the stairs, waving to Connor and Deirdre who were still snuggled into each other on the couch, and my heart caught in my throat. "Grabbing some water," I said, but what I wanted was to be back in Boston in my regular life before Jaime complicated things.

Sitting at the table, I found a piece of paper and pen and doodled around my thoughts. *Why am I so broken when it comes to love? Why can't I open my heart and enjoy the moment?* I knew my shortcomings...I had been living with myself for almost twenty years and had watched myself self-destruct repeatedly.

Jaime didn't come down, and Deirdre and Connor remained in the living room. Jaime's words rolled like a tumbleweed blowing in the wind, and no matter how hard I tried to get away, it kept coming back. It was giant and disruptive and made it difficult to see, but if I just waited long enough, it would disappear. *Could I do that to Jaime? Could I ignore him until he went away?* Tears stung my eyes, and I scrunched them closed. No. That may have been my tactic in the past, but I couldn't do that to Jaime. Not when our time was so limited. Not when tomorrow hung in the balance.

I heard someone stand from the couch, so I rushed to the cabinets. Opening the wooden door, I grabbed the first mug I could find and pretended to drink the emptiness inside.

"Oh, Rory, dear. I didn't realize you were still in here." Deirdre's soft voice brought me back to my childhood when my mom told me to be brave and jump into the pool without swimmies attached to my arms. The same apprehension that swept through me then swept through me now, and I wondered if I could jump to Jaime like I jumped in the deep end, believing the words I heard more than the words I said to myself.

She eyed me up and down, and I dressed my face with my brightest smile. "Yeah, just finishing up."

"Where's Jaime?"

"Upstairs still. I was just heading up." As I walked around her, I ducked my head and escaped up the stairs.

I had to go back into his room.

He remained on his bed with his back against the wall, and a light throw resting over his muscular body.

My stomach flipped, and I wasn't sure if it was a deep attraction, nervous misfires from seeing him again, or buried anger. He didn't look at me, and I closed the door. The click echoed through his room, and I sat on the floor next to his bed, staring up at him. "Jaime."

"Hmm?" His voice lacked any personality, and his face remained flat. His empty eyes looked past me to the pillow on the freshly made sofa bed.

I hated myself for hurting him. The words formed in my mouth like putty, my tongue struggling to manipulate and move. Inhaling, I filled my lungs with courage, and pressed on. "I'm sorry."

"No worries." He shifted on the bed, straightened his body, and lay flat on his back, staring at the ceiling.

"No, Jaime. Look at me."

"Why? There's nothing to say." He didn't sound angry, just sad.

"I'm sorry for hurting you. It took me by surprise. You took me by surprise, and my feelings scared me."

His eyes averted to the left, and his set jaw told me he wanted to say something.

"Jaime, my feelings are complicated. I had a boyfriend when I came here."

A scoff erupted from Jaime's lips. "You call him a boyfriend? He was never your boyfriend. He was using you."

Tears pricked my eyes again, and I leaned away from him, trying to hide my weaknesses. "I considered him my boyfriend, even if he wasn't great." *Why am I defending Scott?* I closed my eyes and shook my head, trying to grasp whatever straw of dignity I had floating around me. "You and I were having fun, that's it. And it evolved into something more. But I'm leaving. I'm leaving to live halfway around the world forever. I'm never coming back here. So whatever we had will be over in a few weeks. I can't open my heart, knowing it will get stomped on because of distance. I'm not strong enough for that."

The floodgates opened, and my confusion and irritation quickly transformed into grief. I knew I was losing him, and I had stupidly let my heart take over my brain.

He grabbed my hands and pulled me toward his bed. "Do you mean that? That this thing—" he waved his arms around us "—is over when you're gone?"

We had never discussed the future, but how could he assume long-distance would work? It wasn't like I could hop in a car and drive to him when I had a bad day. "You deserve more than that. You deserve to be happy, and so do I."

I couldn't allow myself to get hurt again. *What would stop him from seeing girls on the side and stringing me along? How could I know that he was being faithful or that I wasn't making a laughingstock out of myself again?* The words were too painful to speak, so I climbed onto his bed and buried my head in his shoulder.

I could tell by his rigid back and shallow breathing that he was angry. "Do you love me?" His voice was sharp as a tack, and the words poked me.

I recoiled, unsure how to respond or which response would make the next twenty-four hours less painful.

"You told me you loved me that night in the bar. You told me!" His voice boomed and cracked like thunder.

"I was drunk, Jaime. I don't even remember that night."

"People speak the truth when they're drinking. Stop lying to yourself. Stop lying to me!" He jumped out of bed and paced his room. "You love me. You know how I know?"

I couldn't answer, my body frozen in time, afraid that whatever move I made would set him off further and ruin us.

"You bring me chocolate when I have a bad day and leave it on my pillow. You make sure I eat breakfast every morning before school. You give me your umbrella even when you need it. You kiss me every night before bed. You TOLD me you loved me. You make me feel alive, loved, and certain. More certain about everything. You're scared. I get it. I'm scared too, but can't we be scared together?"

"Can I let you know tomorrow?" I sputtered. It was a cop-out, and he deserved better than me, but I needed time. There was too much pressure riding on my future. My parent's loveless marriage destroyed my understanding of relationships, and I hadn't recognized the impact until now. "Please?"

He stomped to the door and threw my bag on the sofa bed. "Fine, but this conversation isn't over."

Chapter 36

When I entered the kitchen the next morning, Connor and Jaime had been outside for over an hour, struggling to put up Christmas decorations around the home's exterior, and I was grateful for the separation. I didn't want to talk, but I had no choice. Deirdre asked me a barrage of questions about my life, and I tried my best to answer politely.

"Rory, dear, tea?"

I held open my hand, and Deirdre handed me an empty delicate teacup. The matching floral teapot simmered on the table. I watched the hot steam escape from the skinny nose and waited before pouring it into my cup. "Thank you, this is great." I blew along the top layer before bringing the cup to my lips.

"When are you going home to America?" Deirdre asked, sitting beside me. She pulled out a shortbread cookie and dipped it in her tea. A smidgen fell into her cup and Deirdre stirred until it disintegrated.

"My flight leaves December nineteenth. My last final is the fifteenth. That'll give me a few days to pack and prepare for my flight home." My stomach lurched, thinking about home, Marty and Scott. And now Jaime. *When I landed in Ireland, I never thought my heart would shatter.*

Deirdre's warm eyes melted my icy exterior, and I felt a sudden desire to confide in her and seek motherly advice, but I couldn't. I barely knew her. "What happens when you all move out? Will Jaime get new roommates?"

I raised my shoulders and frowned. "I don't know. We never talked about that. I assume he'll either request a transfer or he'll get new roommates." I imagined beautiful, interesting women with perky breasts and big hips moving in. One of them would sleep in my bed. A general ickiness settled around me. Back in New England, I would be in my old life with my so-called friends, and it wouldn't be fair to expect him to sit around and wait for me.

Deirdre slurped her tea. "Hmmm."

"Maybe he'll move in with Owen." Aoife's long, blonde locks and boisterous laugh danced through my mind. Irritated at my annoyance, I grabbed a cookie and nibbled on the edge.

"Are you excited to see your parents?"

I choked at the mere mention of my parents and gulped three scalding sips of tea. My eyes watered and I wiped the tears away. I expected my mother to show up at the airport in her prescription-induced haze and explain away my father's absence. "Not really. When I get home, I'm moving into my old apartment with my old friend, Marty." Her name on my lips turned the sweet tea bitter. I took another bite of cookie.

"Do your parents live nearby?" Deirdre wouldn't stop.

"They live about two hours from school. I go to school in Boston and my parents live in New Hampshire, right outside the White Mountains."

"Ah, yes, New Hampshire. I've always wanted to go there."

I looked at her, the invitation on my lips, but the trepidation of her acceptance holding my words inside. I tried to steer the conversation to the beach and touristy things to do in New England, but she continued to turn it back to me.

"Jaime and I don't talk about his love life often," she said, "But you make him utterly happy. I don't know your plans once you go home, but we'll miss you."

I tried to smile, but a grimace settled on my lips.

Deirdre excused herself to use the bathroom, and I stewed in grief until she returned.

Looking out the window, I watched Jaime and Connor huddle around the bushes, planning their next move. He looked so comfortable with his dad, helping, laughing, and working through the chill. *Jaime's such a good guy.* I shook my head to remove the kind thoughts that hovered over my bad mood. *I wish I hadn't felt pressured to say 'I love you.' I wasn't ready for that.*

Deirdre stumbled back into the kitchen and poured more water into her cup. I knew she was prying, but I needed to address her concerns. She didn't want her son to get hurt, and I appreciated that. It was more concern than my parents ever had for me.

Running my hands through my hair, I leaned back in the chair. "Your son is special, Deirdre. He's kind, supportive, loving, and thoughtful. He's patient, and he stands up for the people he loves." Words thrown across the apartment between Jaime and Scott bounced between my ears, and I realized he had believed me and trusted me without even knowing the full story about Scott and I. "I don't know what the future will bring, but he's special, and no matter what, I'll never forget him."

I meant to reassure her, but I felt worse. *I just told his mother that we would not last beyond Galway. That was the truth, right? Isn't that what I had been telling Jaime all along? There was no way we could work.*

Willie Daly's kind eyes and long, white beard appeared before me. His excitement for my future taunted me, and I shook my head. His cheery face disappeared into the Irish countryside beyond the small windows.

Deirdre looked at me, taking in my sadness. "I hope you find solace in your choices, Rory. You're a beautiful girl and you're good with my son. I hope it works out."

I swallowed back the tears that climbed behind my eyes. "Me too."

Chapter 37

J aime and I had said little in the previous twenty-four hours. I feigned illness and went to bed early while he and his family watched a movie. Their laughter echoed through the hall as my mind slipped in and out of sleep. I didn't make it to dreamland, my sleep a black void that kept me on edge all night. I half wanted Jaime to crawl into bed and hold me, but I knew I had ruined any chance of that.

The familiar scent of peat infiltrated my nostrils, and Jaime's rustling body in the bed beside mine kept my alert mind awake. Thoughts about Jaime, my parents, Marty and Scott, Willie Daly, and my upcoming departure back to America rolled around like a lottery machine. Each thought bouncing higher and lower, hitting off each other, until eventually one of them shot to the top, stealing my attention for a few seconds before another emerged.

Jaime had reserved a night at the castle, but we weren't on speaking terms. I didn't know if we were still going or if I wanted to go and be alone with him. He shifted again and I heard the sheets rustle. "Jaime? Are you awake?" He didn't respond right away. "Jaime? I know you're awake."

I saw his shadow shift again. "What?"

"Can we talk? Please?"

He groaned and flipped on the side lamp. "It's two o'clock in the morning. What do you want to talk about?"

"Tomorrow."

"What about it?"

"Are we still going?" My voice was mousier than I wanted and I heard that little girl deep inside who shied away from confrontation.

"Why wouldn't we?"

"Because we had a fight." I felt foolish for stating the obvious. *Was I being immature? Maybe this was a non-issue.*

"Yeah, we had a fight. I still love you."

My heart stopped and I wondered if he meant as a friend or more than a friend. Unsure of his intentions, I played it cool. "Okay, great. Good night."

The next morning, Jaime and I climbed into Deirdre's tiny car and her wild hair flew out the window as we rolled through the Connemara twists and turns. Connor's head pushed against the ceiling and obscured my view out the front windshield. Our backpacks rested between us on the tiny middle seat in the back.

I remained quiet for the thirty-minute drive. Jaime talked with his parents about the weather, neighbors and friends, and the recent development being built off Sky Road. I zoned in and out, expressing obligatory smiles and frowns, depending on the topic.

"Here we are," Deirdre exclaimed. She pulled off Sky Road and traveled down a long driveway.

I leaned into the middle seat to peek around Connor's head. In front of me stood a wall of green. The trees created smooth textures, and they reminded me of giant scoops of pistachio ice cream. Turning a corner, a monstrous castle nestled amongst the greenery jumped out at me.

234

I inhaled deeply, as feelings of excitement and amazement bubbled inside me. I looked at Jaime, wide-eyed and bright, and he cautiously smiled back at me. "Wow," I said.

Deirdre parked the car, and I hurried out, breathing the clean, crisp air. The stone castle walls, partially covered in green moss, looked like something out of The Sword in the Stone. The green growing up the walls blended in perfectly with the green mountains, and parts of the castle disappeared.

Returning to Deirdre and Connor, I watched Jaime gather our items. Connor hugged him and Deirdre kissed him on the forehead. "You be good, aye? Have a grand time. You're getting the bus tomorrow, are ye?"

Jaime nodded. "Tomorrow we go back to Galway. I'll be home in a few weeks for Christmas."

My heart softened at their public display of affection for each other. I adjusted my hat, still gazing at the castle grounds, and Deirdre wrapped me in a hug. Tears leaked out of my eyes, never having felt such love from strangers before. "You be good, ye hear? I hope to see you again. Good luck with everything."

My stomach heaved with the heavy realization that I might never see her again. I squeezed her tighter. "Thank you for everything."

I hugged Connor with less affection, having not connected with him at the same level as I connected with Deirdre. "Thank you for letting me stay with you. It was a great experience."

Jaime and I watched them climb into her petite car and zip down the driveway, beeping the entire way. We waved and grinned until they were gone. Turning to Jaime, I watched his face tighten from joy to unease.

I cleared my throat. "Ready?"

He led me into the foyer and checked us in. A man wearing a black suit handed us the old-fashioned keys and directed us to our room.

"Your palace awaits, your majesty." Jaime turned the doorknob and invited me into a large, Victorian bedroom with a four-poster canopy bed set in the middle.

I gasped, fully transported to another era. I ran to the bed and flopped on it, tossing my backpack on the floor. "This is amazing!" I moved my arms and legs over the silky-smooth duvet and rolled from side to side against the fluffy pillows.

Jaime chuckled and pulled open the floor-to-ceiling curtains, exposing a large window overlooking the gardens. "Welcome to your castle."

I sat up in bed and patted the space beside me. "Come here, Jaime."

He did as I asked and looked at me, crossing and uncrossing his arms, and then finally leaning back and resting on his forearms.

"We have to talk." Those dreaded words I'd been avoiding spilled out of my mouth.

He kicked off his shoes and lay on his stomach next to me, the scent of his cologne strong, and my stomach tumbled.

"Thank you. For this." I knew what I wanted to say, but I struggled with vulnerability and rejection.

A few moments passed, and tension ballooned in the large room. I quickly scrambled to a sitting position and grabbed his hands. "I'm sorry." *Why was that always so hard to say?*

"For what?"

Was he really going to make me spell it out for him? "For being afraid of the future. For not trusting you or trusting my feelings. I told you a little already, but I don't have what you have. My parents aren't in love. They don't love each other…they don't even talk. My dad works while my mom survives on pain medication for non-existent ailments. He broke her and she wasn't strong enough to fight for me or herself. They never emulated healthy love, so I'm sorry that I'm so broken."

His round eyes and persistent attention on me made me squirm inside. He touched my icy hand and my muscles twitched, but I relaxed them and let his warmth pass through me. "I'm sorry you had to experience that."

I waved him away with my other hand, pretending it was no big deal. "I wanted you to know why I am the way I am. If I'm honest with myself, I've never had a boyfriend before that I imagined myself with long term. It was like the risk of turning into my mother and finding a man like my father was too great, so I avoided intimacy, and focused on external things like school. It was a survival tactic to protect my heart."

He rubbed my hands with his large, rough fingers, and I wanted to push him away for feeling sorry for me, but I couldn't.

"I can't commit to anything beyond Galway. I can try, but I can't promise anything and I don't want to feel responsible for hurting you. I care about you, but you need to proceed with caution. My ability to love and fall in love is defective." My hardened voice scared me, and the words I spoke and heard in my ears made me hate myself.

The intense mood of the room wrapped its spiny arms around me, and I needed to get out and breathe again, before my fear crushed me into smithereens.

"I'm sorry. I have to get outside." I hurried from the bed. "I need to clear my head." I kissed him on the lips and grabbed my jacket. "I promise I'll be back. I'll be fine." I motioned to the space around us and grabbed one of the two keys, sitting on the side table. I ran over and gave him another kiss, his eyes blinking with confusion.

He scratched his head and didn't look at me. "I'll be right here." He looked up at the underside of the canopy with his arms folded behind his head.

"I promise, Jaime, I just need five minutes."

I ran out of the room, down the hallway, out the main lobby and into the fresh air, where a barrage of tears finally broke and freed me from my shame.

A few hours later, I settled in front of the fire in the hotel lobby and stared into the flames. After walking the grounds until I couldn't feel my fingertips or toes, I removed my coat and gloves, and warmed under the heat until my skin melted.

Every extreme sensation reminded me I was alive. The man behind the concierge desk offered me a drink, and I refused, trying to maximize the intensity of the temperature hitting my body. My tears had run dry, and it left me an empty shell.

It had been five hours since we'd arrived and I hadn't eaten since breakfast. My tired body didn't want to move, but my brain forced my legs to take one step and then another as I walked back to our room.

Why am I so afraid? I thought back to my relationship with Jaime and how annoyed I had felt on the airplane, followed by shock when he showed up in my bedroom. My heart had softened when he took care of my leg, and my vulnerability grew when he welcomed me into his life. And then I fell in love. I swallowed hard, the ball of spit getting stuck. *Damn it. I've fallen in love.*

My legs shook and my heart rate quickened. *What if he's gone?* I took the elevator to the second floor and ran down the hallway, passing the occasional guests and reached into my pocket. Standing at our door, I grabbed for the key, but the only items I found were my gloves. *No!* I sped up the search, ripping through every pocket on my body, but the key was gone. It must have fallen downstairs when I pulled off my gloves.

I banged on the door, but it never opened. Checking the number, I couldn't remember if this was even our room. Without a key and without the room number, everything looked the same. *Am I even on the right floor? Second floor, I know Jaime said second floor.* I spun in circles, searching for a landmark that would confirm that I was indeed in the right place.

My legs pumped and arms flailed as I ran back downstairs. Nestled under the couch was the missing ornate, metal key, and I grabbed it before racing back upstairs to the second floor. Placing it in the lock, nothing happened. It didn't budge. Tempted to holler his name down the long hallway, I ran back downstairs for help.

The same person who had offered me a drink earlier, stood behind the desk. Seeing me out of breath, he handed me an empty plastic cup and pointed to the water pitcher on the table. "Water?"

"No thanks, I need my room number, and do you have a master key?"

He looked up Jaime's name on the computer and walked around the counter. "Follow me."

He crept slowly along the hallway like a turtle, leading the way. I trailed behind him, motioning with my hands for him to speed up. I needed to see if Jaime was still here and tell him what was in my heart before it was too late. Everything moved in slow motion as the man stopped every few feet to chat with housekeeping, adjust the 'Do Not Disturb' signs on random doors, and pick up trash left in the hallway.

My tightly wound muscles threatened to break at any moment.

"Here you go," he said, pausing outside a door and twisting the key in the lock. "Room two-eighteen."

"Two-eighteen?" I asked. "But we're on the third floor."

"Welcome to Ireland," he said, pushing the door open.

I gasped, my eyes taking in the sight. Jaime wasn't there, but in his place was a bottle of champagne, a dozen roses, and chocolate.

"Excuse me," I said to the man. "Do you know where the other person in this room is? Did he leave, do you know?"

He shook his head. "Sorry, I don't. If you come downstairs, I can check for you."

I didn't want to leave and risk missing him again, so I shook my head and moved toward the champagne. "No, I'm all set, thank you."

The door thudded behind him and the lock clicked, reminding me I had ruined a beautiful night and was now trapped in my choices. *He probably thinks I went back to Galway. I was gone the entire day. What did I expect? That he'd be sitting here, waiting for me?* I dropped onto the bed and sobbed into the pillow. *I blew it. I had an amazing thing, and I blew it.*

I grabbed a piece of hotel stationery and started writing, pouring my heart onto the paper. Jaime's belongings stared at me from the corner of the room, reminding me he'd be back, but I didn't know if our next interaction would comprise love or hate.

Dear Jaime, I'm so sorry. I'm an idiot. An idiot terrified of having her heart broken again. I've been fighting my feelings for you all semester because we live in practically different worlds, but I'm tired of being scared. I'm tired of doing what's expected of me to have a safe, pain-free life. My parents' baggage is attached to me with chains, and I'm tired of dragging it around. It's not fair to you and it's not fair to me. I love you, Jaime. And I'm in love with you. I'm sorry for all the pain I caused. I hope you never felt unloved. Maybe things could be different for us. I guess we have to take it one day at a time. Love, Rory.

By the time I finished, my tears had dried and my body had stilled. I folded up the piece of paper and stuck it on his pillow. Wanting him to read it, I didn't want to be here when he did. Too much pressure to risk losing my heart again.

I stumbled into the bathroom and pulled the plush bathrobe off the hook. Dropping my clothes on the floor, I wrapped the bathrobe around me and tightened the strap. The soft fibers tickled my skin, and an overwhelming sense of home washed over me. Hot water filled the tub, and I dropped a dollop of bubble bath, watching the bubbles transform the bathroom into a day spa.

Climbing in, the hot water zapped my skin, and I sank further down.

Closing my eyes, my pain washed away and all I could hear was my steady breathing. For the first time all day, the tension and panic escaped my muscles, and I took a satisfied breath. *I finally spoke my truth*, even if it came out of my fingertips and lay on the pillow. The hot air around me made me drowsy, and I closed my eyes, listening to the gentle splash of water as I stretched my leg above the faucet.

My mind remained empty until the water turned cold. I stepped out of the tub, dried off, and wrapped the plush bathrobe around my cool body. Pulling the plug, I gathered my clothes and opened the bathroom door.

"Jaime," I gasped. "I didn't know you were here."

"I didn't know you were here." His flat voice matched his flat affect. He sat on the armchair in the corner of the room, his left leg crossed over his right knee, and he stroked the paper dripping with my handwriting. "Do you mean this?" His voice cracked, and he waved the paper in front of him.

I tightened my bathrobe and kneeled beside the arm of the chair, looking straight into his eyes. "Yes." My voice came out breathier than I wanted. "I'm so sorry. For everything." Those stupid tears climbed behind my eyes again, and frustration at myself forced them back. I needed to remain composed. I grabbed his hands in mine. "I love you, Jaime. I didn't want to fall in love. I wanted to come here and have a great time, see the country and learn about the culture, but you showed up, and I fell in love with you." My blood raced throughout my body as I struggled to breathe. The questionnaire from the Matchmaking Festival floated before me. **Taller than me. Healthy/fit. Kind. Thoughtful. Faithful. Motivated/goal-oriented. Good with money. Good with kids.** I had no idea if Jaime was goal-oriented, good with money, or good with kids, but it didn't matter.

His icy hands contradicted his warm eyes. I could tell he was unsure if I was being true. His face didn't respond, his mouth fixed in a hard-set line, and his upright posture kept me on guard.

"I screwed up, and I know that, and I'm sorry for hurting you. I know it might be too late, but this may be the last night we have together alone. Can we take a step back and forget about the history of the last few weeks and enjoy our time together? Please?" I kissed the top of his hand, but he pulled it away. His reaction to me didn't surprise me; I would've been angry too. "Jaime?"

He flipped the paper in his hands, staring at the painting behind me. "Do you promise me you're being honest?"

I nodded. "Yes."

"And do you think you can have an open heart to the future? Or maybe not the far future, but the next week? Let's enjoy our time together. Can you do that?"

"Yes."

He leaned into me and pressed his lips against mine with such a force my body instantly melted. I wrapped my arms around him and ravaged his lips hungrily. All my insecurities fled, leaving pure lust for this man that could easily have been a figment of my imagination.

"Did you get me champagne?" The cart remained in the center of the room.

"Surprise. I ordered it when I booked the room and they brought it up when you disappeared. I thought I'd have to drink the entire bottle myself." He kissed my neck and I gripped his shoulders to intensify the feeling.

He moved me to the bed, and I lay under the canopy feeling like a princess. The environment transported me away from my life and into a dream-like reality where Jaime and I lived happily ever after. "Hey," I whispered, staring up at him over me. "You really are my Prince Charming and I don't deserve you."

He shushed me, placing his index finger over my lips. He unraveled the belt holding my bathrobe closed and treated me like his queen.

I wanted to stay there with him, forever.

Chapter 38

Shimmering rays of sunlight warmed my face the next morning, and I stretched and opened my eyes. I rolled over and placed my arm around Jaime's bare chest. He mumbled but didn't wake up, so I pushed against him, wrapping my leg around his thigh.

"Morning," I said.

"Morning. Do you need anything?"

Despite the bottle of champagne we had devoured, my mind felt clear. "No, I'm all set." I reached across him and grabbed a water bottle from his bedside table. "What time do we have to leave?"

He glanced at his watch. "Check out is eleven. The bus leaves for Galway at half-noon, so we'll get lunch before we go home."

I refused to be sad, even though the days were ticking away and eventually I would have to wake up from this dream. I kissed him on the lips and pressed my body against his. "Thank you for everything. Last night, this, for putting up with me."

We spent the rest of the morning eating the chocolate strawberries that remained in the dish from the night before, talking, and being together without any distractions. I didn't question him or his motives, but stayed in the moment and felt the euphoria that raced through my body.

For the first time ever, I felt loved.

The next week, I swung on a pendulum of emotions. Some days, I was so busy, I could feel my life returning to a list of to-do items and checkmarks. My final projects were due, and I hadn't managed my time as well as I did in the States. Jaime and Owen helped me cram for my Northern Ireland exam, and Deirdre answered some questions for me about the history of women in Ireland. Despite the grades I would receive, I had learned more about the culture from life experiences than any book or professor could have spouted at me.

My mood seemed to match the weather, carrying me from sunny and optimistic when it was warm and bright, to feelings of melancholy and despair when the skies turned gray and dreary. Questions about the future floated in and out of my brain, but I pushed them away, refusing to spend my remaining days in Ireland overthinking.

I tried to spend time with Marissa and Zoey, regretful for not getting to know them better. I knew I'd never forget them, but the bond they shared with each other was something I envied from afar.

Jaime and I moved beyond the friends with benefits stage and outwardly showed our affection. When we were out in public, he held my hand, held me close, and kissed me. At first, confusion about his sudden change in behavior made me uncomfortable, but I pushed my initial reaction away and fell into the moment, cherishing the constant touches of love.

After I turned in my last final, I walked up the curvy streets to our apartment, reflecting on the past four months. Noticing every quaint home I passed, and each gnarly tree growing out of the sidewalk, I embossed the sights and smells of Ireland into my memory. Nothing was too insignificant and I wanted to remember it all.

I stopped at the hotel restaurant next door and grabbed some drinks for take-away. It was my last weekend, and I'd need something to keep me company while I packed my stuff. I cradled four pint cans and walked back to our apartment.

Jaime, Zoey, and Marissa sat at the table eating cereal, and I handed them the tall cans. The tabs cracked open and echoed throughout the room.

"Cereal, milk, and beer. Quite the combination," Zoey said, alternating between the three.

"When does everyone move out?" Jaime asked.

"My flight's Tuesday," Zoey said.

"Mine too," said Marissa. "We're gonna take a cab to the bus station in the morning."

"I leave Wednesday," I said. "Jaime, did you decide if you're moving out or staying here?"

"I went to the office this morning. They told me to stay. I guess some Irish blokes are starting school mid-year or requested a transfer, so I'll be with a few Irish guys."

I leaned forward and scanned the messy kitchen counter. I couldn't imagine what this place would look like without a lady's touch. "That's good. So, you don't have to move out or find a new place. Are you bummed? I know you wanted to move in with some of your football guys."

"Nah, I see them enough. Besides, it's just a few more months. It'll be grand."

I imagined the space without our belongings and recalled the generic, empty shell we had walked into when we first arrived. Marissa spoke my mind. "I'm gonna miss this place."

"Do you miss home?" I asked.

"Yeah, I'm ready to go home and see my friends and family, but I'm gonna miss you guys. We had so much fun this semester."

"What are you two doing once you leave? You live at opposite ends of the country." I didn't have to explain that I was referring to their relationship. The upcoming goodbye weighed us down and I could feel the uncertainty in our apartment.

Zoey leaned back in her chair and placed her hand on Marissa's. "We're gonna see what happens. Try the long-distance thing and make time to see each other whenever we can. We're trying to keep the pressure off, because the pressure to stay together will kill us before we get home."

"Besides," Marissa added, "we're going to stay best friends no matter what. We've shared too many experiences together during this life-changing time. We're part of each other's story. Now, we'll see if the story continues back home."

They made it sound so simple. So natural. I wanted to be like them, to throw caution to the wind and accept the chips as they fell.

"What about you guys?" Zoey asked.

Jaime and I didn't answer. I waited for him to respond because I was curious, but he never did. He looked at me with those amber eyes that contained more green than brown today, and I melted beside him.

"We don't know." I tried to sound upbeat, but my voice fell flat. "We're just taking it one day at a time."

Chapter 39

Tuesday morning, I stood outside our apartment door with Jaime, and we waved as Zoey and Marissa backed away. I couldn't help but cry. We promised to stay in touch and I hoped their relationship would make it. When they turned the bend around the building, I wrapped my arms around Jaime's waist and hugged him. The cold weather settled on his shirt and chilled my cheek.

Walking back into the warm apartment, I grabbed his hand and led him into our bedroom.

"This is it. Our last night together." Pressure to make our last moments perfect hung over me. I stood in the room with my back pressed against his front and wrapped his arms around my torso. Flipping around, I flung my arms around his neck and leaned into his shoulder.

"It's your last night. What do you want to do?"

"I want to go out with a bang," I said. "But not too much of a bang. I have a flight tomorrow so I can't be hungover."

He kissed my lips. "Have you said goodbye to Owen?"

"No. What's he up to tonight?"

"How about this? We'll grab dinner together with whoever you want to say goodbye to. And then you and I will walk around the city one last time. We'll pop into pubs, grab a drink, listen to music, and head home for an early night."

I grinned at him, excited to see how the night would unfold.

"I'm glad we're alone. I'd like to spend some time with you before you leave." He didn't have to say what he hoped to do. I saw the mischief in his eyes and couldn't help but return the look.

"Sounds perfect." I kissed him again, still ignoring the elephant sitting on my chest.

That night, we took a taxi into the city center. The bright Christmas lights hung across the pedestrian street creating a spider web of light. It had flurried earlier, and a light dusting outlined the buildings with glitter.

For a Tuesday night, more people than I expected milled around the pubs and restaurants. "Everyone must be done with school," I said. There was an air of celebration as people roamed throughout the city. "It's beautiful." I took out my camera and snapped a shot of the evening scene.

I turned toward Jaime and snapped before he could realize. The bright flash blurred our vision, and he blinked at me.

"Here." He grabbed my camera, spun me around, and stretched his arm as far as it could go. The viewfinder faced away from us, and Jaime got into position. "I hope we're in the frame. Say cheese."

"Cheese," I grinned, and he pressed his face against my ear, his breath tickling my neck. He clicked the button, and I blinked away the black dots from the flash. Checking the counter, I had twenty photos left.

We met Owen and Aoife at the fish and chip shop. A long line of people spilled out the door and into the street, and I danced in place to keep my blood moving and my toes from freezing.

"Rory, when do you leave?" Aoife asked.

"Tomorrow. My flight is around lunchtime."

"Good luck tomorrow. It was great meeting you."

"Thanks. It was great meeting you, too." I meant it. She wasn't my favorite person at first, but she grew on me. I trusted Jaime when he said there was nothing between them.

We weaved our way into the small chippy and ordered fish. The fried fillet hung over the edges of our take-away boxes and the cook pressed the lid down, forcing it to close. Grabbing a table in the corner, we ate our food. I focused on every bite, not wanting to forget the fresh, delicious food in Galway. Salt and vinegar from the hot, crispy fries attacked my nostrils. A burst of tang attacked my taste buds, craving more.

We settled into a casual conversation about Christmas and the holidays. "You going home?" Owen asked Jaime.

"Yeah, for a few weeks. Then I'll be back until graduation."

"Have you thought about graduation?" Aoife asked. "Have you looked for any jobs?"

Jaime's head shook, his mouth full of fish. "No, I have some ideas, but haven't looked into them yet." Under the table, he squeezed my thigh, and I wondered if I had influenced his ideas.

My lips curled and we made fleeting eye contact.

"What was that?" Aoife asked.

"What was what?" Jaime stuffed a vinegar-soaked fry into his mouth.

"That look. I saw a look pass between you."

"No look, Aoife, just a smile. What about you? What are your plans after graduation?"

"Moving to Dublin."

"How about you, Owen?" I asked.

"Don't know. I want to leave Galway, and try something new. I may head out to Dublin or maybe Cork. Wherever I can find a job, really."

"What are you studying again?" My fish was nearly gone. I couldn't stop eating.

"Commerce, so I can go anywhere, really."

"Good luck, you guys. I know I won't see you, so happy graduation day."

"Thanks." Owen raised his pint can. "What are you doing when you get back?"

I scrunched my face at him. "I don't know. Marty and I are supposed to move into my old apartment, so I guess I'll have to find another place to live." I only had about three weeks before classes started to figure it out. My parents lived too far from school, and I didn't have any other friends to speak of. "I'm kind of screwed." *Don't think about it now. Don't let Marty ruin your last night.* I finished my meal and threw away the box.

As the three of them fell into their own conversation, I brainstormed. My list-making, type A personality was never too far, and with Owen's reminder of the life I was returning to, I couldn't shut it off.

Lost in my own world, Jaime nudged me. "Ready?"

We stepped outside, and I hugged Owen and Aoife goodbye. "It was so great meeting you. Thank you for being there this semester. It's been a semester I'll never forget."

"Anytime you're in Ireland, you have a friend." Owen slipped me a piece of paper with his email address on it. "Keep in touch."

"Good luck," Aoife said. She waved and they both turned, venturing down the street together.

"Want to go home?" Jaime asked.

"Sure. We have an empty house." I waggled my eyebrows at him and rubbed my hands together like I was making a fire.

"Let's go." He grabbed my hand, and we hailed a cab back to our place. Our place for one more night.

Jaime whisked me away to a place full of dreams and fantasies. We spent the night exploring each other like a newly discovered oasis.

Like a tiny delicate bud, I had bloomed into a strong, beautiful flower under the care of Jaime's gentle hands.

A heaviness descended upon me the next morning. Jaime's beautiful pale, freckled skin and red hair peeked out from under the covers and I climbed over him, taking special care not to disrupt his slumber. I checked my armoire and desk one last time, making sure I remembered everything. The ring Scott gave me hid in my desk's top drawer and I dropped it in the trashcan.

My Irish guidebook sat alone on the bare desktop, and I flipped through it, recalling the plane ride. I remembered the jitters acknowledging my unknown future, and the overpowering excitement for the magic of a new adventure. I shoved the book in my backpack, fully aware that I would scour the pages on the plane ride home.

Jaime and I still hadn't discussed our future and the deadline to say goodbye was ticking closer. In approximately two hours, I would sit on a bus, and ride to the airport to restart my life. The quiet apartment, once filled with jubilant laughter, held onto our memories like a novel that was never published.

I carried my suitcase to the door and showered for the last time. The messy bathroom no longer bothered me, and I stepped over a large pile of dirty clothes hiding behind the door. I knelt down beside a napping Jaime and kissed him on the lips. He jumped, his eyes popping open, and he laughed. "Rory." He pulled me close to him until I lay beside him. "You smell lovely."

"Jaime, I have to leave in a few minutes." My nose remained inches from his, and I saw sadness in his eyes.

He sat up in bed and hugged me tight. "I don't want you to go."

"I don't either." I bit my lip and analyzed his face, trying to memorize every finite detail.

He tickled my arms with his fingertips. "Stay here with me."

I giggled and pulled out of his embrace. My courage to talk waned, and I hopped out of his bed, hoping the space would reignite my strength. "I can't. What's going to happen to us?"

"What do you want?" He somehow always put it on me to say the hard stuff.

"I love you and I want to make it work."

He kissed me on the lips. "Me too. Let's do that. We'll email and call and I'll graduate in a few months. Who knows what will happen then?"

My heart fluttered at his openness to an extra-long-distance relationship. I knew it would be impossible to maintain this level of chemistry and closeness, but wasn't life about taking chances? "I have to go," I repeated.

He walked me to the door, where we hugged and kissed one last time. The intensity behind his lips gave me the answer I needed. We were going to make it work. "Love you," he said, hanging onto my fingers as I pulled away.

"I love you. I'll email you when I get home."

As I walked to the main office to grab my cab, I couldn't stop the tears. Even though we were going to try to make it work, my heart still broke in half. Half of my heart remained in Galway while the other half would return to America. I didn't know if the pieces would ever fall together again.

The ride to the bus station was arduous. Thankfully, I didn't have to wait to get on the bus to the airport, otherwise I may have hailed a cab back to Jaime.

Life felt so cruel, falling in love just to shatter your soul.

At the airport, I scavenged the shops, and searched for souvenirs for my parents. Finding a shot glass for my mom that read "FECK IT", and an Irish history book for my father, I figured it was the thought that counted.

On the plane, I searched through my bag for my guidebook. Flipping through, I smiled, recalling all the places I'd been. *There are so many more places to see. Just another reason to come back.*

In between the back cover and the last page, I pulled out a folded piece of paper. Unfolding it, I saw Jaime's scrawl. **Rory, it's been quite the semester, aye? I knew on the plane you were special, but I never thought I would see you again. Funny how life works. I fell in love with you, and I can't believe you're gone. You will always have my heart, and I hope one day we'll see each other again. Even if things don't work out, you will always be my Galway girl. Love, Jaime.**

Behind the letter was a photograph of us from the party at Owen's. Jaime had pulled me close, our faces almost touching. Huge smiles and sparkling eyes caught me by surprise, as I looked at the picture. I recalled feeling annoyed that night, but based on the photo, I was falling for him. Tears fell onto the photograph and I wiped them away.

Underneath the picture was a postcard-sized paper. Staring back at me was me. It was the drawing I caught Jaime sketching in bed. I stared at the face and barely recognized that person. Sad eyes and a half smile reminded me of a woman who was afraid to embrace life.

I compared the drawing to the photo and placed the photo on top. That was the woman I wanted to remember. The woman who fell in love but was too afraid to admit that the annoying man on the plane had opened her heart. All she needed was time.

Exhausted from the night before, I fell asleep for most of the flight. Galway lived in my dreams, and I didn't wake up until the flight attendant rubbed my shoulder, motioning to the active passengers collecting their belongings. My stomach dropped and the ball in my throat grew. I was home.

Back to Reality

II

Part Two

Back to Reality

Chapter 40: February 2003

"Rory, I'm heading to the grocery store. Do you need anything?" My mother leaned into the kitchen counter, and surveyed the contents in the cabinet.

"Do you want spaghetti and meatballs tonight?" I flipped through my textbook. "I can cook while you're shopping."

"Sure." She closed the cabinet and looked at me with empty eyes.

"Can you get some garlic bread?"

My mother snatched her purse off the kitchen chair. "Sure. It's just us. Your father is working late."

I swallowed and didn't look up.

"I'll be home in an hour. Don't forget to swap out the laundry." She walked to the door, and it slammed shut. My mother always walked with heavy feet and sudden movements, the house often shaking in her presence.

I placed a pot on the stove and dumped in sauce and meatballs. As I skimmed the pages of my Educational Foundations textbook, I highlighted important words and concepts.

In the middle of chapter twelve, I called my new friend, Jenny, who was also an education major. She started at the community college a year and a half ago and was applying to Boston schools.

"Hey Jenny, do you want to study tonight? We can meet up at the coffee shop in town. I'm not ready for our exam tomorrow."

"How about seven?"

"Perfect."

I continued stirring the meatballs, and my thoughts moved to Jaime. Checking my watch, I did the calculations in my head. It was ten at night over there. I clicked on my computer and signed into AOL Instant Messenger. His username said he was away, but he was always away. Instant Messenger wasn't nearly as popular in Ireland, and he never got back to me in a timely manner. I sent him a quick hello and returned to the stove.

Jaime and I emailed back and forth a few times a week. I realized the day after my flight landed that things would be different. I had emailed him twice with no response and nightmares of Scott had flashed through my mind. I had felt my walls start to build back up, cursing myself for thinking that what I had with Jaime would be different. But then he called me that night and we talked for about ten minutes before he had to go. It wasn't that we didn't want to stay in touch, it was more that the time change never matched up to our schedules and international calls were expensive.

Living with my parents, I had to be respectful of the time. I hadn't navigated their existence since high school and I felt like a guest, unable to walk around in my pajamas or eat snacks at midnight. I didn't want to upset the apple cart, and for all I knew, the cart had already lost its wheels. My dad 'worked' a lot, and my mother locked herself in her bedroom whenever she was home. I decided the best thing to do was stick to my studies so I could return to Boston and finish my degree.

About twenty minutes later, my mom strolled in with two bags of groceries in her arms. "Rory, help please."

I trudged to the car, grabbing bags and unpacking them in the kitchen. "Dinner will be ready in fifteen minutes," I reported. "After dinner, I'm meeting Jenny to study for my exam."

We ate in silence. The only sounds penetrating my eardrums were the tick of the clock and the hum of the refrigerator.

"Hey mom?" I said, my pulse quickening.

"Yes?" Her big brown eyes looked hollow against her thin face.

"Why didn't you kick dad out? After everything he did to you?"

She dropped her fork on her plate and folded her hands, resting them under her chin. "Why do you ask?"

My inner voice created a monologue of reasons but all I could squeak out was, "You didn't deserve that and you didn't have to live like that."

She cleared her throat. "Like what?"

Annoyed by the game of Cat and Mouse we were playing, I said, "Come on, Mom. He's been cheating on you my whole life. You've wasted over a decade of your life by staying with him. I'd rather get divorced than live a lie. Not to mention how fucked up I am because of the example you two set. Don't you think your life would have been better if you divorced him?"

She jumped to her feet and threw her napkin on her plate. "I will not have you speak to me that way." Redness now highlighted her pale cheeks. "You are living in this house, and I demand some respect."

I cackled under the controversial conversation. "Respect? What's that? You've allowed him to walk all over you while you've suffered for his choices. It's bullshit, Mom. This is not love. This is some fucked up version of keeping up with the Joneses."

She stormed out of the room and I picked up our plates, sighing as I dropped them into the sink. Grabbing my backpack, I left the house without saying good-bye.

Jenny was already waiting, sitting at a table facing the window with her textbook open.

"Hi." I pushed down the aggravation my mother had caused and sat across from Jenny.

"I got you a scone and a cup of tea. I thought it'd be a comforting reminder of Ireland."

Thanking her, I envisioned myself in Deirdre's kitchen, and felt my tense muscles stretch. Jenny wanted to study in Ireland and had been peppering me with questions about my trip ever since we met a few weeks ago.

"Thanks, this is great." I blew on the steaming liquid, taking a sip. "It doesn't taste nearly as good as the cups I had with Jaime."

"Have you talked to him? How's he doing?"

I had confided a little about Jaime, telling Jenny about how we had met and how we ended up together. Marty and Scott were embedded in our story, so I had shared the Thanksgiving debacle, as well. "Um, I don't know. I haven't heard from him in about a week. I feel like the universe doesn't want us to be a thing. The time change, classes, life. It isn't working out the way I hoped."

"Have you talked to Marty? Or Scott?"

"No. The last time I talked to Marty was when I told her I wasn't moving in and she accused me of sabotaging her life." *Like she sabotaged mine.*

"Did you move back home because you didn't want to live with her?"

"She was part of it, but not all. That trip to Ireland was like a dream, right? I had escaped from my life and found myself over there. It felt too soon to fall back into my old life, and I needed time to figure out who I am now. Does that make sense?"

Jenny nodded. "Totally."

"Also, I wanted to live at home to save up some money. Funny thing is, living with my parents brings me back to all the awful reminders of what a marriage isn't. I wanted to escape my life from Marty, yet I'm back with Dr. Jekyll and Mr. Hyde, but it was my only option to save some money. If Jaime and I last, maybe I'll be able to go back to

Ireland. I'm trying to plan ahead."

"If you move back to Ireland, I'll be visiting."

"I have to move back to Boston for fall semester, though. I'm too far into my program to transfer anywhere else."

"Is Marty still with Scott?"

"Who knows? She and Scott can live happily ever after for all I care." I couldn't stop the bitterness from seeping into my voice. "Do you believe in fate?"

Jenny took a sip of tea. "I think so. If you asked me three years ago I would have said no, but weird things happen that don't make any sense. Like my parents getting divorced just to remarry each other. That's gotta be fate."

"If my parents ever fell back in love, I think I'd give up on love altogether."

"Do you believe in fate?"

"I didn't, but then I met a matchmaker in Ireland who told me I'd meet my match within six months. I believed Jaime was my match, but that hasn't worked out the way I imagined since I got home. His prediction of six months is up in six weeks. I'm losing faith...but maybe what happened with Marty and Scott was fate. Maybe that needed to happen to show me that I am worth more than I believed I was. Maybe my match was really about finding me." I shrugged. I knew I sounded stupid, so I flipped open my book. "You ready to study?"

"Yeah. Oh, I wanted to tell you. I've been applying to schools in Boston because I graduate with my associates this semester. I don't know anyone there, even though there are a ton of colleges. I'll be looking for a roommate if you want to live together? I'd rather live with you than a complete stranger."

My heart warmed at her thoughtfulness. I liked Jenny. I'd only known her for a few weeks, but she was the only friend I had here.

Plus, I'd need a place to live and I couldn't afford to live alone. "Sure, that'd be great."

"Awesome." She flashed her straight, white teeth at me and pulled her thick, wavy hair into a ponytail. "Okay, time to ace this test." She flipped open her book, and we quizzed each other on IDEA and FAPE.

When I got home that night, my mom was asleep on the couch and lights illuminated the stairs leading into the basement. I tucked a blanket around her and tiptoed downstairs. My dad sat on the recliner watching the news.

"Hey, Dad. Can we talk for a second?"

He muted the television and turned toward me. "Sure, what's up? Everything okay?"

The talk earlier with Jenny had me thinking and I needed to get a few things off my chest. "Yeah, fine. Mom and I had a fight earlier."

"About what?"

"You. Marriage. Love. I told her she would be better off divorcing you."

He harumphed and crossed his arms over his chest. "We have an agreement and it works."

"Dad, how do you define a successful life?"

Removing his glasses, he rubbed his eyes. "Successful?"

"Yeah, for me. Take you and mom out of the equation. What would my life look like that would make you a proud dad?"

"First, a good career, a nice home, and a husband who treated you well."

"A good career. That's number one on your list? Did you know my entire life you made me feel that if I wasn't the best at school, I wasn't worthy of your love?"

"Rory, where is this coming from?"

I leaned forward, hoping I appeared approachable. "I've had a lot of time to think and reflect on the life you and mom created and how you shaped me. That idea that I was never good enough has stayed with me...and because of that I picked men who didn't treat me well. All because you don't treat mom well and you were my example. Based on your behavior and words toward me, I learned I would never be good enough. So finding a husband who treats me well will probably never happen."

His gaze dropped and he spoke to the floor. "I'm sorry if I made you feel that way. I only wanted you to reach your potential."

"You need to stop." My words cut through the air like a knife. "And you need to let mom move on without you. You don't love her and you're keeping her hostage in this house. I've heard the fights about money and how mom would never make it without you. That's bullshit, Dad. She's a capable woman and she certainly doesn't need your smug attitude. You bring women over here like you're a bachelor. This is not normal, Dad!" I waved my arms frantically around his bachelor pad in our basement. "And you take her to your sister's for Thanksgiving? I don't even want to know what that was about. First, I thought maybe you were getting back together, but when I got home for Christmas, I saw that nothing had changed."

"Just because we aren't together doesn't mean we don't like each other."

"But you don't! Otherwise you wouldn't be living in our basement. You're forty-five years old...doesn't this twisted life get old? You and mom have so much life to live, don't you both deserve to be happy?"

"I am happy. And your mom wouldn't make it without me. She relies on me to pay the bills."

"Oh, please. Don't flatter yourself. You think people don't know we're living a lie? You're a fool if you think people don't know."

I stormed up the basement stairs and to my bedroom. Checking my email one last time, I saw zero emails waiting to be opened. *It's four a.m. over there. What were you expecting?* I opened Instant Messenger and one new sentence sat in my chat with Jaime. **Miss you. Have a good day tomorrow.**

I sighed. *How could I have been so stupid to think this would work?*

Chapter 41: August 2003

❧

"I think that's the last box." I crushed the brown cardboard box and threw it in our new recycling bin. I pulled a spoon from the drawer and a mug from the counter and ran them under warm, soapy water. "Are you up for an ice cream sundae? I went grocery shopping last night. Chocolate java mocha. I also bought caramel sauce, chocolate sauce, and whipped cream. I thought I'd reward myself for unpacking another room."

The weekend Jenny and I moved in, the meteorologists forecasted the hottest week in Boston over the past hundred years. I wiped my brow and mustered up enough strength to pile three scoops of softened ice cream into the mug.

"Sure, that looks amazing." Jenny pulled another mug out of a box and handed it to me. Her armpit stains ran down the side of her shirt and she pulled at her front, waving hot, stale air down her neckline.

"Are you excited? I still can't believe you got into Boston University. That's a great school." The cold ice cream slid down my throat. I took another bite, placing the spoon upside down on my tongue, and let it sit until fully melted.

"Yeah, school starts Tuesday. I jump right in. Somehow, I avoided all early morning classes. I think my earliest is right before lunch. How's it going for you?"

I pulled my sweaty hair into a ponytail and placed my face directly in front of the dusty table top fan my parents had given. "Good. I'm so happy to be out of my house. You could have thrown me in a box on the sidewalk and I would have made it my home. It's good for me to get back into a routine away from my parents."

Jenny leaned against the dresser wedged against the wall. "How are they?"

"It's been a rough few months, but my mom finally filed for divorce. I don't know what she was waiting for."

"Maybe she was scared to be on her own."

I shrugged. "Maybe. I'd like to think it had something to do with me finally speaking my mind. You should have seen her when I was throwing the f-word around. She never expected that. It wasn't funny at the time, but I don't know what got into me! I was so frustrated with everything that went down in Ireland and I was back in that house, stuck and forced to witness the dysfunction every single day."

Jenny sat down, her face in front of the fan. "Good for you for speaking up."

"Yeah, I don't think she or my dad spoke to me for at least a month, but I guess that gave her enough time to throw my dad out. He packed up his stuff, gave me his new address, and told me to keep in touch." I rolled my eyes. "It's been weird but at least they're getting divorced and not living under the same roof anymore. Now, we're a normal family."

"She looked good when I saw her," Jenny said.

"Yeah, she did. I think she's taking care of herself, going to counseling, and figuring out her own shit. At least now I can focus on me."

"Have you heard from Jaime?"

I winced at his name. "Nope. Well, kind of. He sent me this necklace for my birthday. He apologized in his card, saying that the internet in Connemara is spotty, and he'd try to send me letters more often. I haven't gotten another one since." I pulled at the claddagh pendant hanging from my neck. "He overheard me telling Zoey and Marissa how much I loved the symbolism behind the hands, heart, and crown, and how it will always remind me of Ireland. I almost consider it a farewell 'have-a-nice-life' gift, because I haven't really heard from him since he sent it. I keep sending emails, like I did with Scott, because I still love him. Until he tells me he has a girlfriend, I'm going to stay positive. Maybe it really is an internet thing."

"Sorry," Jenny mumbled.

I waved at her like it was no big deal. "I hope he's happy. He graduated, and I sent him a card. Knowing Ireland, it took weeks to get there. Last I knew, he was living with his parents, looking for a job."

"We're in a city with millions of people looking for love. I'm sure you'll find someone."

I threw my empty sundae cup in the sink and guzzled cold tap water. "Yeah, it's fine. I had prepared myself for this. I knew it was too good to last. I sent him an email with our new address, just in case he ever wanted to reach me, but he didn't respond. To be fair, it's only been a few days. Once we get our internet up and running, I'll check my email again. Sometimes he surprises me."

I flipped through my planner, seeing all the exciting events happening on campus. I had taped photos from my trip to the inside pages, so I'd always have reminders of things that made me happy. A picture of Jaime and me in front of the castle remained in the center of the first page. "One year ago today, I was on a flight to Ireland," I said. "I still can't believe it."

"Well, if you never went to Ireland, we never would have met, and you wouldn't be here right now," Jenny said.

I smiled, but my heart still hurt. "Yeah, life can be funny."

Jenny and I had found a one-bedroom apartment off the B-Line in Boston in a four-floor brownstone built in the early 1800s. Gorgeous on the outside, it was barely standing on the inside, but I didn't care because it was mine. Jenny took the actual bedroom, and I converted the living room into my bedroom. In between our two spaces, we shared a small kitchen. It certainly wasn't the Taj Mahal, but for us, it was perfect.

"Do you want to get pizza tonight? I'm too tired to go out."

Plopping into one of our two folding chairs, Jenny said, "Sounds perfect. Let's order a large, so we have lunch tomorrow."

We worked through the afternoon, focusing on our bedrooms. My twin bed from home lay in the corner, and a dresser I found at a yard sale sat beside the door. I still needed a desk, but it was a work in progress. I could go to the library if I needed to spread out.

Feeling overwhelmed by the lack of completeness, I dropped to the floor in front of the bay window and looked outside. From the top floor, I saw the train zoom by. The apartment shook in a crescendo and then stopped just as abruptly. My stomach grumbled, yelling at me to eat.

"Hey Jenny, I'm gonna call the pizza place!" I ran downstairs to grab the restaurant menus that littered the hallway.

I heard a knock on the door and squinted my eyes. *Are the buzzers not working?* We didn't have a doorman, and there were about fifty apartments in our building. Should I let him in? I scrunched my nose and squinted my eyes, debating fate if I opened the door to a stranger.

Bang-Bang-Bang. The knocking transitioned to pounding, and I tiptoed toward the windows. A man wearing a baseball hat looked at the wall with all the apartment numbers and buzzers. He scanned up and down, his finger trailing his eyes.

He looked innocent enough. I trusted someone was expecting him and opened the door.

The man turned, and my eyes locked on his. It had been one year since I'd first stared into those eyes but I still saw him nightly in my dreams. "Jaime." My breath caught and my heart stopped. Instincts took over, and I yanked open the door, throwing my arms around him and pinning him to the wall.

My mouth flew to his, and I felt the familiar curve of his jaw, the shape of his lips, and the softness of his tongue. He reciprocated my assertiveness, and I leaned into him further. The buttons behind us buzzed and random neighbors asked who we were or what we wanted.

I giggled and pulled Jaime into the main lobby.

"What are you doing here?"

He eyed me up and down. "One year ago, I met a beautiful woman on a plane. She slipped through my hands a few months ago, but I couldn't stop thinking of her. I thought if I saw her on the day we met, it would be like she never left." He kissed me and the world stopped.

"How did you find me?"

"Owen and I flew over a week ago. I knew I'd find you. When I got your address, I left our hotel, grabbed a cab, and came over."

"I can't believe you're here. How long were you outside?"

He checked his watch. "I don't know. I wrote down your new address, but not your apartment number and your name isn't listed on the buzzer. I think I've been here about a half hour. I thought someone would come by, but no one did."

I cracked up laughing. Sweat drenched the perimeter of his hat and he smelled like clothes that sat in the washing machine too long. I didn't care. He was here and I was touching him. He wasn't a figment of my imagination.

I led him down the hallway and up the stairs. "How long are you staying?"

"I'm not sure, but Owen and I got an apartment in Brighton. We move in on September 1st."

My jaw dropped to my feet. Frozen on the stairs, I slowly turned. "What?" I grabbed his shoulders, my mouth shaped into a permanent smile.

"We both found jobs in Boston. We're on a work visa. I didn't want to tell you and get your hopes up, in

case it didn't work. I know how you love surprises."

"You're here?" My voice bounced off the stairway. "For good?"

"For at least a year."

I kissed him deeply, my body wanting to pounce on him like a lioness catching her prey.

"Owen's at the hotel now. Do you want to sleep over tonight? We have a hotel suite with a pool and air conditioning. It's not a castle, but it's still rather lovely."

"Yes!" I raced up the stairs, my legs burning.

I bounced into our tiny kitchen. "Jenny, look who I found! This is Jaime. My Jaime, from Ireland."

She waved at him, throwing me raised eyebrows, a grin and a clap. "Nice to meet you. I'm Jenny, Rory's roommate."

"I found him. In the lobby. Jenny, he got a job here! He's here because of me. He still loves me."

Jaime took my hands and kissed them. "I never stopped, Rory. That's why I'm here. I couldn't risk losing you. I'm sorry I wasn't better keeping in touch. I had internet in Galway but not Connemara."

"Of course!" *So he hadn't been avoiding me.* Images of the house nestled between the mountains reminded me that quick internet in homes wasn't common in rural areas. Even here, my parent's cottage in Maine had spotty service.

His beautiful amber eyes bore tunnels straight to my heart and my entire body opened itself up to him.

"Happy one year anniversary, Jaime."

"One year down. And at least one more year together. We'll figure it out after that." He kissed the top of my hand and my body surrendered to his touch.

"Hopefully many more. No matter where we are in the world, I'll be there."

Jaime pulled me close. "As long as you're by my side, Rory Stanley, I'm a lucky man. You're my Galway girl."

"And you're my match." Willie Daly's prediction had come true.

"Huh?"

I nuzzled my face in his neck and kissed his collarbone. "Nothing."

I knew our story hadn't ended in Ireland. It had paused for intermission, and now the adventure of Act Two was about to begin.

The End....for now.

***

When we leave Jaime and Rory, they have a happy-for-now...but will they get a happy ever after? Let's fast forward five years to the summer of 2007 in Promises for a New Adventure at https://dl.bookfunnel.com/boi6ps23bw and find out!

About the Author

E.D. Hackett lives in New England with her husband and two children (three if you count the dog). She loves watching romantic comedy movies, reading women's fiction novels, and planning her next trip to Ireland. She writes feel good stories that dive into family dynamics, self-love, self-acceptance, and personal growth.

You can connect with me on:

- https://www.edhackettauthor.com
- https://www.facebook.com/edhackettwrites
- https://www.instagram.com/e.d_hackettwrites
- https://www.linktr.ee/edhackett
- https://www.amazon.com/stores/author/B08D7QGY2C

Subscribe to my newsletter:

- https://www.edhackettauthor.com

Also by E.D. Hackett

E.D. Hackett writes women's fiction with one foot in romance.

An Unfinished Story

Complete strangers. A bustling B&B. Can two women help each other find their dreams?

Boston. Joanie Wilson has played it safe her whole life. But her fifteen years of loyalty to the newspaper seem like they count for nothing when her boss announces the business's impending sale. And though she doesn't really enjoy her job, the frightened reporter fights to save it by accepting a remote assignment to write articles on local flavor.

Block Island, RI. Carly Davis longs to live on her own terms. But with her father deceased and her mother's dementia dominating her world, the gregarious young woman feels trapped into running the family's bed-and-breakfast. So when a desperate journalist arrives and swaps her rent for assistance with the property, Carly seizes the chance to finally take a deep breath.

As Joanie becomes immersed in the relaxed atmosphere and meets a handsome police officer, she wonders if her need for safety is costing her happiness. And as Carly grows close to her big-city tenant, she sees a new future opening before her.

Will this accidental friendship trigger the changes both women crave?

An Unfinished Story is the charming first book in The Block Island Saga women's fiction series. If you like relatable characters, sweet romances, and beautiful settings, then you'll love E.D. Hackett's escape to paradise.

Hope Hanna Murphy

She sacrificed too much for them. When her real ancestry shatters her world, will she ever reclaim happiness?

Carly Davis was sure getting away from the island would help. Elated after finally freeing herself from running her late family's inn, her fresh start in Maine fizzles in the aftermath of a failed relationship. And her luck sours further still when an innocent DNA test reveals at least one of her parents had been deceiving her for decades.

Furious she gave up the best years of her life to support people she wasn't even related to, the distraught woman returns home to seek answers about her actual origins. But with her dear friend's sister marrying a guy who is suddenly Carly's cousin, the angry adoptee fears the truth could leave her more alone than ever...

Will she find the joy she so desperately craves, or will her true heritage only bring new sorrow?

Hope Hanna Murphy is the enchanting second book in The Block Island Saga women's fiction series. If you like optimistic stories, conflicted characters, and the strength of community, then you'll love E.D. Hackett's tale of courage.

The Havoc in My Head

She had all she expected to achieve. But a surprise hidden in her head was about to change everything...

Ashley Martin has it all. With a high-paying job, a devoted husband, and impeccable children, the ambitious woman is living the dream life she envisioned for herself. So determined to maintain her perfect existence, she hides her odd vision problems, headaches, and confusion... until one morning she wakes up blind.

Diagnosed with a brain tumor, the terrified professional faces two difficult surgeries and a year-long recovery. And as she struggles to cope with her sudden reversal of fortune, Ashley begins to see truths she never had before.

Can this tenacious woman reclaim her health and redirect her happiness?

The Havoc in My Head is a powerful and moving women's fiction novel. If you like deeply personal journeys, overcoming impossible hurdles, and inspirational turnarounds, then you'll love E.D. Hackett's tale of extreme courage.

Reinventing Amara Leventis

She wants everyone to think she's got it together. So where did it all fall apart?

Providence, RI. Amara Leventis craves validation. So when her best friend and roomie gets engaged, the twenty-five-year-old single girl fears she's losing her soulmate... and her apartment forever. Reeling from the sense of abandonment, Amara turns an interview for a work promotion into a shocking pink slip.

Humiliated and effectively homeless, the frazzled woman begrudgingly returns to rural Connecticut and her parents' Greek bakery. But when a fight gets her bounced from the wedding party and she discovers her dad's troubling secrets, Amara wonders if life will always be sour instead of sweet.

Will she ever find the right recipe for happiness?

Reinventing Amara Leventis is a richly drawn women's fiction novel. If you like relatable characters, family dramas, and laugh-out-loud moments, then you'll adore E.D. Hackett's entertaining read.

Farm Cove Bliss

E.D. HACKETT

She's relearning to trust. He's healing his heartache. Can Crystal and Derek fix the farmhouse and mend their fractured hearts?

Crystal Whitman is determined to redefine herself. Pulling double shifts to break free from a cheating ex, the single mom worries her life can't get any more chaotic until her own mother dies. The city gal returns to her painfully rural hometown in the hopes of flipping her vacant ancestral farmhouse fast, but she never expected her hunky hired hand would make her want to slow down and enjoy the view.

Derek Fischer can't shake his grief. Twelve years after losing his wife, the devoted dad's broken heart beats only for his daughter, until a sexy school teacher sparks a different kind of love. But with a dying home improvement business to keep afloat, the contractor fears muddling the line between business and pleasure could only end in financial ruin.

When Crystal hires Derek to fix the old farmhouse, so she can sell it and return to her frenzied life, she moves in for the summer to save some money and give him a hand. Fighting their growing attraction, she wonders if she's destined to be alone and he wonders if his wife will ever forgive him for moving on. When a vivacious blonde sinks her claws into Derek, Crystal relives her ex-husbands betrayal, and her reaction could sabotage their growing relationship.

Can these two shattered souls piece together their future and find a happily ever after?

Farm Cove Bliss is a small town sweet romance. If you like small town settings, relatable characters, and mid-life love, you'll adore E.D. Hackett's Farm Cove Bliss.

Made in United States
North Haven, CT
01 March 2024